THROUGH WARPED SPACETIME

On the flight deck viewscreen, Laura saw the stars redden and dart swirling away, like sparks from a collapsing bonfire. Her hand still gripped the now useless dead-man switch. She lifted her gloved fingers away from the switch: they moved a few millimeters, moved again from the starting point, then moved again—the simultaneous visions overlapping on her retina.

"Time reversal," said Levine. "Twice in a row—backward, then forward again. Didn't seem like backward, of course—our whole universe went with us."

"Have a look at the screens," said Laura . . .

There was a new sun in the sky.

THE GATES OF HEAVEN

Paul Preuss

BANTAM BOOKS
TORONTO · NEW YORK · LONDON

THE GATES OF HEAVEN
A Bantam Book / May 1980

ISBN 0-553-13409-4

Published simultaneously in the United States and Canada

Bantam Books are published by Bantam Books, Inc. Its trade-mark, consisting of the words "Bantam Books" and the por-trayal of a bantam, is Registered in U.S. Patent and Trademark Office and in other countries. Marca Registrada. Bantam Books, Inc., 666 Fifth Avenue, New York, New York 10019.

for Kurt, and for Karen

For their helpful comments, special thanks are due Roger A. Freedman, physicist, Igal Saraf, peripatetic mathematician, and Jerry Rasmussen, connoisseur; mistakes that remain are due to my obstinacy.

Strait is the gate, and narrow is the way, which leadeth unto life, and few there be that find it.

Matthew VII, 14

I

ACTIS

1

Lights come and go in the night sky. Men, troubled at last by the things they build, may toss in their sleep and dream bad dreams, or lie awake while the meteors whisper greenly overhead. But nowhere in all space or on a thousand worlds will there be men to share our loneliness. There may be wisdom; there may be power; somewhere across space great instruments, handled by strange, manipulative organs, may stare vainly at our floating cloud wrack, their owners yearning as we yearn. Nevertheless, in the nature of life and in the principles of evolution we have had our answer. Of men elsewhere, and beyond, there will be none forever.
—Loren Eiseley, *The Immense Journey*

Lynn Nishihara inserted her I.D. card in the automat slot, popped a Thermo-Pak of tea from the dispenser, and walked past dozens of empty tables toward the doors of the brightly lit cafeteria. The place was as deserted as Sunday night could make it.

She stopped outside the entrance long enough to zip up her windbreaker. The desert night was cold. For a moment she considered getting back into the electric tram which had brought her from the BOQ. Instead, she decided to leave it at curbside and walk the half kilometer to the Operations Building. It was easier to think, walking. She was mentally composing the opening paragraphs of the report she planned to submit as her final official act upon resigning from Project Cyclops.

The wind was rising again after the evening calm. A flirtatious breeze distracted her attention by rolling a comical fat tumbleweed across her path, then stole a sandy kiss. She grimaced; two years of life in the desert had not reconciled her to the dust that crept into everything: eyes, nose, ears, hair, clothes.

But in six weeks she would be back in Boston. It seemed an eternity to wait.

Her eyes followed the tumbleweed, now a hundred meters off, as it bounced along the sand and then abruptly tangled itself in a pile of others at the base of the nearest antenna. At night the antenna seemed to loom even larger than it really was, its round central tower and steel armature rising over ten stories to support a mesh paraboloid as wide as a football field. As Nishihara glanced up, the dish obliterated a third of the starry night sky. She became aware of the constant whine that laid a substrate of sound for her every waking and dreaming thought: the sound of the tracking motors which locked the great antennas to the rotation of the celestial sphere.

Like ancient menhirs standing in precise rows, the antennas stretched away to the horizon on every side, beyond counting in the darkness.

Two years earlier Lynn Nishihara, brand new Ph.D., had gazed eagerly from the window of the helicopter which brought her south from Las Vegas. The pilot had a flair for the dramatic, and liked to skim low over the green Colorado River below its flanking cliffs, then turn sharply up and over the Dead Range toward Searchlight Base to the west. The maneuver usually brought a satisfying gasp from uninitiated passengers. Nishihara was no exception; she gaped in awe as the bare rock curtain of twisted mountain peaks dropped away to reveal the whole circular array of radio telescopes suddenly blossoming before her, a thousand silver sunflowers glittering in the harsh sunlight, covering some twenty square kilometers of desert floor.

She had never seen a single human work so vast. She was filled with pride at having been chosen for the staff of Project Cyclops, the ongoing search for extraterrestrial intelligence that was the main business of Searchlight Base.

Now, as she walked toward the Ops Building to start her night watch as Scientific Duty Officer, her eyes registered the dark shapes of the antennas all around her, but her mind ignored them. She was, finally, bored. The silent, heedless Galaxy had humbled her as it had all the other bright and eager young scientists who had preceded her, all of them secretly convinced that they would be the first to hear signals from a distant civilization.

The wind-resistant acrylic doors of the Ops Building swung in to let her pass. She unzipped her jacket to reveal the badge clipped to her tunic, but the Space Force guard at the lobby desk barely glanced at it as she signed in. He was more interested in the holographic *Playboy* he only half concealed below the counter top.

She lifted her thumb from the register, walked to the airlock door, and inserted her I.D. card. The heavy door slid aside.

She stepped into the airlock separating the control rooms and computer banks from the dusty outside environment. The door slid shut behind her, and her ears popped under positive air pressure. Then the inner door slid away, and she walked into the main corridor.

The corridor was dark except for a glowing strip in the floor leading straight to the main control room. In here she heard only the echo of her footsteps in the empty hall and the low hum of air conditioners cooling the computer banks to either side of the central corridor.

Again she had to insert her I.D. card, at the door of the control room. The mahogany door sucked aside to reveal the big amphitheater that was Project Cyclops' nerve center.

She stepped inside. Her vision filled with stars, thousands of white sparks scintillating against a dark field of blue. She seemed to float weightless in a bowl of night.

The star field was merely a projection against the half dome of the amphitheater, an illusion so familiar to Nishihara she no longer noticed it. The striking graphic display showed all the stars visible from Searchlight's latitude and longitude, automatically adjusting itself as the earth rotated and moved through space.

A dozen consoles were arranged on the floor of the dark amphitheater, work stations for the engineers who used them only during the day. Seats for spectators rose steeply on either side. Just behind Nishihara's head, over the main door, was the edge of the rostrum that held consoles for the duty officers and project directors.

"Bless your heart, Lynn, you're early." It was Fred Walker's voice. He had the watch from four to midnight.

Nishihara climbed the steps to the brightly lit rostrum in time to see Walker's wide hands sweeping up the remains of a double-solitaire game from the top of Ted Donner's desk. Captain Donner was the Military Duty Officer, with a watch that ran from eight to four; blond, boyish, and handsome, he lolled in his chair and let Walker sort the decks.

Walker scooped an unruly lock of limp black hair out of

his eyes. "You don't mind if I just go ahead and take off, Lynn?"

"No, of course not."

"It's been a typically thrilling watch. I think I slept through most of it." He unwrapped his legs from the chair he was perched on backward, stood up, and tucked in his shirt tail.

Donner grinned up at him. "Remind me not to play cards with you when you're awake."

Walker snatched his jacket from the rail of the rostrum. "Be sure and call me when the flying saucers land," he said cheerily, as he bounded down the steps. Nishihara heard the door of the control room close behind him.

"Heading straight for the tables," Donner observed.

"That's his business, isn't it?" Nishihara replied primly.

"Sure it is," said Donner, straightening up in his chair. "That's why we're in Nevada, after all. 'Entertainment Unlimited.' "

Nishihara ignored him. She seated herself at one of the consoles at the forward edge of the rostrum. Donner gave up trying to be polite and pretended to find something to occupy him at his desk. She was relieved. With Donner her customary reserve took on an edge of positive dislike.

He was an easygoing young man who made friends readily. If you liked Scotch, Donner would give you a bottle of the best for your birthday; if you liked to gamble, your luck was always better when Donner was alone; if you were a visiting fireman or a lonely bachelor, Donner knew lots of friendly showgirls; and if you were a lonely girl bachelor, he could be pretty friendly himself. Just a humble maintenance officer with time on his hands and loose change in his pockets, so he liked to style himself, but Nishihara knew he was a spy.

All the zoomies were, of course. Spying of one sort or another was the real reason for the Space Force presence at Searchlight Base, although nominally it was strictly an administrative convenience. At one level, Donner and others like him tried to pick up early hints of scientific discoveries that might have military application.

On another level, there were times when the civilian scientists were locked out of the Ops Building altogether, while the Space Force used the antenna array for purposes of its own. These were often childishly simple for the scientists to decipher: when a thousand radio telescopes all swung simultaneously to aim at a particular point in space—on the moon's orbit and equidistant from Earth and moon—it was like a thousand fingers pointing to the space settlement at L-5. Ever since the colony had gained its independence in the aftermath of the *Actis* affair, the Space Force had been nervous about its potential to wreak destruction.

Nishihara considered anyone in uniform to be a child. But so long as Donner and the rest of the zoomies stayed out of her bailiwick, she was content to ignore them.

Nishihara quickly scanned the immense star map in front of the rostrum, reminding herself of the business at hand. Bright green cross hairs framed a region of space in the constellation Cetus, and Nishihara knew the real target was a star invisible from Earth, some two hundred and fifty light-years distant. The K-2 star had been under observation for the previous twenty minutes; Nishihara punched up the results of the observation on the computer screen in front of her.

The close-packed table of numbers held no surprises for her pattern-sensitive eye. Only well-known sources of radiation were present in the radio spectrum from 1 to 10 gigahertz, none of them of unusual interest except to indicate that it was a very good night for listening.

It was now less than a minute to midnight, when the antennas were programmed to swing a few minutes south-eastward to pick up the next star on the Cyclops target list. Although close to the current target as plotted radially from Earth, the next star was actually hundreds of light-years closer. It was the historically interesting Tau Ceti, a G-type single star only a bit smaller than the sun, and a mere 11.8 light-years away.

Tau Ceti had been among the first stars ever singled out for radio observation with the hope of detecting intelligent life; since that first attempt with the primitive equipment of the 1960s, Tau Ceti had been observed on several occasions, without result. There was always the possibility that constantly improving instruments would find what had been previously missed—or that since the last time anyone had looked, some alien Marconi had brightened the radio sky of his planet.

As the atomic clock blinked to midnight, a low rumble penetrated the thick concrete of the Operations Building, the cumulative vibrations of a thousand giant antennas turning and tilting in unison. Solidly as each massive pylon was mounted, the sheer mass of so much steel and aluminum shifting at once—however slightly—was enough to set up a noticeable tremor in the desert floor.

The needles of the power monitors dipped, then swung upright, as the green cross hairs slid a few centimeters on the star map and fixed on the head of Cetus the Whale. As the earth wave passed and the antennas settled, the computer screen in front of Nishihara sparkled with electronic snow, then began spilling out streams of numbers.

Nishira settled into her chair and typed her first entry into the morning's log. She simply reported her presence. The computer knew everything else.

She popped the disposable cup from the top of her Thermo-Pak of tea. The liquid instantly heated; she poured it into the cup. Steam from her first sip fogged her thick glasses. She took them off and put them down on the console, then ran a hand through her short black hair.

She stared at the star map. The stars were all out of focus, circled by little rainbows of chromatic aberration. She imagined they were autumn leaves. It was almost September; she would be back in New England in time to see the foliage at the peak of its glory.

She rubbed her eyes and replaced her glasses. She carefully set down her tea cup, in front of a hand-lettered sign taped to the console: DO NOT SET LIQUIDS ON MACHINE.

As she reached for a notepad and pencil, her eyes fell on the computer screen.

That's odd . . .

It was a routine matter for Nishihara's trained eye to spot the difference of a few decimal places in a familiar column of numbers. A few moments before she had checked the screen and noted the values characterizing tonight's neutral radio sky. Now the value for the 2.2 gigahertz range had changed.

It was a well-used frequency, one of the most common for interplanetary traffic. But the Cyclops antennas were focused on a tiny patch of sky, and any spaceship or satellite crossing the targeted area would have announced its presence with a literal blast of radio noise.

Probably something simple. Let the computer do it in the morning . . .

Well . . . perhaps it's worth checking.

Nishihara switched the display from tabular to graphic.

Although the graph for the current reception was incomplete —the receivers still had a few million channels to work through—she had all she needed.

With the touch of a couple of keys, Nishihara superimposed another graph, representing the average background noise as of the last scan. She tapped the keys again, superimposing a third graph, this one representing the proper spectrum of Tau Ceti as stored in the computer's memory.

Then she typed rapidly for several seconds, instructing the computer to subtract the star's proper spectrum and tonight's background radiation from the real-time incoming signal.

She pushed the key marked "execute." All graph lines on the screen disappeared.

But a tiny pinprick of light remained, gleaming suggestively at that point on the graph's X axis corresponding to 2.2 gigahertz.

It's persistent . . .

She keyed back to the real-time signal and instructed the computer to expand the graph's Y axis.

A range of miniature mountain peaks grew up the face of the screen. Nishihara had to move quickly to stop the expansion—the pinprick of white had stretched into a line that threatened to streak off the top of the screen.

She read the decibel scale: the 2.2 gigahertz signal was millions of times more powerful than the background.

She was unaware that Donner was standing at her shoulder until he spoke. "What the hell is that?" he asked quietly.

She glanced at him in annoyance. "Probably a circuit problem," she said pointedly. Maintenance was his nominal responsibility.

"I don't think so," he replied, resolutely cheerful. "I've been checking circuits all night. Whatever that is, it's really out there."

She could not look at him. She could only stare at the bright white line at 2.2 gigahertz, standing up like a beacon.

Like a beacon . . .

She could no longer hold back her excitement. It surged up to set her heart pounding, to flush her cheeks, to make her tingle with heat under her clothes.

"We've got work to do, Doctor," said Donner, and she knew he shared her excitement. "What star is that, anyway?"

"Tau Ceti." She tried to sweep her emotional turbulence aside and concentrate on the task before her. So much to do, so many possible demons to exorcise. It could be a circuit problem, despite Donner's assurance; she had no faith that he really knew what he was doing. Or it could be an aircraft violating Cyclops' restricted airspace, or a military test of some kind, or a piece of orbiting junk reflecting Earth signals back to the surface. It could even be a deliberate hoax.

Donner, back at his desk, was already on the phone, asking for General Talbot, the base commander. Nishihara was suddenly reminded of her first and highest priority. It wouldn't do for the Space Force to learn of this before Cyclops' own director, Joshua Rosenblum.

She felt in her pockets for the little transmitter Rosenblum had given her when she first started work. She had a moment of panic before she located the almost forgotten device in the breast pocket of her windbreaker.

Rosenblum had winked at her playfully when he handed her the device. "When you press this button, it sets off the screamer I wear right here," he'd said, tapping at his waist. "I wear it *all* the time. So no practical jokes, okay? When this thing goes off, it had better be for one reason only."

The transmitter was technically illegal, as were all transmitting devices in the vicinity of Searchlight Base, but its use was justified under the circumstances. Nishihara flicked off the safety cover with her thumb and pressed the button. And held it down.

All thoughts of autumn in New England had vanished from her mind. She was too excited to reflect that in the last few minutes she had once more become a totally committed member of the Project Cyclops team.

Donner was still on the phone. Nishihara permitted herself a sadistic grin.

If he's lucky he'll have worked his way up to the General's cook by now . . .

Twenty seconds had elapsed; the phone on her console rang.

Donner looked up and cocked an eyebrow at her. She brought the transmitter from her pocket and laid it in plain view as she picked up the phone.

Donner gave her an appreciative grin.

"Doctor Nishihara?" asked the robot operator.

"Yes."

"Professor Rosenblum would like to speak with you."

Rosenblum broke in. "This had better be good, youngster."

Nishihara took a breath. "Professor, we are receiving a moderately strong signal at 2.2 gigahertz from the vicinity of Tau Ceti. I thought—"

"I'll see you in half an hour." The phone went dead in her hand.

2

God does not play dice.

—Albert Einstein

God not only plays dice but also sometimes throws them where they cannot be seen.

—S. W. Hawking

Joshua Rosenblum kept one hand on the bedside telephone while he vigorously massaged the corona of reddish-gray hair on his balding head with the other. He needed time to think; he needed to get the blood circulating in his brain. The fierce impossible hopes of a thirty year career in astronomy had suddenly precipitated in this moment—so often rehearsed in imagination, just as often dismissed as fantasy. Now it had come, and found him unprepared, deep in the night's first dreamless sleep.

He kicked irritably at the sheets that entangled his big feet, and swung his gaunt pajamaed legs over the side of the bed. He expelled a shuddering breath that jiggled his cheeks. Then he picked up the phone again.

"Yes, Professor?" asked the polite robot.

"Confirm my identity," he ordered, and began to recite: "I saw Eternity the other night, Like a great ring of pure and endless light . . ."

The robot chimed in, "Voice print analysis confirms that you are Joshua L. Rosenblum, authorized Director of Project Cyclops, security clearance maximum, under the provisions of National Space Agency administrative order number 18-343 A. Your Social Security number is 1005-525 . . ."

"Store the rest. I'm putting the base on Condition Yellow."

"Condition Yellow in effect as of time code 37:08:31:00: 17:43. Do you require progress reports?"

"I'll query you."

"Very good, Profess—"

Rosenblum hung up and got out of bed. He crossed to his dresser, his long fingers fumbling at the knot of his pajama pants. The loose trousers had twisted around and the knot was on his side. His fingers brushed the dime-sized screamer that had jolted him awake a few moments earlier. It was attached to his hip by an adhesive patch; he peeled it slowly away from his skin, wincing, and at the same time grinning in exultation. The gadget had served its purpose. He tossed it on the dresser.

He got his shorts on frontward on the second try, then turned to consider the wardrobe in his closet: surely something special, in which to receive the first message from the Galaxy? After a moment's thought he gave it up as an insoluble problem, and reached for his ancient tweed suit. Identical to at least three others he had owned, of a style little changed in over a hundred and fifty years, it was the uniform of a certain approach to science; he had worn that uniform almost every day of his working life.

A quiet voice intruded on his racing thoughts: "Promise me you won't wear white socks, dear."

Rosenblum turned to see Miriam smiling at him from the bed. He hadn't even noticed when she turned on the bedside lamp. It was no use apologizing now, since obviously she had been awakened at the same moment he had. He grinned sheepishly.

"I promise."

By the time the electric tram deposited Rosenblum at the door of the Operations Building, fifteen kilometers from his home in the dry foothills of the Dead Range, Condition Yellow was in full swing. Space Police guarded the doors, loaded gas guns slung loosely over their shoulders. Perimeter patrols and guard details at the gates of the base had been doubled.

The robot telephone operators had tracked down most of the day watch technical people and roused them from whosoever beds they were in: the trams were running on close schedule to deliver them to the Ops Building. The building's central corridor blazed with light and echoed to the chatter of the crowd pushing its way into the central control room. As Rosenblum entered the room and mounted the stairs to the rostrum, he wondered at the numerous spectators—technicians and military personnel not on duty—who were rapidly filling the auditorium seats. He had often wondered if he were alone in his enthusiasm for Project Cyclops' goal, but apparently it was not so.

Lynn Nishihara's face told him as much. The young woman was glowing with excitement, although she would have been mortified if anyone had called it to her attention. Rosenblum reflected with satisfaction that Harvard Observatory would have to do without her now; he'd be willing to bet she'd changed her mind about staying on at Cyclops.

Jean-Claude Giroux, the day watch Duty Officer, was also on the rostrum along with Nishihara and Captain Donner. And Fred Walker was not far behind Rosenblum, taking the steps three at a time.

"G' morning, Professor," the young mathematician huffed to Rosenblum. "You guys weren't joking, were you? I—didn't take it seriously at first—I just get my fanny in the chair at the blackjack table, I take the first three hands in a row, and somebody hands me a message it's Condition Yellow. Would *you* have believed that?"

"It's no joke, my friend," the heavyset Giroux told him. "But it is wonderful, isn't it, that Tau Ceti of all stars should prove to be the one we have sought all these years?"

"Yeah. Hello, neighbor," said Walker.

Rosenblum cut in. "Let's hold the chitchat. I'd like to get a look at that signal. And then, since we're all here, we can talk about how we're going to split up the work."

The scientists gathered around Lynn Nishihara's computer console, with Ted Donner hanging on the fringes of the little group. Meanwhile the auditorium continued to fill.

By 12:45 on the morning of August 31st, 2037, the control room was crowded—every console manned by a shirt-sleeved technician, every seat in the auditorium taken. Some of the spectators could interpret the cascading numbers on the computer screens, but to most they were merely electronic babel. They stared fascinated at the green cross hairs of the big star map, slowly tracking Tau Ceti across the arc of heaven.

Almost the last man into the room was General Benjamin Talbot, Searchlight Base Commander. The military people present snapped to quick attention as the General came through the doors and marched up the steps to the rostrum. Every ribbon on the General's space-black uniform was in place, but those close to him noticed that his bloodshot eyes looked a bit glassy. Talbot was accompanied by a short chubby major, his Information Officer.

He headed straight for Rosenblum and the other scientists, but Rosenblum saw him coming and struck pre-emptively. "Good morning, Ben. I hope you'll confirm my order to put the base on Yellow."

"Already have, Josh. You can count on my boys. What's the drill?"

Rosenblum noticed that Talbot was huffing under the exertion of the short climb. Ben Talbot had been a good rocket jockey fifteen years ago, but he was a long way over the horizon. Searchlight Base was a sinecure for him, an easy slide into retirement. Rosenblum searched for simple words.

"Just give me the big picture, Josh," said Talbot impatiently. "I'll get the full briefing later."

"Sure, Ben," said Rosenblum. "We're getting a strong signal from Tau Ceti—pretty strong compared to anything natural on that wavelength."

"Tau Ceti? Where's that? What wavelength?"

"Uh, Tau Ceti's about twelve light-years away, Ben, in that direction." Rosenblum indicated the domed star map and the cross hairs that framed the star. "The wavelength is roughly fourteen centimeters; 2.2 gigahertz." Rosenblum had occasionally wondered how Talbot had made it to flag rank; this was one such occasion. Nevertheless, he was grateful that his own relations with the man had been good.

"How strong?" the General demanded.

"Should be between fifty and a thousand kilowatts," Fred Walker shot back, "calculating the distance against the signal strength at our end."

Rosenblum glared at Walker. The young man's computational abilities were remarkable, but too often he calculated faster than he could think. And he talked too much.

Rosenblum turned to Talbot. "So you see, Ben, we've got a lot of work . . ."

"It's a ship," Talbot announced, without a hint of uncertainty.

The scientists glanced at each other. Walker looked as if he wished he'd kept his mouth shut.

Rosenblum sighed. He'd noticed the rich stew of esters on Talbot's breath, but he'd hoped the General was sober enough to keep a grip on reality. Apparently not: the man had no conception of the vast distances involved, or the laws of evolution which forbade that intelligent life on Tau Ceti—or anywhere else in the universe—should share anything with life on Earth except basic organic chemistry. "We don't have any definite theories yet, Ben," he began, gently.

But the Information Officer hovering at Talbot's shoulder broke in, evidently seeing a chance to make points with the boss. "What the General has in mind, Professor, is that your signal is on a standard navigation channel, and by your own calculation it could have been produced by a standard on-board transmitter." The IO smirked. Q.E.D.

Talbot ignored him. "A ship," he repeated heavily.

Giroux shrugged irritably. "Incredible," the Frenchman rasped. "This so-called ship of yours . . ."

"Yes, and we're certainly looking into every possibility," said Rosenblum quickly, before the scientist's contempt for the military could lead to a disgraceful wrangle. "At this point, though, we're inclined to—"

Talbot bulled ahead: "The message. Are you working on the message?"

Rosenblum took a deep breath. Talbot, out of action for far too long, was snorting like an old war horse at the scent of blood. And before Rosenblum could prevent it, everybody started talking at once.

". . . signal modulation of a complex kind . . ."

". . . pretty fancy mathematical analysis to . . ."

". . . first complete standard debugging procedures . . ."

Rosenblum scowled furiously at all of them, and tried to hide a shake of his head. When they quieted, he turned back to Talbot—smiling. "Ben, as you can see, we have quite a few things to attend to here."

Talbot looked like he was about to lose his temper, but just at that moment, Ted Donner spoke up brightly. "Has anyone listened to this mysterious signal yet? I'd guess not. So why not put the signal over the speakers? Then we'd get a feel for what we're dealing with."

Rosenblum noticed that Donner—on the side facing away from General Talbot—gave Fred Walker a wink, and that Walker winked back at him.

"That's a good idea, son," Talbot grunted, eyeing Donner. "I'll make that an official request." Suddenly the man looked tired. "Then I'll get out of your hair, Josh."

Rosenblum rubbed his balding scalp. "Certainly, Ben.

Right away." He studied Donner for a moment. The Captain had a quick mind; his suggestion was a brilliant way to head off a silly argument.

The scientists—and Donner—realized the signal would sound like pure gibberish. Only the computer, guided by a lot of ingenuity, would be able to make any sense of it, if there was any sense to be had. Once Talbot realized this too, perhaps he would go away and leave them to their work.

Nishihara reached for the keys of her console; Donner's suggestion offered no technical problem. Rosenblum laid a restraining hand on her shoulder. He leaned down to key the public address system. He twisted the filament of the desk top microphone toward his lips. "Ladies and gentlemen, I'd like your attention for a moment."

His flat, amplified voice filled the large room. Everyone turned to look up at the rostrum.

"In a moment Doctor Nishihara is going to patch the signal we are working on through our loudspeakers here. We're probably all pretty curious about just what it sounds like, and I think this will give us a good subjective feel for the nature of the problem we are dealing with."

He flicked off the P.A. system. The room was hushed.

Nishihara whispered, "Professor?"

On her computer screen were displayed a variety of graphic representations of the incoming signal, changing as she twisted the knobs of the CRT's function controls. Rosenblum watched long enough to realize that at least three discrete channels were being received simultaneously, adjacent to each other in the signal band. The wave forms of the outer groups were square and regular, like some form of digital telemetry. The central channel, however, was jagged and irregular, oddly pulsed, like an old movie's optical sound track.

"Try to fix on that one," Rosenblum said.

Nishihara tapped the keys. She flipped a switch that fed the signal through the public address system.

An angry hiss instantly filled the amphitheater, shot through with pops and rumbles and weird phasing whistles, like the echoing roar of a jet plane, or wind in high tension wires.

But underneath the noise, struggling to rise as if from some great ocean depth, there was another sound.

It was a sound so impossibly familiar, so intimate, so heartbreaking, that every person in the room gasped involuntarily.

It was the sound of a woman crying.

The crying went on and on, low and insistent, utterly disconsolate, washed over by waves of static, but always surfacing again to clutch at the emotions of the listeners, gripping their hearts with its tragic litany.

No one said a word.

Finally General Talbot broke the silence. "What in God's name is *that?*"

The room came alive with excited conversation.

What, indeed? Rosenblum wondered. Could there have been some catastrophic error? Surely that human voice was not coming from Tau Ceti!

Then a thought crashed into his brain: *was* it a human voice? Or did it just happen to sound uncannily like one?

As the thought unfolded in his mind, he almost laughed. Why, wild burros braying their hearts out in the middle of the desert night didn't sound much different. Even his own cat sometimes made noises like that. For all he knew, he could be listening to a Cetian love song. Or for that matter, the Cetian version of the six o'clock news.

The same thought must have occurred to others in the room, for now he heard laughter amid the excitement.

Walker, Giroux, and Donner were all grinning at each other in self-congratulation. Only Nishihara seemed to be paying serious attention to the alien sound.

General Talbot looked ill.

"Ben——" Rosenblum began, but he was cut off by young Donner.

"General, I think it would be a good idea for you to have this transmission piped to your office, in case you need to handle any queries from HQ." Donner gave the Information Officer a flat stare. "Don't you agree, Major?"

"Right," said the Major, belatedly catching on. "Definitely, General. I think we should get to work drafting a statement for the press."

Talbot nodded. "I'll do as these two suggest, Josh. You know where to reach me." He turned a bit unsteadily, and started down the steps toward the door. The Information Officer followed.

Rosenblum watched them go. He knew there was a well-stocked bar in the General's office. He wondered if Captain Donner's suggestion had been kind. Never mind; it had been effective in clearing the room of potential interference and embarrassment.

Rosenblum turned back to the microphone. "Okay, ladies and gentlemen, back to work." His commanding voice rode over the stellar signal. "We're not going to learn anything more by listening."

He switched off the microphone, and half turned toward Nishihara. Her hand was already reaching for the switch that would kill the speakers.

And then they heard it.

"I'm sorry," said the voice from the stars.

Rosenblum, shocked, allowed his long body to crumple into the chair beside Nishihara.

"I'm sorry," the voice said again. It *was* a woman's voice! "I didn't want this to happen. I promised myself I'd be brave. I'm sorry."

Rosenblum stared at Nishihara. She was expressionless behind her thick glasses.

He turned to look at the computer screen. Jagged lines bounced and squiggled with each word from the speakers.

"Can you hear me?" the woman asked.

Rosenblum almost answered her.

"Arnold says you can't, but I don't think he knows what happened any more than we . . ." A great roar of static drowned the words.

Rosenblum snapped out of his trance. "People—please!" he shouted.

Technicians flinched and began tapping keys to tune the computer-controlled receivers.

The voice emerged from the static: ". . . Anton has located a star he thinks is you, so we're beaming in that direction. No matter what Arnold says."

There was a long pause, not caused by interference. The woman began again, her voice stronger now. "If this transmission does get through, maybe you'll be able to figure out what happened. We can't. All the information we can give you is on the telemetry channels."

Another pause, a shorter one. "My own impressions, subjective: the new star looks a lot like the sun. A bit pinker, maybe. We've already located at least two wanderers, objects pretty certain to be planets. Marston tells me one of them may be earthlike. That would be interesting, I guess. I have no idea what we're going to do with that knowledge."

Another pause. ". . . God, how far away are you? How many years into the future?"

Rosenblum kept his attention on the computer screen, but

from the corner of his eye he noticed Fred Walker suddenly reach forward to a nearby desk and begin scribbling something on a scrap of paper. Walker stepped over to Rosenblum and handed him the note, with just one word scratched on it: "*Actis?*"

Rosenblum stared at it: an incredible suggestion.

In the hushed, semidarkened room, where all eyes were transfixed by the green cross that floated in the glittering void, the woman's soft voice resumed, filling every nook. "We're all still healthy. All life support systems functioning just fine. The fire didn't touch them. It's out now, completely dead. Everything's gone back there . . ." She swallowed a sob. "As if any of that matters to you anymore." It took her only a beat to recover. "I'll come back on later. I like to think you're out there somewhere, even if you don't hear me."

Then she spoke rapidly, professionally, as if suddenly bored. "Rebecca Meerloo, Third Officer, *Actis,* 26:03:28, ship time 20:51, end transmission."

The channel went dead, except for the hiss of empty space.

The spectators in the room began to murmur, but no one moved. Rosenblum stared at his hands, his long fingers kneading Fred Walker's note into pulp. He looked up at Lynn Nishihara, but she did not meet his gaze. He turned to Giroux, but the burly Frenchman merely shrugged. What was there to say?

Rosenblum looked back at Fred Walker. The young man brushed his hair from his eyes. His black eyes sparkled.

"Well, spit it out before you choke on it, Fred," Rosenblum demanded.

"Forgive me, Professor, but this silly little thing just keeps running through my head." Walker looked almost embarrassed.

"Yes?"

"We have met the aliens, and they is us."

3

The human brain is the most public organ on the face of the earth, open to everything, sending out messages to everything. To be sure, it is hidden away in bone and conducts internal affairs in secrecy, but virtually all the business is the direct result of thinking that has already occurred in other minds.
—Lewis Thomas, *The Lives of a Cell*

Michael Ward was making coffee when he heard the news. He was doing it in a way very few people bothered with these days, using an antique Chemex given to him by his colleague Roger Crain. The slow process suited Michael just fine, providing ritual busy work to keep his hands occupied while his reluctant brain made the transition from sleep to his normal edgy alertness.

It took five seconds to boil the water in the flash-boiler, another fifteen seconds to grind the coffee beans in an old electric hand grinder. Then Michael folded the paper cone, feeling the rough dry texture of the filter paper as he pressed his fingers along the crease. At this hour of the morning the filter paper felt like a dusty chalkboard, making his fingers tingle and sending an involuntary shudder through his body.

In that moment, Michael was vulnerable. Twenty minutes later he would have been psychologically armored against the booming, buzzing confusion of the world, impervious to suggestion, resistant to creative thought. He would have been "rational." Instead, his mind now floated freely in the phenomenal universe, each particle of experience charged with equivalent energy—free to collide between the halves of his brain with explosive effect.

As his fingers ran down the fold in the paper cone, as his skin prickled, his ears picked up the voice of the announcer on the television set in the living room of his apartment: ". . .

monitoring a signal from the direction of the constellation
Cetus the Whale . . ."

The words did not register consciously. Years later, when
he wondered how he had ever gotten himself in so much
trouble, it would never occur to him that the source of it was
the simple congruence of those words from the TV set and
the act of making a paper cone.

Michael plopped the folded cone into the flask of the
coffeepot, dumped in the ground coffee, and poured in the
hot water. Not waiting for the dark liquid to collect in the
bottom of the pot, he wandered into the living room to watch
the news.

The newly risen sun lanced across the haze of the Colorado
Plains to the east and washed the interior of his sparsely
furnished apartment with searing light. He had to polarize the
picture window in order to see the wall screen.

The announcer's familiar face was two feet high, glowing
with phony health captured in sharp, 2,000-line resolution.
Michael was vaguely irritated (as always) that anyone should
presume to look so awake at so uncivilized an hour. Did
those TV guys really think that thick pink makeup looked
real? Then Michael noticed that the announcer was looking
even more awake than usual—in fact, he seemed downright
excited.

Michael glanced at the digital time display in the lower-
right corner of the wall screen. It read 7:05 and a few
seconds—Mountain time, of course. The morning news
would have been recorded two hours earlier in New York.
Unless something of really extraordinary interest were happening.

"We are waiting to bring you live coverage from Searchlight Base, Nevada, of the news conference called for 6:00
A.M. local time—that's nine o'clock here in New York—by
the National Space Agency . . ."

Six in the morning? What's going on?

". . . when the Agency's representatives will presumably be
able to tell us more about these mysterious signals from deep
space."

Michael grunted. This *was* interesting.

The announcer continued, "At the moment we can only
repeat the very brief item which reached us on the satservice
less than an hour ago."

The announcer picked up a scrap of fax paper from the
desk in front of him. He had obviously memorized its

contents, but he handled it with the reverence due a Message-from-the-Great-Beyond. "For the past five hours the radio telescopes of the National Space Agency's Project Cyclops, located at Searchlight Base in southern Nevada, have been monitoring a signal from the direction of the constellation Cetus the Whale. With the cooperation of the U.S. Space Force's Automated Planetary Environment facility at Farside Base on the moon, this weak radio signal has been definitely identified as a coherent message of interstellar origin."

As the announcer put down the paper, his gaze flickered away to the side of the television camera in front of him; he was receiving a message of his own from the studio's floor director. "Now here's correspondent Peter Gray at Search-light Base," he said smoothly.

The scene switched to the newsman, posed in front of one of the huge antennas, its stark white paint glowing pink in the dawn light. "Thank you, George," said the reporter. "Behind me you can see one of the giant radio telescopes—and it's just one of more than a thousand here at Searchlight Base—that at this very moment are receiving this mysterious message from the stars. Now the dedicated staff here at the base has been working literally all night to bring us this truly epochal event, right over here in the Operations Building . . ."

The camera panned away from the reporter to frame the Operations Building, guarded by self-consciously spiffy Space Police. "Now I've been informed that the Space Agency people won't actually be getting this conference under way for a few minutes yet," the reporter went on, "and we'll be right on the spot when that happens, of course; but while we're waiting we'd like to remind our audience of the history of Project Cyclops, and introduce some of its staff, that little-known group of dedicated scientists who are responsible for this truly stunning discovery."

The image of Searchlight's Operations Building dissolved, to be replaced by a view of the desert landscape spreading across the full width of the television wall screen. Men and machines worked in clouds of blowing dust to erect the scaffolding of a row of antennas that stretched to the horizon.

Michael sighed, scratched the stubble of his beard, and returned to the kitchen to check on his coffee. The reporter's voice droned on in the background, narrating the twenty-year-old file tape of Searchlight's construction, reciting facts that were familiar to Michael.

Michael dropped the soggy bag of coffee grounds into the recycling chute marked ORGANIC, poured some of the hot coffee into his cup, sipped, and felt the welcome stimulation spread from his midsection. He walked back into the living room.

The documentary was still playing, and the time was 7:12. Michael, fully awake now, began to feel uneasy. If the Space Agency news conference didn't start soon, he was going to be late for work, and his boss was going to be very unhappy. As Dr. Franklin Muller never tired of reminding his staff, work was a privilege—and Muller delighted in withdrawing privileges on slight provocation.

Michael turned up the gain on the TV speaker and went into the bathroom. He pulled his chemosonic shaver from its wall receptacle, ran it once over his stubble, and rubbed his fingers over the smooth skin the razor left behind. Too easy, he thought. Maybe one of those antique razors would be more interesting, if he could learn to use it without cutting his throat. It would be a waste of water, though, and besides, antiques like that were frightfully expensive.

A beard, perhaps? Keeping it trimmed would present a diverting challenge, though Michael knew Muller would never put up with his scruffy appearance during the weeks it would take to grow a presentable beard.

At the recurring thought of Muller, Michael's face flushed, and his stomach lurched—involuntary anger and fear mixed in the precise proportions of cowardice. He despised Muller, but he was genuinely afraid of losing another job. With the sharp downward slope of his career visible on his work record to any prospective employer, his post with the Mathematics Instructional Committee run by Muller might well turn out to be his last anywhere.

Nobody needed to work to live, that was the problem. Jobs were scarce because they were a luxury. The sense of doing something useful with your mind (or even more rarely, with your hands) was so infrequently available that people with personal wealth were known to bribe employers to hire them. The alternative was to go quietly mad while staring at your wall screen, your every basic need tended by quietly efficient machines.

These thoughts more and more formed a kind of solemn *basso continuo* to the daily play of Michael's mind; bothered that they had started so early this morning, he frowned at his even-featured, innocuously handsome face in the bathroom mirror. He decided to quit feeling sorry for himself and get to work.

Ten minutes later he stood in front of the wall screen in the living room, juggling his still hot breakfast Thermo-Pak. He was dressed conservatively in gray denims and white cotton shirt, ready to dash for the escalator as soon as the news conference had made its point.

The conference had been going for five minutes now, and the point seemed a long way off. Behind a big folding table, which looked as if it had been scrounged from a high school cafeteria, sat a row of uncomfortable scientists and military people. They were perched on a narrow stage hung with blue curtains, facing an auditorium full of impatient reporters. Michael realized most of the reporters had been put on magneplanes and helicopters in the wee hours of the morning and rushed to this assignment without a chance to change clothes or eat breakfast. Red-eyed and jittery, they were in no mood for elaborate technical explanations of the arcana of radio astronomy.

Yet that's all they'd gotten so far; history and details of Project Cyclops' construction, specifics of Tau Ceti's classification and distance from Earth, and an intricate description of the signal itself, its strength, amplitude, frequency, and so on.

Much of this information had been delivered by a young woman introduced as Lynn Nishihara—Michael recognized the name from articles in the mathematical journals. Clearly she was not practiced at public speaking: she kept her head down and hid herself effectively behind dark bangs that hung low to meet the rims of thick eyeglasses. She held a fat sheaf of notes close to her round face and read from them in a mumbled monotone.

After a few minutes of this an irritated voice rang out from the auditorium: "What's the point? Let's get to the point!"

Nishihara looked up from her papers questioningly, as the television camera panned away from her and zoomed in on a florid chubby fellow slouched defiantly in his seat. A chorus of low mutters filled the air.

Gray, the TV reporter, spoke over the scene, his voice low and conspiratorial. "George, as you can see, the media people here at the conference are getting a bit impatient. It looks like there may be something more to this story, but for some reason it hasn't all come out yet."

The anchorman's voice replied. "Yes, Peter, and I have a

feeling those of us who are watching can sympathize with the press. Though the lack of decorum is certainly regrettable."

The scene had switched to a close-up of Joshua Rosenblum, who had leaned forward and was tapping the filament of the desk microphone in front of him. Loud pops filled the auditorium.

"Professor Rosenblum has their attention now," said Gray.

"At four o'clock this morning, local time, I spoke to the President of the United States," Rosenblum said, and instantly there was silence in the room. "I persuaded him of the need for this press conference," said Rosenblum, with the merest hint of regret in his voice, "on the grounds that the news we have is of such significance that it should not be withheld from any member of the human race an instant longer than necessary."

Rosenblum's gaze was sad as he took a moment to look around the room. "This press conference was not arranged for the purpose of entertainment," he resumed, "but rather for the purpose of disseminating vital information as quickly as possible. Since not everyone present is capable of understanding the nature of this information, I will ask Doctor Nishihara to save the remainder of her remarks until later."

Rosenblum paused again, daring any who would to cheer his decision. None did. With long delicate fingers he held the thin slab of a microcorder up before the microphone. "This is a recording of the first part of the message we have been receiving from Tau Ceti. Before I play this recording, however, there's something you *must* understand," he said. "It's a point Doctor Nishihara has already made, but I will make it again. The star Tau Ceti is almost twelve light-years away. Radio waves travel as fast as light, but no faster. What's on this tape happened twelve years ago. *Twelve years.*"

Rosenblum looked slowly around the room, as if reading the minds of the reporters, judging their deportment. They were as silent as a classroom full of scolded children.

His thumb bent, and with an audible click he pressed the stud of the microcorder.

Rebecca Meerloo's voice was rebroadcast to the assembled reporters and to the listening world.

Michael Ward's half-eaten breakfast grew cold in his hands.

Several minutes passed before Meerloo said, "Rebecca

Meerloo, Third Officer, *Actis*, 26:03:28, ship time 20:51, end transmission."

"*Actis!*" Michael said aloud, startled, and simultaneously the whole group of reporters rose to their feet and began shouting questions.

"Please remain calm, ladies and gentlemen, be calm," Rosenblum was saying. "A complete transcript will be distributed . . ."

The digital time display in the corner of the screen read 7:30; Michael was absolutely late! His attention wavered between the TV picture and the door. Finally, with reluctance, he dropped the tray of neglected instant breakfast on his coffee table, grabbed his briefcase from the couch, and bolted from his apartment.

As he ran down the escalator three steps at a time, he realized he had forgotten to turn off the television set. He would have to phone his apartment's computer from the office and tell it to turn off the set; otherwise it would play all day long unattended, bringing talk shows and game shows and soap operas and prehistoric movies to an empty room.

The last word he had heard the TV set utter still lingered in his ears: "*Actis.*"

It was a name to conjure with. Twelve years earlier the interplanetary research vessel *Actis*, adrift with crippled engines and rushing headlong into empty space, had been sucked into the maw of a monstrous black hole.

And had disappeared from the known universe.

4

Testimony before the Senate Space Committee, Special Sub-committee to Investigate Political Unrest on the Space Settlement at L-5; 119th Congress, 1st Session; October 31, 2027 (popularly known as the *Actis* Committee).

Senator McCord: Now I want to be sure I understand what you're telling this Committee. It's your contention that these unfortunate people were actually justified in attempting to seize resources that legally belong to all the people of Earth . . .

Mister Slater: Senator, I—

Sen. McCord: Just a minute, Mr. Slater, you'll have a chance to answer my questions just as soon as I get finished asking them. Now then—these resources, these asteroidal resources, are administered by the United Nations through their Space Advisory Board, isn't that true?

Mr. Slater: Of course, Senator, but I—

Sen. McCord: And the treaties establishing that board and governing the use of these resources were signed by every member of the Security Council including the United States of America, isn't that true too?

Mr. Slater: Certainly, Senator—

Sen. McCord: Damn right, certainly! I'm not the only senator in this room who remembers what a hell of a struggle we had, putting those treaties in shape so you people over in State wouldn't give away half the solar system. You probably remember those hearings yourself, don't you, Mr. Slater?

Mr. Slater: Indeed I do, Senator.

Sen. McCord: I thought you might. So you know damn well who the asteroids belong to, and it's not L-5, is it? You know, Mr. Slater, I'll let you in on a little secret: I'm mighty surprised to find you sitting in that chair and still wearing that fancy title of yours, whatever it is, Under-assistant Secretary for Space Giveaways, or whatever the hell it is—

Mr. Pritchard: Point of order, Mr. Chairman! I object to

28

this—this browbeating of Mr. Slater. His qualifications to hold his post and to be a witness before this committee are beyond question, and in any event are not the subject of this hearing.

Sen. Gardner: The senator from Missouri will kindly stick to the matter at hand.

Sen. McCord: Mr. Chairman, I agree that the witness's qualifications—or lack of them—are properly the subject of a separate hearing. And I intend to move that we hold such a hearing at an early date.

Sen. Gardner: You'll have the opportunity, Senator, in due course. Now, is the Senator finished with the witness?

Sen. McCord: Not yet, sir. No, sir. Though I'll be brief, Mr. Chairman, for I know we have a lot of work to do before we can get to the bottom of this whole disgraceful affair. But I just want to be very sure I understand the witness. I understand him to say he knows about the United Nations treaties; that he knows the United States is party to those treaties; and presumably he knows that the space habitation called L-5 was built, paid for, and is owned and operated by the United States of America. You *do* know that, Mr. Slater?

Mr. Slater: I am not ignorant of the simple facts of law, Senator McCord. My testimony has not concerned the legality of the actions of the crew of *Actis,* but the actual causes which motivated them to—

Sen. McCord: Which *justified* them. Which *justified* them, I think you want to say, Mr. Slater, and you would say that, except you know that to say that would be tantamount to condoning treason!

Mr. Pritchard: Mr. Chairman! Objection . . .

(and several voices, general commentary in the room, unintelligible)

It was the autumn of 2024 when *Actis* left the space colony at earth-moon libration point 5, on her voyage toward the outer planets.

"Autumn" was a fiction still preserved on L-5, whose American colonists had attempted to recreate the north temperate zone in the null climate of space. Thus Captain Arnold Pratt, Ph.D. (astrophysics), could look back on an acre patch of aspens turning green-gold in the filtered sunlight of the station's interior as he rode the escalator toward the docking hub where *Actis* waited for launch. Pratt was the last crew member to leave the interior, having lingered to attend a last-minute secret meeting of the colony's Resources Management Board.

Pratt was old enough to have memories of autumn on Earth, but his feelings about that little grove of aspens, had he allowed them to surface, would have been mixed. The trees nudged at an insistent ache for the lost world of his childhood, a world that no longer existed on the surface of the Earth itself. He could not know that all humans, no matter where they had been born or raised, shared that ache: after some certain age, no one goes home again. But Pratt did know that such emotions were inefficient, counterproductive. He sternly suppressed them.

Pratt had been ten when his parents left their home in Connecticut and migrated with him to the space station, then under construction. He was forty-three now, a dour tight-lipped man who rarely shared the processes of his active mind. His reticence was congenital, not acquired—and it had survival value.

From the escalator Pratt had a commanding view down the five-kilometer length of Cylinder A, one of two counter-rotating cylinders that formed the bulk of L-5. What he saw resembled nothing so much as a late twentieth century "New Town," its upper-middle-class houses, apartments, office buildings, shopping malls, hospital, schools, lawns, parks, even a lagoon with sailboats—a total area of 25 square kilometers—all stripped neatly away from Earth and rolled up like a map. It was "midafternoon," the time determined by the bright image of the sun reflecting through the immense glass skylight that capped the far end of the cylinder. The sun never actually set on L-5; its disk remained centered in the huge Mylar mirrors that floated some distance away from the cylinder ends. Dawn, midday, evening, and night were mimicked with the aid of polarizing filters covering the skylights.

Pratt considered this bit of stage managing a luxury. Earthborn, space-matured, Pratt was a member of the colony's transitional generation, caught between two realms of experience and two political extremes.

The Founders of L-5 were spiritually bound to Earth. They had laid out the twin cylinders with towns and artificial countryside modeled after the best they knew of Earth, and set the cylinders to spinning at the exact rate needed to produce a functionally normal Earth "gravity" inside the skin. They had pressurized the cylinders with a mix of gases, notably nitrogen and oxygen, which approximated the earth's atmosphere at an altitude of 4,000 meters. The cylinders were not quite airtight; a few cubic centimeters leaked away into space each day. Oxygen was easily replaced by processing moon rocks, but the precious nitrogen had to be hauled up from Earth.

To Pratt, this was folly. Humans didn't need nitrogen, only plants did. The plants that counted were in the agricultural units that ringed the station. Inside the cylinders, the grass and the flowers and the few trees that would grow were intended for recreation. They helped to keep the air fresh, but Pratt knew there were more efficient ways to accomplish that end.

And yet, though Pratt would not admit it to himself, there was a large part of him that sympathized with the vision of the pioneers. As the escalator carried him past a cascading brook on the landscaped conical "mountain" that formed this end of Cylinder A, his eyes were distracted by the waterfall that fed the stream. Up and away it curved, falling from on high in slow motion, a graceful spiral that bent smoothly in midair like the curve of a nautilus shell. The notion of a waterfall was an earthly thing, but its unique shape was a gift of space, crafted by the vectors of the spinning cylinder. As the cool spray of water brushed his cheek, Pratt forgot to calculate that better than a tenth of its chemical weight, hydrogen, had come up from Earth.

Perhaps if the pioneers had been allowed to realize the full scope of their original vision things would have been different for Pratt. The colonization of space had begun in the 1980s with clearly stated economic goals. Earth needed energy. She was running out of fossil fuels at a frightening rate, fouling her air and water in the process. With a large pool of labor comfortably housed in space, solar power stations could be constructed to convert sunlight to microwaves and beam the energy to Earth. Within a few short decades this free and inexhaustible supply of nonpolluting energy would supply most of the world's needs. Its value would far outweigh the cost of building and maintaining the space colonies.

The colonies would grow and multiply; they would act as a long-term ecological experiment, showing what precise mix of resources and controls might be used to maintain life under the harshest possible conditions; they would manufacture exotic products cheaply in their zero-gravity, total vacuum factories; they would mount scientific experiments of a variety and scale hitherto impossible; they would care for the world's sick and aging; eventually they would even relieve Earth of her excess population. Such was the vision.

But the first large colony at L-5 was never even finished. L-5 as Pratt looked on it was only a third of its designed size, having been truncated and modified in midconstruction. The dozens of solar power satellites the colonists had already completed and put into operation were shut down. A new generation of colonists came to maturity in isolation, in resentment—and no new colonization was planned.

What had gone wrong? Nothing . . . something had gone right down on Earth, for once. Earth scientists had achieved practical large scale fusion power at the turn of the century. It was a cosmic good news, bad news joke. Earth no longer needed or wanted energy from space, which only compounded her waste heat problems. L-5's grandiose ecological experiment was rendered irrelevant. On Earth, survival under deprived conditions was no longer the question; survival with abundance, with exploding expectations, was the new challenge, and a stern one.

Pratt neared the top of the escalator. He looked out at the station's interior for the last time. From up here near the hub, the cylinder's essential nature was clear at a glance: a fragile bottle of humanity, endlessly barrel-rolling through space, with no up or down, only a delicate inside and an immense, hostile outside.

Pratt turned and lightly grasped the handrail leading into the hub structure, allowing his momentum from the escalator to propel his now-feathery weight into the padded wheel of the reception lobby.

There was no one on hand to greet visitors, for there were few casual visitors to L-5 these days. Pratt eschewed the VIP entrance to the station, a long cushioned tube that debouched in the dead center of the dome-shaped padded bulkhead of the lobby. Instead, he caromed gently off the lobby's floor/ceiling rim and steered himself toward the auxiliary personnel hatch on one side of the bulkhead. He punched the call button of the vidphone beside the hatch.

Quinn Thatcher's lined, sunburned face appeared on the screen. "At last, Arnold. Come on in," said the worried-looking launch controller.

"Trouble?" Pratt asked.

"Meet you upstairs," Thatcher replied.

Keyed by Thatcher, the iris of the hatch dilated and Pratt dove through head first, into a big hexagonal prism of a room, the cylinder's main cargo bay. The visitors' tube ran down the center of the room; steel mesh catwalks ran up and down and sideways. Elevator shaft heads studded the walls, the real working entrances to the interior. The shafts themselves radiated from the hub in six spokes that were hidden with a lot of other plumbing inside the artificial mountain Pratt had just climbed. Weightless men and women maneuvered weightless cargo in and out of the elevators, standing and walking at every conceivable angle, steering themselves and their burdens by occasionally tapping the catwalks with the electromagnets in the soles of their shoes.

To a first-time visitor who did happen to see this room, the scene was a queasy reminder of Escher's lithograph "Relativity." To Pratt, it was a familiar and natural place.

Over Pratt's head, seen through the hub's main ring bearing, the bulk of the docking terminal seemed to revolve. But it was Pratt who was spinning, along with the rest of Cylinder A. The terminal was always pointed toward the sun, its six floors stacked perpendicularly to the cylinder's axis. Inside the terminal it was always high noon and zero-g.

With a kick, Pratt launched himself "upward" through the twenty meter ring, slowing rotation by sliding along the handrail of a balcony that surrounded the wide open shaft, and letting momentum carry his legs in a graceful vault over the railing. The pressure of his heels on the steel floor activated tiny electromagnets in his shoes—toe pressure as he walked forward turned them off. The gait was almost natural. Through long experience, humans in space had learned to establish conventions for "up" and "down" in weightless areas. It made no physical difference, but it saved frazzled nerves when many people had to work together in an enclosed environment—upside-down facial expressions are not pleasant.

Pratt met Quinn Thatcher coming out of corridor E-2, which led to the launch shackles where *Actis* waited.

"What's the problem, Quinn?" Pratt asked him.

"It's not with the ship, Arnold, you can relax on that score. She's all checked and ready, and the boys and girls are all suited and waiting for final briefing." Thatcher leaned his close-cropped gray head close to Pratt, lowering his voice as he did so. "But the Space Force is with us."

"Zoomies?" said Pratt, with sour surprise.

"An inspection detail's crawling all over *Actis* right now."

"What the hell do they expect to find?"

"Frankly, I hoped you'd be able to tell me, Arnold," the older man said. "I don't like zoomies any better than you do, but I don't have any call to confront them."

Pratt looked irritably at Thatcher, then walked past him down the corridor. Thatcher was a Founder; though he might speak contemptuously of zoomies he had no political differences with them, and he knew Pratt did.

Thatcher persisted, following close behind Pratt. "Arnold, if there's more to this mission than I've been told, I think it's your duty to let me know now."

Pratt bit off his words. "Don't let your imagination run away with you. You already know the precise nature of this mission. You know more than I wanted you to. But that was the committee's decision."

"I haven't said anything about the destination of *Actis*, Arnold. As far as I'm concerned—as all of us are concerned —this is a test flight." Thatcher hesitated. "But it's your wife—"

Pratt cut him off. "She's the best navigator in the Cylinders."

"She was Rudi Nabokov's aunt," Thatcher blurted.

Pratt's mouth tightened. "That's over and done with. You're wasting my time, Thatcher. I intend to get my ship away on schedule, Space Force or no Space Force. That's all there is to say."

Thatcher's hand darted forward and plucked at Pratt's sleeve, and suddenly Pratt was floating free of the steel floor, momentarily helpless. "I'm still the launch controller here," said the space-wise old man. "That ship goes nowhere without my say-so."

Recovering from his surprise, Pratt adroitly rolled away from Thatcher's grasp. He spoke calmly. "Quinn, you don't know what you're saying. You don't know the ship. You don't know the FPC." He held up the gloved fingers of his right hand. "I can let it loose with one hand, Quinn, and when I do there's nothing in the solar system that will ever be able to catch it. And I will do it, right here if I have to, if I can't leave with your cooperation. The blast will take the docks away. But the Cylinder will survive." Pratt pushed himself closer to Thatcher. "I don't need your say-so, Quinn, and I won't allow you to get in my way."

Thatcher's face was flushed with frustrated rage. "You people can't take the Cylinders away from us, Pratt. You didn't build them. We did."

Pratt stared at him, surprised. "We're trying to give L-5 back to you, you fool," he snapped. He grounded a heel and spun away from Thatcher, launching himself down the corridor—toward the invading zoomies.

Thatcher, miserable, stared after him.

5

Now that the truly independent man of wealth has disappeared, now that the independence of the academic man is fast disappearing, where are we to find the conditions of partial alienation and irresponsibility needed for the highest creativity?

—Garrett Hardin, *Nature and Man's Fate*

The wheel of Michael Ward's beat-up Ford Flyer tried to wrench itself out of his hands as he turned, too sharply and too fast, into the parking lot of the Mathematics Instructional Committee. One of the car's flywheels had a sticky gimbal; if he didn't get it fixed it was going to kill him one of these days. This time, however, he escaped. The gyroscopic action of the faulty flywheel threw him into a sideways skid that ended, luckily, in a double parking stall.

He leaped out of the little Flyer, noting with disgust that the car was neatly trapped fore and aft by the cars of employees who had arrived on time. He decided to abandon it until lunchtime. He loped toward the door.

The MIC building was perched on the lip of a mesa east of Boulder, Colorado, where it commanded a view of the whole Front Range of the Rockies. If he had been interested Michael could have picked out his own apartment in the soleri that bridged the mouth of Boulder Canyon, arcing high above the old center of the town. A greenbelt of farms and ranches separated Boulder from the sprawling suburbs of Greater Denver to the east. Downtown Denver, fifty kilometers away, was easily located by the huge permanent thunderheads that loomed over the city's fusion generators. The two-story Mathematics Instructional Committee building was plunked down in the middle of some of the rare open space east of the mountains, a tribute to the political skill of its founders. Director Muller's office on the second floor was situated to take full advantage of the spectacular view.

But Muller was not in his office this morning, unhappily for Michael. As Michael entered the lobby, he caught sight of the director's gaunt figure lurking behind a potted rubber plant on the second-floor balcony. The route to Michael's office lay up the broad staircase to the second floor, and for a split second he contemplated turning hard right and seeking refuge in the library. But with a sinking heart Michael realized that Muller was beckoning him.

Michael trudged up the stairs as if to the guillotine. Was this the end of his job? His mind was boiling with fear, frustration, and self-contempt, all focused for the moment on his hatred of Muller. A more detached observer might have seen in Muller a sad-looking man whose distinguished features were marred by the traces of a long-gone case of severe adolescent acne. To Michael, Muller looked like one of Dr. Frankenstein's rejects.

Muller had effectively retired from the arena of active scholarship thirty years earlier, his reputation established with a proof that demolished hopes of ever solving one of the remaining Hilbert problems. In retrospect, it was a highly characteristic achievement—Muller seemed to delight in fixing the limits to knowledge, rather than in trying to expand them. Michael was certain that he was rabidly jealous of anyone who might still harbor ambitions of a real contribution to knowledge—like Michael.

The director regarded Michael coolly, and the younger man struggled to keep his own features expressionless. "When do you expect to finish the module you are developing, Dr. Ward?" asked the demon.

"It's coming along on schedule, sir." (A craven lie, thought Michael.) "The end of the month should do it."

"I'll count on it," said Muller. He gave Michael a searching glance, his dark eyes glittering. "And then we'll have to see whether we can find something else to keep you occupied, won't we?"

Sweat sprang up on Michael's forehead. "I've sent you a number of proposals, sir . . ."

"Oh, of course. They will be carefully evaluated. A number of factors must be taken into account. For example, the personal qualifications of the staff member involved."

Neither of them said anything. Michael could only stare at the floor, miserable.

"I hope I make myself clear?" Muller asked, with an unvoiced sigh intended to demonstrate how painful he found these disciplinary sessions.

"Perfectly clear, sir," gulped Michael.

"Oh, good. I'll let you get on with your work, then."

Michael could feel the director's eyes on his back as he moved toward his office, trying not to scurry away.

As he rounded the corner of the corridor his unexpressed anger curdled into a wave of guilty depression. He had no one to blame but himself for having floundered into the scientific backwater that was the Mathematics Instructional Committee. He had always lacked the mental and emotional discipline he needed if he were to make that contribution to knowledge he pretended to aspire to. His mind toyed with one subject after another, discarding each before he'd dug deeply enough to make any real headway. His arrogant manners (held precariously in check these days) had alienated even those former bosses who'd recognized his brilliance. In short order he'd lost an instructorship at a major university, an associate professorship at a community college, a consulting job with an insurance company—and finally he'd come to this: he was a translator of work others had done a century or more before him. He was a popularizer, a hack.

He opened the door to his tiny windowless office and flicked on the overhead fluorescent light. Its pallid imitation of natural skylight picked out the disorganized piles of papers on his cluttered desk, the books lying haphazardly on every flat surface (some bristling with scrappaper page markers, others sprawled open, face down and exhausted), and finally that awkward edifice surmounting his file cabinet—the focus and only visible evidence of his current work—a fish tank full of soapy water. A superstructure of bent coat hangers was rigged over its open top. Suspended from the coat hangers on strands of fishing line were several delicate geometrical shapes made of thin copper wire; when lowered into the soap and gently withdrawn, the wire shapes formed shimmering jewels of curved intersecting surfaces, elegant little topologies.

Michael's current assignment, the project that held him to his salaried position by a thread finer than the monofilament suspending his soap-film frames, was to lead high school students from the contemplation of these lovely analogues, with their direct appeal to the brain's geometric intuition, toward some ability to manipulate symbols expressing the same spaces abstractly (along with others that could not even be visualized). He had hardly made a good start.

Michael threw his briefcase unopened onto his desk, and sat down in the desk chair, hard. He leaned his elbows on the desk and planted his chin between his palms, staring morosely at the soap-film contraption. He knew that as his deadline approached he could cobble together some amusing parlor tricks, with Möbius strips and interlocking paper rings for example, and throw in a few definitions so a kid could tell a one-holed donut from a two-holed donut, and he could call the mishmash an instructional unit. What depressed him was that Muller would probably be delighted by the result. The MIC tended to peddle curriculum by the kilo; the more hardware the better.

But the basic tools that might allow a student to transform imagination into experience would be lacking. If there was no royal road to the learning of mathematics, there was no royal road to the teaching of it, either.

Michael caught himself thinking of his student audience with sympathy, even with respect. A dangerous tendency, utterly without survival value in this profession.

For a moment Michael saw himself clearly, free of the grip of stormy emotion, of ambition, aggression, and guilt. It was plain that if he really wanted to hold onto his job he could do so easily, simply by giving Muller what the man wanted and nothing more. It was equally plain that the job would become worse than useless to him if those were the conditions for keeping it. The solution seemed simple enough: he would attempt to do a good, honest piece of work, fulfilling his responsibilities to his employer, his consumers, and his own ability.

But there was the rub. For while translating topology's rudimentary principles might be a worthy challenge to a good teacher, it was not one to engage the powerful mathematical engine now rusting in Michael's brain. He might try with good conscience to do the work society was willing to pay him for (as he did now, bending over a scratch pad with pocket computer in hand), but the dreamer in him would not let him concentrate. Lately the dreamer's dreams had bubbled up again.

He caught himself staring at his soap-film apparatus. He got up from his desk, leaned over the fish tank, turned the little wire crank that lowered and then raised the frames. The shapes glistened wetly in the cold blue light, their curving membranes trembling in invisible currents of air.

And then he knew what it was that called to him—the far deep thing that had awakened his sleeping dreams and now tugged at his imagination.

Twelve years ago, when he was still in his late teens, it had consumed him with enthusiasm. Eventually he had forgotten about it, though the books he'd devoured and the courses he'd crammed had stayed with him, had in fact set him on the course of his wayward mathematical career. It was invisible, this thing of mystery and horror, though his mind's eye could detect its faint quantum radiation, and the coordinates of collapsing spacetime, which vanished somewhere in its hidden center. The black hole—the whirlpool in space that had swallowed *Actis,* and as he and the rest of the world had learned this morning, spit her out again—now had him once again in its inexorable grip.

Michael went to the door of his office and pulled it open a crack. He glanced surreptitiously up and down the hall to make sure Muller was not stalking him, then stepped out and quickly made his way toward Roger Crain's office.

6

Testimony before the Senate Space Committee, Subcommittee to Investigate Political Unrest on the Space Settlement at L-5; 119th Congress, 1st Session, November 4, 2027

General Hamlyn: Senator, I wish I could give you a better answer, but I can't. All I can do is repeat something we all learned as cadets: "God's universe is vast, and man's ships are slow."

(pause)

Senator McCord: General, I'm familiar with your excellent service record; I'm familiar with the duties of the high post you now hold. Perhaps you will be good enough to recall that I have, in the past, given you my support when I thought your plans and recommendations were in the best interests of the service and our nation.

Gen. Hamlyn: I sure as hell do remember, Senator, and I appreciate it!

Sen. McCord: Please don't quote nursery rhymes to me when I ask you serious questions.

Gen. Hamlyn: My apologies, Senator.

Sen. McCord: I ask you again: how did the Space Force fail to detect and prevent the illegal activities of the ship *Actis,* whose activities resulted in tragic loss of life and numerous other casualties, which it was your sworn duty to avert?

(no response from the witness)

Sen. McCord: General?

Gen. Hamlyn: Senator, I hesitate—

Sen. McCord: That's not your privilege here.

Gen. Hamlyn: Well, sir, then I respectfully suggest you ask your daughter. Major McCord was the last Space Force officer on that ship. She was the last of us who saw any of those people alive.

(general commotion in the chamber, unintelligible)

Sen. Gardner: Order! Order! If we can't have order I will adjourn this hearing.

(general discussion continues, unintelligible)

Sen. Gardner: Senator McCord?

Sen. McCord: Just a moment, Mr. Chairman.

(Sen. McCord confers with Chief Counsel Levine, privately)

Sen. Gardner: Senator McCord, are you through with the witness?

Sen. McCord: Mr. Chairman, before I excuse the witness I wish to remind him that—his high rank notwithstanding— he is subject to proceedings for contempt of Congress just like any other man or woman who testifies before this Committee . . .

(general loud commotion in the chamber, unintelligible)

Sen. Gardner: Order! Order!

Gen. Hamlyn: Mr. Chairman . . .

Sen. Gardner: General Hamlyn, the Chair must advise you . . .

Gen. Hamlyn: Sir, I just want to say that I'd like to withdraw my last remark . . .

Sen. Gardner: It will remain on the record, General.

Gen. Hamlyn: . . . and I want to apologize to the Senator from Missouri. I realize I spoke improperly.

Sen. Gardner: I'm sure the Senator will accept your apology. This hearing is adjourned for one half hour, or until we can all get a rein on our tempers and proceed more calmly. The witness will hold himself available.

Seconds after he had left Quinn Thatcher fuming, Arnold Pratt reached the double bulkhead that separated the corridor from the E-2 ready room. Through the thick glass port he could see the other members of the *Actis* crew, pressure-suited but helmetless, waiting for his arrival. He pressed the com button beside the hatch.

"Let me in, Pat," he said.

Pat O'Connor, his co-pilot, drifted across the room and released the hatch's magnetic locks from inside. The double doors moved aside, and Pratt floated into the room.

The ready room was crowded with unhappy people. Pratt mentally called the roll: the co-pilot O'Connor; Rebecca Meerloo, communications officer; Marston Smith-Jones, engineer; Anton Meerloo, quartermaster; Louise Chew, physician; Nancy Wilson Duquesnes, programmer; finally, Pratt's wife Angela, the navigator. Also on hand were the assistant launch controller and the launch bay crew chief.

Pratt was oddly struck by how young everybody looked.

He and Angela were a decade older than all the rest; they were the only two members of the crew of *Actis* who had not been born in space.

There was one more figure in the room: a space-suited guard with helmet down and sealed. He stood beside the airlock door, which opened into the tube leading directly to the ship. He held a gas gun.

Pratt went to his pressure suit hanging on the wall. Slowly and deliberately he began to put it on, keeping his eyes on the guard as he did so. The guard shifted uneasily, but said nothing.

The crew chief, a kid named Sanchez, came over to help Pratt with the bulky suit, while O'Connor stood by.

"How long have they been out there, Pat?" Pratt asked in a low voice.

"About an hour now. There's three of them, besides that punk by the door: a major and two noncoms."

"We tried to call you, sir, but the committee said they couldn't locate you," said Sanchez.

"Just as well," said Pratt. He straightened up and reached for his helmet.

"They won't let you put that on," Sanchez warned him. "They don't want anybody going outside."

"Stay out of this, son. You too, Pat." Pratt picked up his helmet and started to lower it over his head.

"No helmets, those are my orders," the Space Force guard shouted through his helmet speaker.

Pratt's estimate of the situation was confirmed by the guard's tinny, amplified voice: he was a nervous youth whose superiors did not even trust him with a dart gun, which could penetrate a space suit and was therefore potentially lethal. Pratt stared at the guard steadily as he fastened his helmet in place.

"Sir . . ." said the guard uncertainly.

Pratt yanked at the helmet seal and simultaneously launched himself toward the guard. He clicked magnetic heels to the floor a few inches away from the boy.

"Sir, I respectfully request . . ." the guard quavered.

"Your warrant," Pratt demanded, his voice booming from his helmet speaker.

"What, sir?" Inside his helmet, the guard was sweating. Pratt saw that he was indeed a boy, no more than nineteen.

"You are detaining my crew against their will. If you have a legal warrant to do so, show it to me now."

"Sir, I'm acting on the orders of Major McCord. She said—"

"Bring her here," Pratt ordered.

"Sir, she said no one was to enter the ship until she had completed her inspection."

"Bring her here within fifteen seconds, or I will disarm you and place you under arrest."

The look on the young soldier's face showed he believed Pratt could do it. He lowered his useless gas gun, tabbed his helmet radio with a nervous thrust of his chin, and said something muffled into the microphone.

A few seconds later the tense group in the ready room heard the outer hatch of the airlock clang shut. A few seconds after that, the heavy inner hatch swung open. Inside the airlock stood three space-suited figures, all with dart pistols at the ready. A major's gold pentagons emblazoned the helmet of the smaller figure in the lead. The face inside that helmet was calm, totally concentrated on the moment, prepared to take action.

It was also a beautiful face. Major McCord was a woman no more than twenty-five, with deep green eyes, a full mouth, and soft dark red hair longer than regulation length.

Major McCord took a moment to look around the room. Seeing no threat, she smiled and holstered her gun, signaling the noncoms behind her to do likewise. She stepped out of the airlock.

"You shouldn't frighten my men, Doctor Pratt," she said, as she began to unfasten her helmet. "Accidents happen that way."

She pulled the helmet away and her long hair, loosely restrained by a green ribbon, floated out around her head.

Pratt tugged at the latch of his helmet seal and took it off. He looked at the young woman. "Children have no business playing with guns."

McCord turned to the men in the airlock. "Secure everything as you found it and report to level C." She looked at the young guard. "You go and meet them. Use the corridor."

The guard leaped to obey, flying across the room and crashing awkwardly against the corridor bulkhead in his haste.

"Are you admitting this is an unauthorized search?" Pratt demanded.

"I've seen enough. *Actis* is a very interesting vessel, Doctor Pratt."

"Tell me why you're here," said Pratt.

"Ostensibly, because Moon Base Command is nervous about your FPC. Oh yes, we have some idea of its capabilities," McCord said quickly. "We keep our ears open around here; I'm sure that comes as no surprise to you."

"We've made no secret of our hopes for the device," Pratt replied calmly. "If you'd asked, we'd have given you a guided tour. You didn't have to muscle your way in."

"A guided tour is not what we had in mind. It's a very impressive device, Doctor. Did you have a hand in its design?"

"No, I didn't," Pratt replied shortly.

"Even so, you must know it well. Our pet scientists think you people might have the know-how and the technical capacity to rig it as a hydrogen bomb. Given your crew . . ." McCord glanced at Angela Pratt, "they also think you might have a motive for doing so."

Pratt's taciturn expression threatened to dissolve, flickering between outrage and laughter. Angela Pratt, the least political person he knew, was condemned to guilt by association with her dead nephew Rudi Nabokov—the infamous revolutionary who may or may not have tried to blow up Moon Base two years before.

Tempering Pratt's instinct to defend Angela was his delight: the mission's "test flight" cover story seemed to be serving its purpose. It had never occurred to him that the Fusion Product Collimator could be converted to a bomb, but he was glad the Space Force was concentrating its attention on the experimental FPC propulsion system.

McCord smiled at the play of fleeting expressions on Pratt's face. "Of course, I agree with you, Doctor—that's all nonsense. A theoretical possibility, maybe. Not a practical one, as anybody who knows as much about ships as you and I would recognize at once."

"Good," Pratt said. *How much do you know about ships?* he wondered. "Then you'll get out of our way and let us proceed with the countdown." He signaled the crew to board.

"Go ahead. But if you like I'll tell you what my inspection *did* reveal."

Pratt stopped, trying to look impatient.

"First," said McCord, "you're supplied for a voyage of up to two years. That's excessive for a test run of a few million kilometers."

"Normal precaution," said Pratt. "New engines don't always turn off when you tell them to."

"Second," said the woman, "the midsection of your ship is beefed up for reasons that aren't at all apparent. What kind of stresses are you expecting? Or are those stringers something more than they seem?"

"Talk to the designers."

"And your crew," McCord continued. "Your co-pilot and your communications officer are both also geologists; your quartermaster is a cartographer, your engineer is a physicist, your doctor is a chemist, your programmer is a working astronomer. That's a useful set of specialties for, say, an asteroidal prospecting and mining operation."

Pratt sighed. "We're all miners and the children of miners on L-5, Major. That's how we built the place, remember? Nobody qualified for space flight lacks a similar range of abilities. Now I'm out of time . . ."

Pratt lifted his helmet to his head, and the other crew members did the same.

McCord made no move to stop them, but as Pratt reached for the airlock controls she spoke over her suit radio so that all could hear her. "I think you misunderstand me. I hope your mission will be successful. That's unofficial, of course. But if you have any notion of keeping what you find to yourself, forget it. You're still citizens of the United States, and subject to its laws. It's my duty to enforce those laws, and I intend to."

Pratt looked out of his helmet at the beautiful, arrogant Space Force major, and knew that he had met an enemy. As he turned to enter the airlock, he also knew it would not be the last time he confronted Major McCord. He was right in a way he could not possibly have imagined.

Eight hours later the countdown drew to a close. Pratt sat cushioned in the command seat of the control module of *Actis*, closed in by banks of tightly clustered dials, CRT screens, diode arrays, switch panels, nested levers, knurled wheels, banks of potentiometers. He looked forward through the small quartz window in the ship's nose at empty space before him. In the left side of the window a small portion of the Cylinder A docking terminal was visible, its stark white paint glaring against the black of space, all that Pratt could see of the home he was leaving behind.

Behind him, hidden from view, stretched the two-hundred

meter length of *Actis,* a maze of exposed pipes and cables, pumps and valves, access tubes and beams, supply bays and solar panels, antennas and sensors, fuel tanks and rocket nozzles.

As "T" reached zero, the automatic sequencer fired the auxiliary chemical rockets; Pratt was pushed gently down into his contoured couch. The visible scrap of the docking terminal slid smoothly away.

Amid the clamor of data demanding his attention, Pratt found time to reflect with amusement on the surprise that awaited Major McCord and anyone else who tried to track his ship.

Actis was outbound.

7

Escape velocity. The minimum velocity that a body must attain to overcome the gravitational attraction of another body, such as the earth.

—*American Heritage Dictionary*

It was 10:30 A.M. Eastern time when Colonel Laura McCord finally turned off her desk-top television set. The news conference at Searchlight Base had ended fifteen minutes before, and the television commentators on all five networks were beginning to repeat themselves. McCord touched the com button on her desk. A young man's face appeared on the screen.

"Yes, Colonel?" the sergeant asked.

"Any luck reaching Captain Donner?" asked McCord.

"No, ma'am, he's been unavailable," replied her secretary. "I'll keep trying."

"Okay. What have I missed so far this morning?"

"Well, Colonel, at 8:30 there was a conference call scheduled with General Olsen and General Wilbur. They canceled. At 9:00 you were supposed to go to a faculty meeting. You canceled."

"Nothing ever happens at those things anyway."

"Yes, ma'am. At 11:00 you're scheduled to review the Levine case with the Cadet Honor Representative."

"Where's Levine now?"

"Should be in his quarters, Colonel."

"Get him over here right away. I want to see him alone before I meet with that other little prig."

The sergeant smiled. "Right away, Colonel. Is that it?"

"For now. Don't forget about Donner."

"Yes, Colonel." The picture blinked off.

McCord got up from her desk and went to the picture

window. She was thirty-eight now, but one had to stand very close to notice any difference between the Laura McCord of today and the Laura McCord who had confronted Arnold Pratt on L-5 almost fourteen years earlier. A long tour of duty at Moon Base does that for people: in one-sixth gravity the aging processes slow down. McCord was more a beauty than ever.

She had long been aware of the expectations aroused by physical beauty, and, perhaps because of her relatively carefree childhood, she had never been uncomfortable with her looks; she had grown wise and practical enough to use them to precise advantage. She had no idea why people persisted in believing that a handsome man or woman was also a worthy leader (despite repeated evidence that there was no correlation), but in her case they were not mistaken. It was one of the factors that seemed to have fated her to command.

She had only once, and briefly, tried to escape her fate. Her father managed to annul and conceal her disastrous marriage before the press or public learned of it. Since that short escapade, the summer after she graduated from the Air Force Academy, her career had been an uninterrupted rise to prominence.

Until the last few years . . . There was little she could do to object when she was assigned as Provost to the newly formed Space Force Academy, but she knew the post was intended to keep her out of action. She had not been near the controls of a ship, except to maintain her pilot's rating, in over five years. She was forcefully reminded of her agonizing boredom every time she looked out the window of her office at the dreary quadrangle of the temporary campus several floors below.

The Academy looked its grimmest on days like these, miserable wet drizzly days that seemed to melt the old brick buildings. Rain was almost constant in New York since the earth's mean temperature had risen a few degrees, a condition that was aggravated locally by the microclimatic effects of the city's huge fusion generators. But to McCord it hardly mattered that the Army had a castle on the Hudson, the Navy had a lovely Georgian campus on Chesapeake Bay, the Air Force had a glass box and a whole mountain behind it, while the Space Force had a collection of old office buildings in midtown Manhattan. They were all on earth. Her heart was in space.

She would do almost anything to get back, even if it meant calling on her father for help one more time.

The com unit buzzed. She crossed to the desk.

"Yes?"

"Cadet Levine to see you, Colonel."

"Send him in."

Levine opened the door of the office and almost immediately snapped into a brace, his chin developing a couple of extra wrinkles as he pushed it into his chest. His arm bent stiffly into a salute.

"Cadet Levine reporting as ordered, ma'am!" he barked.

McCord returned the salute. "Ease off a little, Levine. You don't have to shout in here."

Levine dropped his hand. "Yes, ma'am," he said more quietly.

"Sit down. Over here, by the table."

McCord took a seat on the couch in front of the coffee table in the corner of the room, and directed Levine to a comfortable chair close to her. She noticed the gold stars on the collar of his black tunic: a scholar. His thinning black hair belied the youthful nervous features of his face; he looked like an old man trapped in a boy's body.

She picked up his file from the table and pretended to glance through it, although she had already studied its contents. She put it back down on the table and stared at the miserable cadet.

"So you were caught using a computer during an exam. Why did you do that?"

"No excuse, ma'am."

"Don't use that bullshit with me, Levine." Her voice stayed even, but her green eyes blazed. "I want every detail."

The cadet looked at her, then down at his hands. "Geometrodynamics. Take home, closed computers. One of the problems involved Penrose twistors. I'm pretty familiar with those operations, but I couldn't seem to get a result that made sense. It occurred to me that perhaps the problem might have had an—a misprint."

"You think the instructor goofed, you mean," McCord prompted him, amused.

"Uh, yes, ma'am. So I retrieved the equations. That's when Cadet Prinz came in."

"And were you right?"

"In fact, Colonel, I was," said Levine.

She smiled and shook her head. "Did you explain this to the Honor Board, or did you just try that 'no excuse' crap?"

"I did explain it, Colonel. It was their view that the rules of the exam were explicit. Calculators, but no computers."

"Well, next time guard your rear, Levine. It looks to me like Prinz was laying for you."

The cadet was surprised, but cautious. "You think so, Colonel? I admit the thought had occurred to me, but —"

"Never mind. Forget I said anything. I'm dismissing the Board's recommendation."

Relief spread over Levine's face. "Thank you, Colonel. I don't—"

"Store it. You're aware I know your father?"

"Yes, Colonel, he's mentioned it."

"He's been very important to the Space Force. Many people will undoubtedly assume that's why I'm letting you off. It's not, but you'll just have to deal with it on your own."

"I can handle it," said Levine, sounding much more confident.

McCord reflected that unless his father chose to tell him, the cadet would never know just how important the elder Levine had been to the Space Force, or to Laura's own career. She was intensely relieved that the boy was in fact innocent of the charges against him, for if he had not been, she would have faced the bitter choice of betraying her old friend, or her own honor.

"Well, I suppose you'll be in touch with your father soon?" she asked casually.

"Oh, yes, I'll phone him right away to tell him the news."

"Ask him to call me, will you? I appreciate the fact that he hasn't wanted to interfere, but now that the matter's cleared up I'd like to speak with him."

"I'll be glad to tell him—"

"Privately," McCord cut in. "Outside of channels."

"Whatever you say, Colonel."

"Good. That will be all, Cadet. Keep out of trouble."

She and the young man stood up at the same time. He saluted, and she returned the salute. He turned stiffly and left the room.

McCord walked to her desk and pressed the com button. "Is Prinz here?"

"Yes, Colonel."

"Send him in."

Cadet Colonel Prinz, the Wing's Honor Representative, stepped through the door and snapped a salute. "Cadet Prinz reporting . . ." he began.

"Store it," McCord rasped. "If I informed you that you were relieved of your duties as a cadet and reassigned to a radar station in Greenland pending reduction in rank, would you know *why*, Prinz?"

Prinz said nothing, but his fair skin blushed red to the roots of his blond crewcut.

"That's right," said McCord, "don't say anything. It would have to be either a confession or a lie. But remember I've got my eye on you, Prinz. Don't ever try to get rid of a rival with a cheap stunt like that again. Clear?"

"Perfectly clear, Colonel," he said sullenly.

"Now go cry on the Commandant's shoulder."

"Is that all, Colonel?" said the rigid cadet.

"That's all."

This time she returned his salute. She grinned to herself as she watched him leave. She was sure the little snitch would go straight to her superior, General Wilbur. Good. Anything was a plus if it helped convince the General he could do without his present provost.

The com unit buzzed. "Yes?"

"Captain Donner on the line from Searchlight, Colonel."

"Put him on."

Donner's smiling face came on the screen. "Good morning, Colonel. How are you getting along with that horny bunch of graduate students?"

McCord laughed. "I remember now—you were the last man through these rusty gates who tried to give me any trouble, Captain."

"And you fixed my wagon quick enough," Donner sighed. "Well, what can I do for you?"

"Ted, I'd sure like to get my hands on the telemetry data from that signal you people are picking up."

Donner's eyes widened with interest, but then he assumed a look of regret. "Gee, Laura, I'd really like to help, but that information is being handled on a need-to-know basis. Have you put in a request through Talbot's office?"

"I'd rather not get turned down. You're clever at these things, Ted. Can't you think of something? You know, in the interests of higher education?"

Donner hesitated. "An aging captain in a backwater base doesn't have a lot of pull, Colonel."

McCord smiled. Down to brass tacks. She said, "I have something in mind, Ted, and if it develops the way I hope, it will give all of us a chance for some action. And visibility."

Donner came back fast: "And if it doesn't develop?"

"I'll get you out of there in any case, Ted. Depend on me."

"I will. I'll get back to you later. I have a number in my little black book that says 'Laura McCord, private' . . ."

"It's still good," she said.

"Nice talking to you again, Laura."

"Good-bye, Ted." She keyed off the vidphone.

McCord leaned back in her chair, looking at the rain through the window. It was going to be tricky to fit all the pieces together. There were the political aspects, both inside and outside the service—those could get messy. There was the money, a lot of it, though with the politics solved that should be easy. And then there was the little matter of nature: what McCord wanted to do was physically impossible, according to all the scientists and mathematicians. At least that was the assumption until this morning.

But where *Actis* had gone, another ship could follow. And—presumably—come back to tell the tale.

8

Testimony before the Senate Space Committee, Special Subcommittee to Investigate Political Unrest on the Space Settlement at L-5; 119th Congress, 1st Session; December 2, 2027

Senator McCord: Sorry if I sound dense, Professor, but I'd just like you to go over that last part again, in layman's terms, if you don't mind. So that we can all get a clear picture of what happened.

Doctor de Giulio: I'll do my best, Senator. Basically the L-5 people didn't realize their device would set up powerful secondary lines of force due to resonance effects caused by the particular crystalline structures of the rock. That happened with the result—excuse me, Senator, I mean we think that's what happened, but of course we can only guess at the true sequence of events.

Sen. McCord: We understand that, Professor. So the result was an explosion, then?

Dr. de Giulio: No. A sustained thermonuclear reaction, Senator. You see, these lines of tremendous magnetic force squeezed the hydrogen fuel together, causing fusion of the nuclei—and at the same time this force prevented the rock from being vaporized. Analogous to what goes on in any ordinary power plant or rocket motor, but scaled up by orders of magnitude greater than anything ever imagined before. It must have been horrible for them, really.

Sen. McCord: Well, just as an added comment, Professor, I suppose your people are working to prevent that sort of thing from happening again, eh?

Dr. de Giulio: Oh, no sir, we're doing our best to make it happen!

(laughter in the chamber, and general commentary, unintelligible)

Dr. de Giulio: "I'm sorry, Senator, I did not mean to make a joke.

Sen. McCord: I understand, Professor.

Dr. de Giulio: I only meant this new and unexpected effect

is of great theoretical interest. We wish to understand it better.

Sen. McCord: This effect has potential use as a weapon?

Dr. de Giulio: Weapons are not my specialty, Senator.

Sen. McCord: That will be all, Professor. Thank you.

March, 2026: In the year and a half since *Actis* had left L-5 she had undergone a space-change. Never an elegant craft, she was now an unrecognizable hybrid monster. The blunt white nose of her command module was still there, and the ring of ejection pods immediately below—six two-seaters, their ceramic heat shields staring blindly out at the stars. From there all resemblance to a spaceship ended. Her once compact crew quarters had spread laterally into a pile of boxes, something resembling a cheap apartment house on Earth. Beneath the crew quarters *Actis* simply disappeared, swallowed up by a vast cancerous growth of black and pitted rock that swelled around her and stretched away behind for almost twenty kilometers. Like some great wasp in the grip of reproductive urges, *Actis* had burrowed tail first into an asteroid.

Asteroid 2L-5 2394 was a carbonaceous chondrite, a storehouse of carbon, hydrogen, rare metals, dozens of compounds and elements condensed billions of years ago out of the primitive nebula from which the solar system had formed. Its millions of tons of raw materials were those on which L-5 depended for survival, which the colony could not get from its mines on the moon, and therefore those on which Earth held a monopoly. The asteroid was the rock on which the independence of L-5 would be founded.

Seen from the asteroid's horizon, only a few hundred meters away from what was left of the old *Actis*, the ship's remains rose like a medieval keep against the eternal night sky. The squat tower was silhouetted against the squashed disk of Jupiter, as big and red as a harvest moon. A warm yellow glow shone from one domed window, a touch of life in the frozen dark.

Inside the ship, a party was in progress.

"Happy birthday, Arnold. Let me give you a kiss," said Nancy Duquesnes, leaning, with lips puckered, toward Arnold Pratt.

Pratt turned fractionally away, and the kiss glanced off his cheekbone. "You'll spill your champagne," the gaunt captain warned. "Besides, my birthday was a month ago."

"Who keeps track of time?" Nancy retorted. "Unbend a

little. Have some fun. You deserve it, we all do." The expression on her long, elegantly horsy face was playful, as if she were wondering how far she could push him.

Pratt was conscious of Angela's eyes on both of them, and he felt a stab of guilt. He had done nothing to warrant suspicion, but in the close confines of the ship even thoughts were enough. And to thoughts he must confess.

Angela Pratt turned back to her conversation with Pat O'Connor. Angela's makeup gave her a false high color, and she had done her graying blond hair in lopsided curls. She was laughing a bit more than the level of gaiety in the room could explain; the handsome, wavy-haired copilot seemed uncomfortable. Arnold Pratt's guilt turned to sadness.

"Excuse me, Nancy, I want to check on something with Marston," said Pratt, sidling away from her.

"Stick-in-the-mud," she accused, but she was smiling at him.

Pratt stepped around a rattan armchair—the cramped wardroom of *Actis* had been furnished with three of them in a misconceived attempt to relieve the monotony of padded plastic and polished aluminum. He ducked under a Boston fern, which was splayed like a sea urchin in the minimal gravity, and drifted up to Marston Smith-Jones just as the gangling young physicist was uncorking another bottle of Moët-Chandon, '13. The cork fired out of the bottle and a stream of bubbles flew clear across the room.

"Don't waste it!" Pat O'Connor yelled in mock alarm. "It's the only thing made on Earth that's worth a damn."

"Hear, hear," agreed Marston, while he aimed the foamy stream at a plastic cup held at arm's length. "Hold this, Arnold," he ordered, shoving the full cup into Pratt's free hand and grabbing another from the bar top. The champagne filled that cup too, and kept on flowing. In desperation Marston stuck the end of the bottle in his mouth. His rosy cheeks bulged and his eyes popped, but somehow he managed to contain it.

Everyone in the small room turned to watch the show.

"Some physicist you are," jeered Anton Meerloo, one arm around his wife's waist. "Don't even know Boyle's law."

Marston came up for air; with great dignity, and with champagne dripping from his chin, he glared at Anton. "I'll have you know I am a *theoretical* physicist. The *real* world is a total mystery to me."

"Obviously, or you wouldn't be here," Nancy observed dryly.

"Hear! hear!" said Anton, mimicking Marston. "Just like the rest of us."

"What's Boyle's law?" asked Pat O'Connor.

"You remember. Champagne boils in low gravity," drawled Nancy.

A chorus of groans mingled with choked laughter.

"All right, I apologize," Nancy shouted. "Just hand me another glass, and I promise to shut up."

Arnold Pratt looked at her, and then at all of them, and for a moment he was flooded with love. Must be the champagne, he thought; but the emotion refused to go away. It was nothing short of a miracle that they were all still here, four men and four women who had transformed one small world and were about to transform another.

The Committee planners on L-5 had warned him there was a high probability of one death, and that they had been prepared for two. Yet in the long year of exhausting, critically sensitive work only recently completed, there had been just one really close call. Pratt stole a glance at Louise Chew's twisted left hand, and was pleased to see she no longer tried to keep it out of sight as she had for many weeks after her accident. The hand had been crushed under a weightless but massive valve that ground into her with relentless inertia as she tried to guide it into place. Her suit had ruptured, but the others had reached her before she lost consciousness; the young doctor had directed her own emergency surgery.

Arnold Pratt was not the sort who agonized over past errors, or who congratulated himself on past accomplishments, not when the major goal still waited to be won. The goal was close, now—soon the asteroid, four times as long as L-5 itself, would rest in orbit beside the space colony, and Earth's economic hold would be broken. As he reviewed the past eighteen months, Pratt's rigid self-discipline yielded to pride.

Actis had eluded the Space Force with ease, although the maneuver required the vast number-crunching power of the ship's outsized computer and the expenditure of almost all her fuel. After delicately easing herself into position, *Actis* had fired her FPC at full thrust for several hours, and then cut off her engines. Aboard *Actis*, Rebecca Meerloo received the probing radar beams of the Space Force's searching antennas. But the ship maintained radio silence, and could not be tracked. Soon the ship had made it impossible for watchers in Earth orbit to determine her true velocity, her position, or her target. Vanishingly small in cross section, *Actis* effectively disappeared into the cosmos. And before she reached her final destination she had interposed the sun between her target and Earth.

The mineral riches of the asteroids were known to all; that L-5 had not tapped them earlier was a matter of politics, not of practicalities. The United States government was an absentee landlord on L-5, preferring to maintain the colony as a useful site for dangerous experiments, and other activities impossible to pursue on Earth. The U.S. had no desire to see the "protectorate" of L-5 grow in size, or gain its independence. Therefore the United States hypocritically held to the concords that prevented any nation from appropriating the resources of space to its own use. (Earlier, when L-5 had been seen as more important—even vital to the country's future—the U.S. had brushed aside objections to mining the moon. Things had long since changed.)

Speed was the essence of *Actis'* mission. She must capture an asteroid and start toward Earth before the government could interfere, and the asteroid must arrive at the space colony weeks, or even months, before it was expected.

When the truth finally dawned on the Space Force, L-5 would rise up and revolt. It would be a swift, forceful coup, with at least half the population in support. And then, worldwide opinion, a determined revolutionary militia, and hoarded resources would be sufficient to hold the Space Force at bay until the asteroid was in position. Once L-5 could not be starved into submission, it would be free.

Actis had already done her part to make the audacious plan a success. Aided by the enormously powerful FPC drive, *Actis* had arrived among the lead Trojans in only four months. She surveyed asteroid 2L-5 2394 and confirmed the colony's hopes (based on long-range photometric studies): the asteroid was prodigiously rich in hydrocarbons.

Weeks of painstaking measurement and mapping followed. Sensitive gravitometers determined the precise axis of mass through the length of the asteroid. *Actis* positioned herself, sank great bolts into the rock, and turned on her main engine. The first drilling beam was needle-thin, shaped by the magnetic nozzle of the FPC. Searing blobs of molten rock gushed from the drill hole—finally the shaft was sunk clear through the rock.

Radioactive lava began escaping through the slender shaft into space, at the far end of the asteroid; finally the shaft was widened enough to permit some steering of the FPC through the tube. Now the top of the shaft was widened still further; *Actis* settled into the hole.

The precious hydrogen fuel loaded aboard *Actis* at L-5 was long gone, most of it consumed in the escape from Earth orbit. *Actis* now worked with fuel refined from the asteroid itself. Lasers powered from the ship's MHD generators carved a honeycomb of chambers into the asteroid. Solar mirrors built from empty fuel tanks distilled crushed rock into water, and the water was electrolytically separated into hydrogen and oxygen. The process became virtually automated, and the stony tanks of the asteroid filled with pressurized hydrogen until they held enough for all the power plants and rocket motors of L-5 for a siege of years.

Actis reconnected her plumbing to the interior of the asteroid; the asteroid became part of *Actis*.

And all these many months the exhaust of the FPC fled down the long central tube, gently but persistently nudging the asterioid out of the comfortable berth in gravity's cradle she had held for billions of years.

It was all part of an intricate battle plan drawn up by the clandestine efforts of a hundred L-5 scientists and engineers, nourished by L-5's thirty years of experience mining the moon, inflamed by the revelations of the Nabokov affair, and now, finally, executed by four men and four women working around the clock for a year.

The mighty FPC was the key to the plan, but except for its scale it was the least experimental part of *Actis;* only now that she was bound in symbiosis with the asteroid was *Actis* truly complete.

There came a day when the full power of the new *Actis* was unleashed.

Liquid hydrogen flowed into the combustion chamber at the rate of several grams per second; if it were not expelled on the instant a thermonuclear explosion would have consumed the asteroid in the blink of an eye. But the FPC crushed the hydrogen into helium in its fiery womb at a temperature greater than that at the core of the sun, hurling the newborn particles away with the energy of their own creation, amplifying and focusing that titanic progeny into a massive beam of light that lanced across the stars.

Actis could not hope to hide herself now; the light that blazed from her was brighter than a thousand comets. Instead, she hoped to deceive and surprise her adversaries.

Deception first: her thrust vector was chosen to maintain the asteroid in the orbit of Jupiter while moving closer to the giant planet—or, depending on one's frame of reference, to slow down the rock in space until Jupiter caught up. It was a seemingly senseless route back to Earth, for the asteroid had to be dragged almost twice the distance of a direct trajectory home.

Yet Jupiter was the linchpin of the plan. As the asteroid fell into that planet's gravity well, which was shaped by a mass more than two and a half times that of all the other planets and asteroids together, the rock would be whipped out of orbit and slingshot toward Earth with all the speed it had accumulated and more.

And then, surprise: the FPC would blaze out once more, braking the onrush of the asteroid. Only then could the true position of the hybrid *Actis* be plotted, and by then she would be only days from Earth, while the revolt on L-5 would be at its height.

Pratt stood alone now in the darkened wardroom, having made some excuse to stay behind while the others wandered off to bed one at a time. The party was over at last—it had gone on and on, the crew apparently unwilling to let go of the first real party they had allowed themselves since before leaving L-5.

Even without them the unsightly vessel, ninety-nine percent rock, was functioning perfectly; its homeostatic functions were routinely monitored by the exceedingly competent computer; the miniature sun at its core was self-sustaining, driving the largest object in the history of the solar system ever to fly under human guidance.

As Pratt gazed from the room's plastic dome, the misshapen disk of Jupiter, low on the asteroid's horizon, seemed to grow perceptibly closer. The emotions which earlier had taken him out of himself were suppressed now, and cool logic tinged with wariness had possessed him again.

Tomorrow he would put the ship on radiation alert; that meant wearing bulky suits twenty-four hours a day, and shielding all the windows, but it was a minor discomfort compared to what they had already been through, and they could not afford to take chances with Jupiter's intense radiation fields.

Pratt studied Jupiter as if sizing up an antagonist, wondering what nasty surprises the planet might hold in store. Its angry red face, silently shrieking with supersonic winds, was the face of a failed star, a beaten rival to the sun. Ringed by fourteen moons, it was a solar system in itself, and the resonance effects of those orbiting masses on the curvature of spacetime could not be calculated by any straightforward probabilistic mathematics. The fate of *Actis*—and thus of L-5 —hinged on Pratt's ability to play cosmic pinball with a malevolent Jove—and win.

"Are you going to be up all watch, Arnold?" asked a plaintive voice.

Pratt turned to see Angela, silhouetted against the dim glow of the corridor on the far side of the room.

"No. Just trying to calm down. It was quite a party." He moved toward her.

"Do you want to come to bed?" she asked, fearful of his answer.

"Of course," he answered, too heartily.

She would not look at him. He came up to her and stood for a moment, then awkwardly put an arm around her shoulders. The motion lifted them a few centimeters from the floor; imperceptibly they began to fall back downward.

"I love you," he said.

"Do you really?" she whispered, doubting.

"Yes. Really," he said, and he meant it. He tugged her gently toward their cabin.

In the middle of the night Arnold Pratt woke up. Angela lay beside him on the bunk, her breath quiet and shallow and warm. He could not place what had roused him. All was quiet. The ship hummed and gurgled as it always did—no flashing lights, no clamoring alarm bells. Yet he was wide awake, and he knew that something was wrong.

Carefully he pulled back the blanket and the restraining netting that kept people in their beds in negligible gravity. As he swung his legs to the floor, he realized . . .

A flash of cold fear ran through him. He lurched to the intercom, and keyed it.

"General alert," he barked. "Pat, Marston, control deck on the double."

At his home on L-5—at one gravity—Pratt weighed eighty-one kilos. For months in space he'd weighed nothing. For the past two weeks, under the thrust of the FPC, he'd weighed a mere four kilos. Until now.

Suddenly he was his normal weight again. *Actis* was moving at twenty times its supposedly maximum acceleration.

For four days, as Jupiter loomed up and then reeled drunkenly off and away to stern, the crew of *Actis* tried every desperate measure to turn off the holocaust in the heart of the asteroid.

At the end of three days, half the asteroid's mass was gone, devoured by the insatiable flaming cancer that ate it from within.

At the end of the fourth day, it was gone completely.

Actis had streaked across 800 million kilometers of space, crying her agony to anyone who could hear her Doppler-shifted radio, and then, somewhere below the sun, she vanished.

9

In the nature of the case, an explorer can never know what he is exploring until it has been explored.

—Gregory Bateson
Steps to an Ecology of Mind

Roger Crain didn't look up when Michael Ward crashed into his office unannounced—it couldn't be anyone besides Michael, since no one else would dare interrupt the imposing old man. Crain continued to jot neat rows of symbols and numbers, his leathery dark hand moving across the creamy white paper, his brown eyes seeing nothing but the abstract infinities his equations described. Crain's big head was bent in concentration so that Michael saw only his tightly-curled, snowy hair.

"Be with you in a moment, Mike," he murmured. The thin lead of his pencil snapped. If it was a sign of irritation, Crain was too polite to draw attention to it, and Michael too distracted to notice. Crain thoughtfully selected another needle-sharp pencil from a battery of a dozen similar instruments, which stood at attention in the ceramic University of Chicago mug on his desk. He continued his calculations.

Michael stood rocking on his heels as he glanced around the familiar office, not really seeing it. Two walls were solid with books, cassettes, and computer program files. The titles covered developmental psychology, philosophy of science and education, every field of mathematics and physics. One section was devoted to Crain's private passion, the history of technology. All the books were lined up by descending height within their categories—free of dust, backs unbroken, hardly betraying their frequent use.

The wall facing Crain's desk was taken up by a standard

graphic display screen, now dark. A well-worn hand keyboard and light pen hung at the ready beside it.

Against the fourth wall stood a rosewood cabinet, displaying ancient coffeemakers and accessories restored to almost new condition. Most of this wall was glass—a floor to ceiling window that provided a spectacular backdrop of mountains and sky to Crain's desk. The picture window was the only visible sign of Crain's value to the institution: it gave the second best view in the building, after the director's.

The old man had been with the Mathematics Instructional Committee almost as long as Director Muller, and fully ninety percent of whatever reputation for excellence the Committee could still claim was due to Crain's work. The fact was not apparent to the user of the MIC's textbooks, tapes, programs, and packages, for each of these was introduced by a long-winded essay from Muller, illustrated with the director's carefully lit holographic image. But if the thing were any good, Crain's name would be found in the fine print with the list of authors.

Muller did not love him for it. Crain was slow, methodical, logical, and insistent upon sound research. As a result, the programs he worked on used up all their grant money, with no funds left over to be squirreled away into the hidden profit accounts of the nominally nonprofit Committee. But without Crain, the MIC's market and its access to government funding would eventually shrivel and die. Muller knew it, and left Crain alone.

For his part, Crain turned a blind eye to the Director's extracurricular financial schemes. Whatever its method, the MIC reached into most of the schools in the land, and therefore had access to young minds. That was all that mattered to Crain. Social reform might be desirable, but he left it to others.

Crain laid the sheet of paper aside and looked up at Michael. "What's got your brain seething today, boy?"

"See the news this morning?"

"Oh, yes. *Actis*. Josh Rosenblum'll be tearing his hair out . . . what he's got left of it."

"How much do you know about black holes?" asked Michael intensely.

"No you don't," Crain said with a shake of his head, leaning back in his chair. "I'm not going to help you run off on some wild goosechase that'll just end up with you getting fired."

"Just give me twenty minutes, okay? Or else I'll spend the whole morning in the library, and Muller will catch me for sure."

"Don't try to blackmail me, Mike," said Crain, eyeing him skeptically. "Look, it's none of our business—we're supposed to be educators, not scientists. Rosenblum's got some of the best brains in the country out there, worrying about *Actis*. When they come up with something, maybe you can have a shot at translating it for the kids. Until then, forget about it."

Michael flushed. "Okay, so you're not responsible for me. And I promise I'll try to forget about it, if you'll just help me understand what's going on."

Crain glanced at his watch and sighed. "Okay, twenty-minute break for adult education. Then you go back to work. But don't look for understanding, because you won't get it. Want some coffee?"

"I'll make it," Michael said. He went to the sideboard, selected an old copper kettle, filled it with distilled water from a beaker, and set it on a 1952 GE hotplate.

Crain watched him a moment. "Where do you want me to start? Seems I recall you know a bit about black holes already."

"Start at the beginning. I haven't thought about the subject for ten years."

"Just about the time all the best theoretical models went out the window," Crain mused. "*Actis* did one thing for black holes—proved they exist. After that the science stopped and the politics began."

"You mean, what happened to those expeditions?" asked Michael.

"An expensive form of suicide, I think one Senator called them. The government doesn't like to see scientists fail so spectacularly, Mike," Crain said. "Kind of shakes people's faith in the system."

Michael grunted. From his point of view the system was *too* effective: the warm blanket of technological utopia was smothering him.

"Well, they collected some interesting information before they disappeared, and before the government put a stop to any further attempts," Crain went on, "and most of it contradicted accepted theory. But they just didn't get enough to give us a *new* theory."

"Maybe those ships will turn up later, just like *Actis*," Michael suggested.

"Could be—wouldn't hold my breath if I were you," Crain drawled.

Michael scooped coffee beans out of an aluminum canister, into Crain's rewired Braun grinder. He waited patiently for Crain to resume talking.

When Crain did speak, his voice was hesitant, as if he were tentatively picking his way through vague words, trying to find those that would not completely betray the mathematical concepts they stood for. "In general, in the classical theory, a black hole is what's left when a massive star burns out and collapses under its own gravity. The dead star vanishes inside its Schwarzschild radius . . . that radius is the event horizon: you can't see past it. Nothing inside the horizon can get out . . . not even light. Anything crossing the horizon disappears . . . at least as far as we're concerned."

Crain paused, seeming to consider elaborating; but he changed his mind and continued: "There's no way to tell one star corpse from another—the only thing left of the star is its mass, angular momentum, and maybe a bit of charge, if it had any. Now the star has no material existence—it's just a point mass of infinite density, infinitely curving the spacetime around it . . . a singularity, hidden inside the black hole created by the collapse. Universe should be littered with them—at least ten to the ninth in our Galaxy alone. Gravitational collapse goes on all the time."

"But there's another kind of hole, right?" Michael probed, testing his own memory.

"Maybe, maybe not. You mean primordial holes, presumably formed in the turbulence of the big bang—like bubbles in spacetime. They could be just a mathematician's pipe dream. If they're real and if they've been swallowing matter all this time . . . well, by now they've grown big enough to swallow whole galaxies. None right around here, lucky for us. Or, on the other hand, maybe they didn't all grow. If that's the case, they'd be tiny, subatomic in dimension. Either way, we don't have to worry too much about them."

Crain paused, on the edge of real complexity. "Talk's not much good from here in, Mike." He got to his feet and slowly crossed the room toward the wall display.

"Before you start on the numbers, tell me what it is about the *real* black hole that doesn't fit the theory," Mike said.

"In a nutshell, it's an odd size and an *impossible* shape," Crain exclaimed, turning to eye Mike over a hunched shoulder. "It's only about a third the mass of the sun. A star corpse should be two or three times the mass of the sun, at the very least. Anything smaller would have stopped short of total collapse. Degeneracy pressure—you'd have a white dwarf or a neutron star instead."

"Is that why it was never detected before *Actis* ran into it? Because it's so small?"

"Partly," Crain assented. "It's definitely tiny. Schwarzschild radius is less than half a kilometer—the thing's no more than a kilometer around. But even an ordinary black hole isn't all that much bigger. What really hid it was the extreme eccentricity of its orbit, and the fact that the plane of its orbit is oriented almost perpendicularly to the plane of the ecliptic."

"It doesn't come around very often . . ."

"Only about once in twenty thousand years," Crain confirmed.

"And when it does, it comes in from . . . ?"

"From the south, actually . . . it caught *Actis* on its way in, we think."

"So the chance that it will perturb planetary orbits is—"

"Practically nil. Meaning there's been no evidence to tip us off to the sun's dark companion during all the history of human astronomy."

"And what about the impossible shape?" Michael asked.

"Look at this," Crain said abruptly. He picked up the hand keyboard of the wall screen and began to punch its keys furiously. Signs and numbers flowed across the screen.

Michael watched as the old man became entranced. As so often happened when Michael got Crain to join in one of his crazy enthusiasms, Crain caught hold of Michael's excitement and appropriated it to himself.

Crain kept muttering as he worked: "Event horizon ought to be spherical. According to Shipman and Berry, ours isn't—they got some starlight displacements before they disappeared—ours looks like *this*."

A string of equations blazed into existence on the board.

"Ergosphere ought to have an elliptical cross section," Crain mumbled excitedly. "National Geographic expedition said 'no'—they got some red shifts from probes—a lot of uncertainty here—could be *this* . . ."

A formula for a hyperboloid appeared.

". . . or *this* . . ."

Equations for a four-dimensional fold appeared on the board.

". . . or something even stranger . . . which is one reason why the beast is deadlier than anyone imagined. Never know when it's gonna grab you."

Crain wrote more signs and numbers, then stood back, looked at the board, and shook his head in disgust. "Does that make sense to you?" he demanded irritably—but he was questioning himself, not Michael.

"How could *Actis* survive a trip through *any* black hole?" Michael asked. "No matter what the shape . . ."

Crain didn't answer. That was the critical question, all right.

Michael remembered that he was supposed to be making coffee. He turned on the little cylindrical coffee grinder; the blades inside whined as they pulverized the coffee. Michael could feel the gyroscopic inertia of the whirling blades as he tilted the grinder in his hand, coaxing the coffee to an even texture. A few seconds was enough.

"Couldn't," Crain grunted. *"Actis couldn't* survive. Tidal forces should have ripped her to atoms a long way off— maybe three hundred kilometers from the hole. Not much at her speed, of course. *Actis* never knew what hit her. Her gravitometers must have gone crazy a split second before it happened, but too late for anybody to notice."

"But she did survive," said Michael. "And turned up twelve light-years away. She must have gone straight through the hole and out the other side."

"Impossible!" Crain sneered. "You're talking like a TV show. The camel can't go through the needle's eye. The eye of this needle probably has a dead star in it. And what's on the other side should be another universe altogether, not our own backyard. Not Tau Ceti!" Crain was belligerent, as if single-handedly holding the universe together by the force of his conviction.

Then he softened, perplexed. "But of course, *Actis* did get through." Crain's eyes misted over, and he smiled ruefully at Michael. "You know that about the camel's eye I just mentioned? That was my mother's favorite Bible saying: 'Easier for a camel to go through the eye of a needle, than for a rich man to enter into the kingdom of God.' I think the old lady took some comfort in it, thinking herself poor the way she did." He grinned mischievously. "Mom wouldn't have approved of *Actis*, not at all. Too easy. Sets a bad example."

"Think *Actis* found heaven?" asked Michael.

"One way or another," said Crain, but his smile was fading. He turned to gaze at the figures on the wall board.

Michael let Crain study the equations in peace. If anyone could make sense of the paradox, Crain was the only man Michael knew personally who had a chance.

Michael picked up a circular paper filter from the sideboard and folded it into a cone—just as he had that morning when the news of *Actis* had first come on the air. He set the cone into the top of Crain's Chemex and poured in the ground coffee.

Some coffee powder remained in the grinder; Michael reached in and dusted it out with his finger. Then he ran his finger over the inside of the paper cone to brush off the clinging grains. In doing so he left a light smear of oily powder across the fold on the cone.

Michael stared at the brown mark curiously. His mind went blank.

He looked up at Crain. The old man's back was to him; he was hunched tiredly, as if he were on the point of giving up.

"Roger, I know what happened to *Actis*," Michael said. He could hardly believe the sound of his own voice.

10

There is no spacetime, there is no time, there is no before, there is no after. The question of what happens "next" is without meaning.

> —Misner, Thorne, and Wheeler, *Gravitation*
> (on incompatibility of the concept of
> spacetime with the quantum principle)

"I know what happened!" said Michael, suddenly sure of himself. "It was a catastrophe!"

Crain turned away from the wall board filled with equations and stared at Ward, as if the young man were mad.

"A mathematical catastrophe, I mean," Michael went on hurriedly. "Catastrophe theory; you must know about that, Roger. Some Frenchman invented it in the seventies or eighties . . . comes out of topology; a way of graphing discontinuous phenomena."

"Yes, yes, of course," said Crain impatiently. "Useful in medicine, social science. I suppose there's some analogy—"

"More than an analogy. Look at this." Michael snatched up a fresh sheet of filter paper, and waved it at Crain. "This is spacetime," he said grandly—and laid the universe flat on Crain's desk. He snatched up a pencil and sketched a quick hatchwork of lines, covering the circle of paper with an open network. "Now if this was a normal flat graph you could plot some curve on it with nothing more complicated than, at most, differential equations. You can't use those to explain jumps, though. But now look!"

Michael quickly folded the filter paper into a cone with the graph lines inside. He was becoming rather nimble at this exercise in origami.

He laid the cone on its side, on the desk top. He took a pencil, held its sharp point against the inner surface of the cone, and began to draw a line around the circumference of the cone . . .

"This line is the path of a ship moving through spacetime near a mass. Suddenly . . ." Michael moved the tip of the pencil across the fold in the cone, still drawing a straight line. ". . . the ship encounters something irregular. Far as the ship's concerned, it's still going straight. But if you look at the path in the whole of spacetime . . ."

Michael dropped the pencil and unfolded the cone:

The pencil line was in two parts. The first half stopped abruptly where the edge of the fold had rested.

On the opposite side of the circle of paper, starting at the crease that had been the fold, the line continued in the opposite direction.

"The ship jumped right across the universe. A mathematical catastrophe."

Crain puffed out his cheeks, looking a bit irritated. "I suppose this cone of yours is supposed to represent an embedding diagram?"

"Right," said Michael. "Gravity well. Distortion of spacetime coordinates near mass." Michael looked at his handiwork, then added ruefully, "Of course this model is sort of reversed—the amount of folding gets smaller here as you get closer to the bottom; it really should get bigger. The graph of spacetime surrounding our black hole has a kind of hyperfold, I'd guess."

"Oh, you would?" Crain looked sourly at the marked and folded filter paper. "There are so many things wrong with that idea I hardly know where to begin."

Michael laughed. "I'll finish the coffee. You tell me about them." Michael poured the hot water into the waiting coffeepot.

"Where does the fold come from?" Crain demanded. "Gravity wells don't have folded sides. You don't fold up a flat sheet of paper to make an embedding diagram, you use a rubber sheet. Poke your finger into a balloon: you get a smooth depression."

"What else?" asked Michael, continuing to pour.

"Tides," said Crain. "No ship would get far enough down your 'hyperfold' to change its position before the tides tore it apart. And what about the singularity? The geometry still has to go through the—" Crain stopped himself. "No. I guess I've got to give you that one, don't I?"

Michael grinned fiercely. "Right. That's the beauty. Doesn't matter what the singularity is, dead star or whatever . . . the ship doesn't have to go through it to make the jump! It crosses the fold before reaching the singularity, and makes a hell of a leap even so."

For a moment Michael regarded the coffee pouring through the filter with satisfaction. Then he looked up at the wall board.

"As to the existence of the fold, Roger, look at your own equations." He pointed to the board. "Forget where it comes from for a minute. See if it's there. Look at the distortion in the ergosphere. Look at the shape of the event horizon. That's no simple funnel of coordinates into a gravity well."

Crain frowned at the intricate pattern of lighted diodes on the board. "Maybe. Maybe," he grumped. "I'd need a couple of hours of computer time—"

"Will Muller give you the time?" Michael interrupted eagerly.

Crain avoided the question. "You haven't explained away the tides," he reminded Michael. "Not much point in squirting a pulverized ship across the universe."

"Look at the ergosphere again," said Michael. He moved to the board, picked up the light pen, and drew boxes around terms of the glowing equations. "Got at least three possible solutions for this, maybe more. Some of 'em are no good to me, but one is a moving lobe . . ."

He tapped values for the equation's constants into the keyboard, and the wall board's built-in processor confirmed his approximation.

". . . or that could be a toroid, looked at skewed." He started rapidly tapping more numbers. "This will take me awhile—"

"Never mind," Crain snapped. "You'll be there all day. What are you driving at?"

"What if there were another mass, Roger, as big as the first?" Michael looked at the equations again. "They orbit each other. They create a curved behavior surface of null tides. A ship could ride that surface almost to infinity and never feel a thing. And—"

"And the second mass folds up the spacetime of the first," Crain finished for him. "Two black holes . . ."

"Two black holes," Michael repeated, and then grinned. "It really fits, Roger. Even the size—could be a primordial black hole that never grew up—'cause it threw up everything it ate!"

"No, wait a minute," said Crain, disgusted with himself. "Two masses that size, orbiting that close, should be spiraling in toward each other, radiating enormous energy in the form of gravitational waves. A configuration like that shouldn't survive more than a fraction of a second!"

"But if each is spinning on its own?" asked Michael.

"What of it?" Crain demanded.

"Each would have its own ergosphere. And the ergospheres would interact—they could be locked in equilibrium."

"I'm sorry, Michael, you're just not making sense to me," Crain said impatiently.

"Look," said Michael, excited by his vision and determined to make Crain see it as he did, "energy can be extracted from a spinning hole, right? That's where the 'ergo' in ergosphere comes from—from 'work!' "

"Yes," Crain said. "By choosing an appropriate orbit close to the hole and ejecting matter at the right moment, a ship could gain more energy than it had going in. But how does that help you?"

"Forget ships, Roger. I'm suggesting that spacetime itself has some of the properties of matter, that the interlocked ergospheres of the two holes are *extracting energy from each other*." Michael grinned even wider, slapping his palm with his fist. *What a wonderfully outrageous idea!* he thought. Aloud he said, "Enough energy to balance the loss due to gravitational radiation, Roger. Enough to maintain a stable orbit around each other, indefinitely!"

Roger Crain was silent, not sharing Michael's good humor. "Isn't that coffee ready yet?" he asked curtly.

Michael's smile faltered. He walked back to the sideboard, crossing in front of Crain's unseeing eyes. Crain stood with his hands behind his back, staring at the equations on the board. Michael plucked the filter full of soggy grounds out of the coffeemaker, and threw it in the wall chute. He poured coffee into a mug and handed the mug to Crain.

Crain accepted it and held it up to his face, letting the steamy vapors warm the brown wrinkled skin around his eyes before he sipped.

Meanwhile Michael poured another mug. He looked at Roger Crain, and smiled tentatively.

It was a pretty little bubble while it lasted, he thought—*but*

*Roger's going to prick it full of holes as soon as he gets it on
the big computer; you can see he's already working out the
line of attack.*

Michael told himself that none of his grand ideas had ever
amounted to anything, and that this was just another that fit
the pattern: offbeat, intriguing, probably worthless, but suffi-
ciently entertaining to get Crain's attention. *Maybe that's all I
really want, he thought; just for somebody like Roger to think
I'm worth talking to.*

Crain's emotions were far more complicated than Michael's—and far different from what Michael assumed. Black
holes, the fate of *Actis*—these had nothing to do with Crain's
life. Many years ago he had decided to devote his talents to
education—and making easy for others what had been made
hard for him—instead of to the basic science for which he
was qualified. It was a decision compounded of self-sacrifice
and, perhaps, fear of failure as well.

But he had built himself a position of respect over the
years . . . and now came this wild young misfit Ward,
threatening to entangle him with Muller, and worse yet,
arousing his own long-suppressed ambitions.

Ward was no idealist's dream of a starry-eyed, dedicated
youth, innocently seeking the kind of knowledge that Crain
could hand out from afar (meanwhile avoiding the daily
indignities of the classroom). Ward was a troublemaker, full
of aimless enthusiasms; he deserved no breaks—he had
squandered plenty of opportunities.

Yet Ward laid a claim on Crain's honor, if there was any
truth to his commitment to education. Crain knew better than
Michael could that there just might be some substance in this
madcap theory of the black holes.

If anything was to come of it, though, Crain would have to
involve himself deeply, supplying the discipline and the depth
of training that Ward lacked.

Crain looked at Michael. It was a stern look, as if he were
weighing a man's fate. It may have been Michael's fate; it
may have been his own.

"Good coffee, Mike," he muttered. He reached over to his
desk and keyed the vidphone.

"Yes, Doctor Crain?" asked the robot operator.

"Please put me in touch with Doctor Joshua Rosenblum,
Project Cyclops, Searchlight Base, Nevada. He'll be hard to
reach, so keep trying. Every hour. Business hours, that is.

Until I call you off. Tell his machine that it's personal and urgent."

"Yes, Doctor Crain," said the robot.

"That's all. Thank you." Crain keyed off.

Roger Crain is the only man I know who's so polite he says "please" and "thank you" to robots, Michael thought idly.

And then the realization of what Crain had done took him, in a rush of excitement.

11

Estimate of the Situation
1. Mission
2. Situation
3. Enemy Capabilities
4. Own Possible Plan
5. Decision
        —*Contrails,* USAF Academy
        Handbook

A rush of warm dry air sucked the last drops of moisture from Laura McCord's pale smooth skin. She vigorously combed out her thick copper hair until it fell softly over her bare shoulders, dried by artificial wind from blowers ringing the shower stall. As she switched off the blowers, she heard a phone ringing.

She slung a dark blue terrycloth robe around her naked body as she ran into the study of her apartment. Three phones rested on the desk. The red one was a direct line to the Space Academy's underground command post; the yellow one went through the academy switchboard. The white phone was the one that was ringing—it was her private number. As she keyed it with her right hand, her left instinctively reached to trigger the room's shutters from a switch mounted in the desk top console.

A color mural of the Pleiades slid across the window, shutting out the towers of Manhattan with their thousand watching windows gleaming dully in the feeble sunset. The pretty mural was backed by a centimeter-thick sheet of steel; electronic sound baffles were etched in its surface.

The screen of the phone was glittering like a shower of colored sequins. A block of code letters appeared in the corner of the screen, advising those who could read it that the call was scrambled. An unscrambler was built into her phone; she cut it into the circuit and tapped out the proper code.

Ted Donner's face appeared in the screen, in front of a poster that advertised the LAST CHANCE SALOON AND CASINO. "Good evening, Laura," he said, and his eyes widened. "Say, you're looking delicious."

"Thanks, and I've barely started." She looked at his haggard features. "Wish I could return the compliment."

Donner rubbed the bridge of his nose. "Yeah, I'm up way past my bedtime, and I'm supposed to be back to work in an hour." He sighed. "Afraid I've got bad news for you. I slipped an authorizing memo past Talbot for that dope you wanted, but not a half-hour later HQ in Washington clamped a maximum security lid on the data banks! The only access terminal still hooked in is inside a vault with a ring of SpaPo's around it."

"Is that the reason for the mumbo jumbo?"

"Yeah. That's why I'm calling from a casino. I don't think I'm supposed to be talking to you, and I'm afraid to ask."

"Well, thanks for trying, Ted. I won't forget you." Laura was already calculating other means of getting what she needed. She'd go over General Hamlyn's head, if she had to. Her hand was moving to the off key.

"Not so fast," said Donner, alarmed. "I can't get at the raw data, but I can still make myself useful. String me along for a minute."

"Certainly, Ted. What's your proposition?" Laura's voice was cool, challenging Donner to make it good.

Donner dropped his bantering manner. They both realized his further value to McCord lay in what he knew—what he knew about others that she wanted to know, and what he knew about her that she wanted to conceal. He was an accomplished broker in this sort of commodity. "I came to the conclusion after our talk this morning that you might be planning a little expedition. I think you're going to need help. You've got the connections to get the ball rolling, but you've also made some—well, let me put it another way. There are some highly placed people in our branch of the service who aren't going to go out of their way to help you win any more medals."

He paused to gauge her response to the opening gambit.

She met him boldly. "I assumed you were smart enough to figure out that much when I called you, Ted. But where do you come in? Our highly placed friends are a little out of your league, wouldn't you say . . . Captain?" She gathered the folds of her robe around her throat, and leaned away from the screen.

She was still listening, though. It was enough to satisfy Donner. "You don't need raw telemetry, Laura, you need a flight plan. If Congress backs anybody it'll be the first bunch who shows them a plan for getting into that hole and back out again in one piece. The Space Force is already in the game, and you're not on the team—which means you won't get anything out of Searchlight through channels." He paused to let it sink in. "On the other hand, Rosenblum's whiz kids are trying to crack the same nut, and with them it's pure science. Anybody who tries to put a muzzle on Rosenblum is likely to get his hand bitten off."

"Sorry, Ted, but I still haven't figured out—"

"Where I come in? Rosenblum likes me, isn't that weird?" he asked ingenuously. "I happened to be hanging around this morning when he got a call from some old crony—outfit I never head of, Mathematics Curriculum Committee or something. Surprised me that Rosenblum took the call; he's got enough to keep him busy. Anyway, ten minutes later he comes blasting out of his office shouting for a staff meeting. I was included out, but I picked up some scraps later." He stopped.

"And?" she prompted. Her eyes narrowed with impatience. "Ted, you know better than to play games with me—"

"No game, Laura," he said seriously. "Only I'm a mile out on a limb on this, and I'm beginning to feel kind of lonely. I'd like to get some kind of a commitment from you."

"I've already promised to help you any way I can," she replied.

"I mean something specific. If you get the ship you want, I want to be on it. Space Force or no Space Force. I mean it. I'm going crazy out here."

"I give you my word I'll do everything in my power to see you're aboard. Is that good enough?"

"Yes. It has to be. I have to start trusting somebody sometime." He took a breath. Strain and fatigue dragged at his features.

He's in lousy shape, thought Laura. By the time I've gotten him in condition to go with me, he'll wish he'd never asked.

"Okay, the upshot of this meeting . . ." Donner continued, ". . . I'll keep it simple. Rosenblum thinks these math people have an angle on solving the geometry of the hole."

"Can you give me details? Names?" Laura leaned closer to the screen.

"I don't have any of that yet, but I can get it. Wait a minute, I've got the right name of that outfit written down here somewhere . . ." He fished in his breast pocket and came up with a scrap of paper. "Mathematics Instructional Committee," he read. "Listen, Laura, this line makes me nervous; every G-2 in the country has this code. Let me get back to you tomorrow or the next day. You'll know it's from me."

"All right, Ted. You've been a big help already. Get some rest if you can." Again she reached for the off key.

"Good night," he said, just before she made him disappear.

Laura looked at the wall clock. She had less than an hour to make it to Grand Central Station.

Twenty kilometers outside Washington the magneplane began to decelerate. At a top speed of over five hundred kilometers an hour, the trip from New York took less than an hour. Laura sat in the observation lounge at the front of the plane watching the onrush of lights, and the blurred streak of the aluminum trough that disappeared beneath the plane, only a few feet below her perch. The conductive track simultaneously powered the wingless fuselage and levitated it on magnetic fields. The sensation of speed was thrilling to some, like Laura, for nothing on Earth or in space normally moved this fast this close to a fixed surface. Others with more delicate stomachs sat back in the body of the plane and kept the windows shut.

Laura had selected a lounge chair close to the plastic nose dome, facing outward, so she could avoid the approaches of lonely fellow passengers. Offers of a drink, and more, were inevitable whenever she dressed as she was dressed tonight: her gown was of dark bronze, and a rain cape of black wool covered her bare shoulders. High heels were back in fashion, and she enjoyed the extra height hers gave her—but inside her purse was a military issue dart gun; the disadvantage of high heels was that they made unarmed combat awkward.

As the magneplane slowed and slid smoothly into New Union Station, Laura could see two of the police tactical squads that patrolled the city's perimeter. Free-lance terrorism was endemic where people had too much time on their hands—any cause would do—and the Capital was a favorite target. She knew she would be electronically searched as she left the magneplane, as she had been upon boarding. She counted on the gun's built-in Kirlian generator to produce a false outline, disguising it as a harmless compact. If worse came to worst, she could show identity and prove her right to carry the weapon, but she preferred to leave no official record of her visit.

As it happened, Laura managed to avoid inspection altogether. Daniel Levine's dapper figure was visible on the platform as the plane slowed to a stop; he gave her a discreet wave of the fingers when he spotted her through the dome. As she got up from her lounge chair, she saw Levine turn to the platform guard and show him an open wallet. The guard nodded deferentially.

". . . For your own safety, please remain seated until the magneplane has come to a complete stop," the ceiling speakers were murmuring, at a level of volume guaranteed not to attract attention. Meanwhile, the already-queued-up passengers stood waiting for the doors to open.

Laura was carried along by the press of people leaving the plane when the doors finally slid apart, and Levine snagged her by the arm just as her feet touched the platform. He hustled her toward the terminal, past the taciturn guard who glanced at her with only mild curiosity.

"Wonderful to see you again, Laura." Levine looked at her sidelong, raising bushy eyebrows on an otherwise bare scalp. "And I must say, wonderful is the word. Didn't you say you were traveling incognito?"

She gave him a quizzical look. "Do I look like a Space Force colonel to you?"

"Not unless things have changed considerably since I last visited the Pentagon," he assented. "This way—I persuaded the authorities to let me park at the side entrance."

He guided her through the vaulted station interior to a side door. Outside waited a long black Cadillac. A muscular young man in a business suit helped them into the back of the limousine, and then got into the driver's seat.

The gas turbine whined as the car pulled smoothly away from the station. In the back seat, Levine took Laura's hands and gave her a proud look.

"How 'bout a kiss for your Uncle Dan, Laura? It's been a long time."

She leaned toward him and chastely pecked his bald dome. "It's been too long," she said. "It almost feels like coming home."

"Speaking of home, what's all this hush-hush about?" he

said briskly. "I'm not even supposed to tell your father you're in town? And every time he sees me he complains that you never visit him. What's this about?"

"Nothing personal, Dan, no problems. I'll tell you all about it—you'll understand." She looked out at the rain-slick Washington streets and the floodlit public buildings sliding by in the wet darkness.

She frowned. "Where are we going, Dan? This isn't the way to Chevy Chase."

Levine seemed puzzled. "Didn't Davy tell you?"

She looked at him blankly.

"I suppose you don't see each other outside the office," he continued. Suddenly he was struck with dismay. "Goodness, Laura, how stupid of me. I haven't thanked you for what you've done for him."

"Hush," she said, "You thanked me more than enough on the phone. And I was doing my duty, not doing you a favor. He was innocent. But what didn't he tell me?"

"Rachel and I are divorced," Levine said, with the faintly over-assertive tone so many people in his situation used to fend off pity. "Been coming for years, of course. Final a month ago. I have a new place now."

"I'm sorry to hear it, Dan," said Laura, with straightforward warmth. "I guess I *have* been out of touch."

"Well, we handled it without a lot of publicity. Anyway, we're heading for my apartment in Georgetown. I'm a lot closer to the office now."

Laura thought for a moment. "Uncle" Dan was perhaps a dozen years older than she, certainly no more; he was a vigorous, charismatic man, and a new bachelor. A certain degree of familiarity between them was essential to her hopes and plans, but too much could wreck them. She came to a decision.

"Listen, Dan, this cloak-and-dagger stuff is silly—I don't really have anything to hide. Why don't we make a night of it? Let me take you to dinner. I didn't have time to feed myself before I left New York, and if I know anything about bachelors you probably haven't had a decent meal either. What do you say?"

Levine brightened. "You've got yourself a deal. And I know just the place: new private club I've joined. Rather special. Terrific view of the city—but it's on me, understand?"

"Dutch," she countered.

"Well fight over the check," he laughed, and leaned forward to give the driver new directions.

Laura smiled to herself. Levine was obviously relieved they weren't going to his bachelor apartment—he had no more desire to change the nature of their relationship than she did.

Laura was smiling again, when, after a relaxed and sumptuous dinner, coffee and brandy finally arrived at their table. In Levine's company she had relived many of the good and exciting times of her past, events in which Daniel Levine had so often played an important part.

She had also done her best to persuade him to help her with her plans for the future. So far he had committed himself to nothing. He was a shrewd man, one who could play hard-ball politics when he had to, but he was an honest man before all. She knew that whatever decision he came to, they would remain friends.

At the moment he was busy chatting with the waiter, whom he seemed to know well—he was obviously taking the opportunity to delay answering Laura's proposition. She recalled their first meeting at her father's home in Washington, shortly after she'd been ordered to take a leave from her first tour at Moon Base.

She'd been a twenty-three-year-old first lieutenant in the Air Force; the year was 2022, only a few months after Rudi Nabokov's infamous attack on Moon Base. She was in Washington to testify before the Senate Subcommittee investigating that affair—the committee then chaired by her father, Senator Benton McCord. Dan Levine was a new member of the committee's investigative staff; he and the senator had formed an instinctive partnership that was to ripen into a lasting friendship.

Even at twenty-three Laura McCord had a sure grasp of political reality. The trouble leading up to the Nabokov affair had been brewing for years, ever since the first generation of L-5 colonists actually born in space had come of age and realized their impotence. All the colonists were automatically citizens of the United States, and as such had the right to vote for the President, but that was a meaningless courtesy. The colonists had precious little support on earth, no real constituency, and they had no vote in Congress. Even their voice in local government was limited to an "advisory" committee to the Space Agency's appointed administrator. The Space Agency bureaucrats who were assigned the Administrator chore never stayed beyond their two-year tours of duty: the Space Agency was an absentee landlord.

The spaceborn children began to talk of independence, of a free "Nation in Space." Talk led to demonstration; demonstration led to agitation, which gave way to provocation, which finally erupted in sabotage.

Space Agency scientists engaging in delicate experiments suffered power failures at critical moments. Zero-gravity factories manufacturing products for Earth sprang air leaks, and were seized with sudden and unprogrammed accelerations. The military garrison on Cylinder B was a favorite symbol of repression: communications links to the Air Force Satellite Command Center were interrupted so many times in one month that a whole end of Cylinder B was cordoned off, and guards were ordered to gas civilians first and ask questions later.

Perhaps no more than twenty or thirty individuals were responsible for these acts, out of a total population in excess of a hundred thousand. Until the summer of 2022 the embarrassed Founder elders tried to dismiss them as adolescent pranks. Then, in July of that year, a youthful rebel stole a lunar transport from the main industrial docking bay and headed for the moon.

Rudi Nabokov was a twenty-year-old utility shuttle pilot; the underground Organization for a Free Nation in Space considered him an irresponsible exhibitionist, and had shunned him ever since one cell meeting where he had brandished an old-fashioned lead bullet revolver, threatening to assassinate the Space Agency Administrator. The OFNS wasn't ready to see anyone killed in the name of freedom, yet.

The day before the hijacking, Nabokov had been suspended from his duties ferrying personnel to and from the agricultural stations that ringed the Cylinders. He had argued with one of his passengers, an ultraconservative Founder farmer, and in his distraction had come close to colliding with one of the satellite farms.

Nabokov used up most of the fuel in the stolen transport blasting straight for the moon. There was no question of intercepting him—it was impossible to board a spacecraft that didn't cooperate. Tracking computers established that

the stolen shuttle would fall into a tight orbit bringing it only
a few kilometers north of the joint Army-Navy-Air Force
Moon Base in Copernicus Crater.

Long before reaching the moon, Nabokov broadcast a
manifesto from the shuttle, announcing that he and unnamed
others in the "Action Arm" of the OFNS were prepared to
die for the liberty of L-5. He threatened unspecified reprisals
unless a long list of demands was met. Notable among these:
the Space Agency Administrator and all military personnel
aboard the Cylinders to immediately depart for Earth; the
United States to recognize the colony's independence; the
Secretary General of the United Nations to call Nabokov
personally and assure him that the sovereign status of L-5
would be recognized. Less notable: a demand to talk to his
ex-boss, and a demand to talk to his mother. The last demand
was met.

A long day passed while Mrs. Nabokov and various negotiators tried to reason with the lad. Angela Pratt, Mrs. Nabokov's sister, was one of the negotiators; no one had any luck.
Meanwhile, the less-responsible newspapers and television
networks screamed "Communist plot," and took to calling
Nabokov "Red Rudi," ignoring the fact that his ancestors had
been U.S. citizens since 1920.

The lunar transport went into orbit around the moon. As it
rose over the eastern horizon, it sent back to L-5 what was to
be its last message. Nabokov had renamed his spacecraft; it
was no longer Lunar Service Vehicle 19, but was to be known
as the *Divine Wind*.

Five minutes later, according to reports of witnesses on the
lunar surface and observers who were watching through
telescopes on L-5, the *Divine Wind* began to oscillate strangely, as if its steering thrusters were firing out of phase. Then
there was a brief burst of flame from the main rocket, hurling
the craft out of orbit. It vaporized in the Sea of Serenity,
twelve hundred kilometers northeast of Moon Base.

It was assumed that Nabokov had intended to crash the
Divine Wind into Moon Base but had lacked the skill to do it
properly. Six months later, Senator McCord's investigating
committee uncovered a startling truth. Under relentless questioning from young staff counsel Daniel Levine, Lieutenant
Laura McCord reluctantly told everything she knew of what
had gone on at Moon Base during those crucial hours. The
key revelation: a nervous Army captain, jumping to the

obvious (and no doubt intended) conclusion about the meaning of the name *Divine Wind*, had irradiated the ship with an intense particle beam from a top-secret weapon that was illegal on the moon. The beam had scrambled the ship's on-board control computer. In effect, the Army had shot Nabokov down.

Repercussions were international and cislunar. L-5 was put under martial law to quell riots that erupted in the wake of this proof of Nabokov's "murder." Russian and American troops went on the alert around the globe.

Culminating a long history of interservice rivalry, the joint Army-Navy-Air Force military jurisdiction in space was abruptly terminated by the President, and a new service, the Space Force, was created by a swift act of Congress to take its place. The United States reluctantly agreed, in the face of global condemnation, to United Nations inspection of its facilities on the moon.

Although Senator McCord, out of a delicate sensitivity to his daughter's feelings, absented himself from chambers on the day she delivered her testimony, it held no surprises for him. It had been carefully planned in his own living room, by himself, Laura, and Dan Levine. She had no need to lie or even to exaggerate; she simply volunteered the truth, more fully than the military establishment could tolerate. The eventual results, which included the founding of the Space Force (and the Space Force Academy) and Laura's rapid advancement through the ranks, had all been part of the plan.

But there were unplanned effects as well. The Nabokov affair was only a prelude to the *Actis* debacle two years later. Although the revolt of L-5 was a nominal failure, the mounting pressure of worldwide opinion succeeded in convincing even the Congress of the United States that the country would be better off without the burden of L-5's maintenance. The space colony achieved its independence.

This act of Congress was a repudiation of Senator Benton McCord's expansionist policies, and a death blow to his presidential hopes. He had already begun campaigning for the election of 2028; he was ignominiously defeated in the primaries.

Major Laura McCord's failure to predict the fate of *Actis* (after having personally inspected the ship)—and her involvement in putting down the abortive revolt on L-5—

became factors in her father's defeat. Laura's rising career abruptly slowed. It did not come to a complete halt, for her father was still a powerful man and one who mightily influenced the destiny of the Space Force (and its budget). But eventually Laura was shunted off to the academy she had helped to establish, to the satisfaction of senior officers who had always resented her; although these generals owed their present positions to the existence of the Space Force, and thus to Laura's burst of honesty, they considered anyone who blew the whistle on any branch of the military, under any circumstances, to be disloyal and dangerous.

Now, a decade later, as Laura glanced sidelong at Dan Levine's dapper figure nestled in his red plush armchair, she reflected that only he of all of them had emerged unscathed from the brouhaha of those years. His career had suffered no check; if anything, he had profited from his knowledge and his intimate contacts with all the principals, without allowing himself to be caught in the direct glare of public attention.

A soft yellow light filled the Victorian-style dining salon where Laura and Dan Levine sat looking at each other across the damask-covered table. The light came not only from the candles in their massive silver candelabra, but from the glow of the city's lights, reflected from the bellies of the lowering rain clouds.

During dinner the great airship that carried the salon and the other rooms of Levine's "rather special" club had made a slow circuit around Washington, hovering just below the cloud cover, a thousand meters above the lights of the capital. The ship had turned slowly as if tethered by an invisible cord to the gleaming dome of the Capitol. Throughout the evening, whenever Laura glanced out the windows, she saw shining in the night the symbol of the power she sought to bend to her own ends.

She broke the silence, speaking cheerfully. "This was a wonderful idea, Dan. We were certainly lucky to make the flight."

He held a finger to his lips. "Don't tell anybody, or next thing you know, reporters from the *Post* will be digging into my bank account: but I'm a charter member of the Fogg Society. One of the investors. Had them hold the flight for us."

She smiled knowingly. "You always did have a knack for making your own good luck."

"Yes, I suppose you're right." He looked at her seriously. "Well, Laura, it's been a delightful evening, and you're as full of exciting ideas as ever. But now I suppose you'd like some kind of a reaction from your Uncle Dan."

"That's right, Dan." She sipped at her coffee, waiting for him to go on.

He sighed. "Laura, I know you. I know your abilities. I know you're being wasted where you are now. No one knows that better than I do." For a moment his expression was one of pained regret. "But this black hole thing—it's been an embarrassment in the past, and there's no evidence to suggest Congress will see it any differently in the future."

"We can neutralize that, Dan," she said urgently. "Maybe they want to forget about *Actis;* I can understand that. But if *Actis* survived, there's a chance the other expeditions survived as well." She hesitated an instant. "In fact, it wouldn't be hard to start some 'well-founded' rumors to that effect—"

Levine held up a hand. "Hold off on the strategy. I want you to look at the political situation." He folded his arms across his chest and leaned back into the recesses of his overstuffed armchair. "So what if *Actis* got through the black hole, Laura? So what if the others did too? What happened to them then? They just died an even lonelier death than they might have otherwise. A slower, more agonizing death. With no way even to communicate their pain, except posthumously. Granted there might be some renewed interest in sending a very cautious scientific expedition out to the hole . . ." Levine's tone of voice indicated that he was dubious of even this limited possibility, ". . . what reason under heaven would Congress have for trying to send another ship *through* the damned thing?"

Laura's face flushed. "Because, Dan, that black hole is the gateway to the stars. Or to Tau Ceti, at least. If I were a loyal Spacer, I'd give you a military argument." She grinned bitterly. "I can hear Hamlyn now," she said, launching into an imitation of the Chief of Staff's nasal midwestern drawl: "Who's gonna' control the objective, us or them? Us or those dirty Reds? Us or those sneaky Fivers?"

Levine squirmed uneasily. "Remarkably good imitation," he muttered.

"I've had time to study him," she said. "But as it happens, the Space Force hasn't done me any favors lately, Dan, so I'm not going to peddle their line for them. The reason to explore that black hole is that it leads to the universe. That's all the reason anyone could ever need."

Levine pushed his fingers together as if in prayer, and pressed them to his lips. "The problem is, you think in centuries, Laura. Congress only thinks ahead to the next election." He dropped his hands to his lap. "And then there's this whole business of your involvement with *Actis*."

"*I* didn't send them out of the solar system, Dan. If I'd guessed how foxy Arnold Pratt really was, I'd have stopped him." She shifted in her chair impatiently. "But let people talk. I was the last to see them—I'll be the first to follow. And the first to come back and tell about it."

Levine reached for his brandy snifter. "I'm not arguing the justice of your position, Laura. You know I'm on your side. I'm just telling you how I see the situation. What do you think you can do about it?" He sipped at the amber liquid, and looked at her over the rim of the bubble of glass.

"With your support, I can do plenty," she replied. "I'll start a nationwide public relations campaign to put pressure on Congress and the Administration to back an expedition. The people of this country *will* back it, Dan. We're all dying of boredom; we'd all like to see some tangible proof that there's more to life than this damned suffocating cradle-to-grave security. I'll have myself touted as the logical choice to lead, and I *am* the logical choice: I've got more command experience than anyone my age. I've seen more action than anyone, period."

Levine interrupted. "My sense of the thinking at Defense is, they'd rather have just about anybody but you."

She stared at Levine. "So you already know they're planning an expedition?"

Levine returned her gaze coolly. "I was planning to tell you about it. Yes, they're planning an expedition. No, I don't think they've got enough to persuade Congress. They sure haven't got enough to persuade *me*. And frankly—so far—neither have you."

"Well, to hell with DOD," she said angrily. "Defense works for the President, and he reads his mail."

"Perhaps. But he won't be stampeded. You'll need something solid to assure him he's not involving himself in a fiasco. The same goes for Congress, of course."

"Dad will help me, Dan. If I can persuade *him* I'm not going to kill myself, he'll bring Congress around."

"But, since you come to me first," Levine observed dryly,

"I deduce that you're not quite ready to try to convince him of your . . . immortality."

"I don't have to be immortal to survive the passage, Dan. I believe that with all my heart." For a moment she looked distracted. "I'm sure I'll be able to prove it soon." Her expression brightened. "Dan, do you know of a group calling itself the Mathematics Instructional Committee?"

He raised his bushy eyebrows, surprised at the apparent change of subject. "Sounds vaguely familiar," he said. "What does that Mathematical whatsis have to do with your problems?"

"I just remembered something a little birdie told me before I got on the plane tonight. What kind of a place is it?"

"Must be one of those educational consortiums, I would guess. Lots of them cluster around Boston, Boulder, San Francisco Bay—places like that." Levine seemed genuinely puzzled by her interest.

"Dan, the grapevine has it that Rosenblum is excited by their approach to the geometry of the hole," said Laura. Her eyes were flashing. "That could be the key to the whole thing."

"Sounds a bit wild to me," said Levine, shaking his head. "Those outfits aren't exactly hotbeds of original thought. But I can look into it, if you want."

"Would the Space Agency be willing to support their research?" Laura asked.

"Shouldn't be any problem justifying that. I think the agency gives those educational groups a bit of money now and then, anyway. Seems to be useful public relations," Levine said lightly.

"Good. I want them tied up anyway you can think of, Dan. I want them drowning in money, if need be. I want them working for me," Laura said with determination.

Levine was amused. "Don't overestimate my influence. I expect Josh Rosenblum will have something to say about who these people are working for. But I'm pretty sure I can get you on the need-to-know list. Under the table, if that's the way you want it."

"Thanks, Dan. And . . . I'm really reluctant to presume, you know . . ."

"But could I get on it right away, like tomorrow?" He grinned. "Sure, Laura." Then he waved his hand in a little negative motion, and his features grew serious again. "But not so fast. Even if that part eventually works out as you hope, my instincts tell me you haven't got enough to pull this off. For one thing, I'm not as sanguine as you about the adventurous yearnings of our warm, well-fed citizenry."

Laura said nothing. She looked at him, and her eyes burned with conviction, but her expression could not fully conceal an undercurrent of anxiety. She knew Levine was telling her the truth, and that she had not yet convinced him to support her.

A club official dressed in a fanciful nineteenth century airship officer's uniform approached their table. His manner as he addressed Levine was a suave blend of deference and authority. "Terribly sorry to disturb you, sir, but your driver has relayed this message from your office. Urgent priority." The man inclined his head in a minimal bow, and clicked his heels smartly, as he held out an envelope of rich, thick-laid paper.

Levine took the envelope. "Thanks, Commodore," he said, raising quizzical brows at Laura. "Carry on," he added, in a faintly mocking British accent.

"Very good, sir," said the "Commodore." He retreated.

Levine neatly gutted the envelope with a forefinger and pulled out the message. He read it quickly, glanced up at Laura, and then handed it over to her.

"Perhaps we should have been home watching the news," he said.

The message read: "Audio reception from *Actis* received Searchlight Base 10:41 EDT reports captain and all crew abandoning ship. Ejection pods launched in attempt to reach planetary surface, Tau Ceti Five."

Laura read the message three times, rapidly. She looked up at Levine. "It's damned hard to convince yourself this isn't happening right now, isn't it, Dan?"

Levine took a long sip of brandy. He set the snifter down carefully. "They've been . . . dead . . . dead for twelve years, Laura. Perhaps now we can finally say good-bye for good."

Laura read the message one more time. When she again looked at Levine, her eyes smoldered with conviction. "Maybe not, Dan. Maybe they made it to that planet. Maybe they're still there. Waiting. Waiting to be rescued."

Levine's expression was grim. "You don't really believe that, Laura."

She smiled, but it was a feral smile, frightening in what it revealed of her naked will. "It doesn't matter what I believe, does it? What matters is what *people* will believe."

Levine looked down at his drink, swirling the amber liquid in its bubble of glass. Laura did not shock him; he was too old a Washington hand not to understand and even sympathize with ambition.

It was just that the Secretary of the Space Agency had to remind himself that his adopted "niece," the daughter of one of his oldest friends, was not only charming and warm—she could also be as ferocious as a lioness.

Under the circumstances, it seemed likely that Laura would get her way by one method or another. Since he could not save her from her desires, he might as well see to it that she went to her fate with the best support he could give her.

12

Already for thirty-five years he had not stopped talking and almost nothing of fundamental value had emerged.

—James Watson, *The Double Helix*
(guessing at Sir Lawrence Bragg's opinion of Francis Crick)

"I'm disappointed in you, Roger. Deeply disappointed," Franklin Muller intoned. He stood with his back to Roger Crain, hands clasped behind him, staring through the sweeping curve of window behind his desk. To the north, forty kilometers away, a plume of snow blew eastward from the tip of Long's Peak. To the south, sunlight glimmered on Pike's Peak, almost a hundred and fifty kilometers distant. But the crenelated wall of ice and granite that stretched between the two watchtowers could not contain the looming storm that pressed in from the west. Already, ragged chunks of black cloud had broken free and were racing closer across the clear vault of the afternoon.

Crain waited impassively. He was comfortable in one of Muller's chrome and leather armchairs, his feet snuggled deep in the thick carpet. He could sit there as long as Muller saw fit to waste his time.

Muller turned, giving Crain the darkest glance the old man could recall ever having received from the MIC's director. "Don't you have anything to say?" Muller demanded.

Crain smiled sadly and shook his head. "Please, Frank . . . what can I add to what's been said already? The boy hasn't called me. You've checked with his parents—they haven't heard from him. The police are no help. That's all there is to it."

"Why in God's name did you have to get him involved in the first place?" Muller whined. "Don't you realize this is the richest contract this Committee has ever been offered? Do you have any *inkling* of the prestige we stand to reap? And it's all slipping through our fingers because we can't produce this—this madman Ward!"

"Sit down, Frank," Crain snapped, showing a rare temper.

Muller gaped at him, taken aback.

Crain instantly attempted to soften the blow of his impatient words. "Men our age have to watch our blood pressure, you know . . ."

Almost humbly, Muller obeyed, collapsing into the soft swivel chair behind his desk.

"We need to clarify a few things," Crain continued, leaning forward. "*I* did not involve *Ward* in anything. This idea that's got everyone so excited is his idea, his alone. I have no claim on it, you have no claim on it, the Committee has no claim on it . . ." Crain grinned despite himself. "Since if he'd been doing Committee work the idea never would have occurred to him in the first place."

"Precisely!" Muller interjected. "And that's why I was perfectly justified—"

"Let me finish, Frank, or I'll surprise myself by walking out of here," Crain threatened.

Muller shut up.

"Now in the second place, Josh Rosenblum assures me he didn't say anything to the higher-ups in the Space Agency about this. It's much too preliminary. It was and is an inspired hunch that has about a ninety percent probability of being wrong. Josh would never—"

"Well, who . . . ?" Muller started to interrupt.

But Crain ploughed on. "I am at a loss to explain the call you received from the Space Agency. I'm at even more of a loss to explain all this irresponsible publicity. And in the *third* place," he continued, before Muller could interrupt again, "I'm afraid you know exactly who's responsible for Michael Ward's not being in this office with us right this minute. Please think about that for a moment."

"How was I to know the insubordinate little bastard was some kind of genius?" Muller snarled. "He certainly never gave any indication of it to *me* . . ."

Muller suddenly blinked in panic as Crain disgustedly started to rise from his chair. "Hold on, Roger, I take it back." The spectacle of a belligerent Roger Crain threatened his sense of reality. "I'll raise his salary. I'll double it.

I'll . . ." Muller almost choked, ". . . *apologize*, if it will do
any good."

Crain relaxed, breaking into a grin. He'd never seen the
director in such a dither. It was a strangely satisfying sight.
"Oh, I doubt you'll have to go that far," he drawled. "And as
for Mike's being a genius, don't let it get you down—he isn't.
He just happend to bring some fresh insight into a particular
branch of science he knows nothing about. It happens all the
time. He's probably not much brighter than you are, Frank,"
Crain observed with cheerful malice. Abruptly he became
serious. "If I were you I wouldn't let myself be blinded by all
this money—and 'prestige,' as you call it—the bureaucrats
are suddenly throwing at your head. It looks pretty obvious to
me that we're only pawns in some deeper game."

Muller sulked. "You have no call to argue with my administrative policies, Roger."

"I have plenty of arguments," Crain shot back. "I don't
think you really want to hear them."

"All right, all right," said Muller, waving the unpleasant
prospect aside. "Just tell me if you're willing to work on this
project until we can put Ward back to work on it."

"If that's what you want," Crain said carefully. "It has
nothing to do with education, this black hole thing. To my
mind, this is all a temporary flap that's going to blow over
pretty damn quick. But I'll do what you want. Getting the
Space Agency to give you the time of day, unless Ward is
back on the project, is your problem. Ward's free to go
elsewhere, you know."

"You're the mathematician, here," Muller protested.
"You're the man who's going to do the real work."

"Under no circumstances will I reveal anything I discover
without Michael Ward's cosignature," Crain said simply.

Muller stared at him aghast.

Crain went on: "But if I were you I wouldn't worry about
me right now. I'd worry about finding Michael Ward."

Muller hissed in frustration. He swung his chair around to
the window to brood on the building storm.

The last of the hail rattled in the yellow aspen leaves, a few
pellets bouncing from branch to branch and finding their way
down the back of Michael Ward's neck. He straightened
painfully from his stiff half-crouch against the big aspen's
papery bark. A feeble ray of sunlight crept through the grove

of golden trees. Michael knew it would not last. He started walking down the steep trail.

His boots squished as he walked. He could hardly feel his frozen toes. His jeans were soaked up to the middle of his calves, and a cold wet patch of cloth rubbed against each knee. Drifts of tiny white hail spheroids had collected in the creases of his windbreaker, on the top of his pack, and in his hair. Drops of ice water ran into his ears. His misery was so complete he forgot to feel sorry for himself.

Three days earlier he had been driven into the mountains by an urge to escape his fellow humans—an attempt he should have known was foredoomed to failure. Some romantic vision of a pristine wilderness lured him on, some dream of lonely crags and barren tundra and empty vistas. A fifteen-kilometer hike on that first afternoon—made doubly long by the breakdown of his little Flyer, which he had been forced to leave in an isolated recharge station by the side of the two-lane road—had brought him to a tiny lake tucked just under the Continental Divide.

Perhaps eighty people were there ahead of him. They were camped in groups along the stream from the lake, where it meandered through the high alpine meadows on its way to lower elevations. Too tired to look further, and with night coming on, Michael had set up his bubble tent in the lee of a wind-blasted spruce, on a knoll overlooking the tent city. All night long he was serenaded by music sucked into the campers' radios from satellites orbiting high overhead—as the hours wore on and the shadow of night raced westward around the globe he heard everything from koto to sitar to tuba. At 3:00 A.M. a fight broke out, and most of the encampment took sides. By 5:00 A.M. he knew much more of the nomadic village's ethnography than he wanted to know: who was sleeping with whom, and who objected; whose brats belonged to which moiety; who's turn it was to trek into town to pick up the monthly guaranteed income check.

By 6:00 A.M. he was already packed and walking, his head swimming with fatigue and high altitude. He reached the crest of the Divide as the sun struck across the plains, and he heard the distant whine of the Forest Service helicopter, come to collect the garbage and empty the chemical potty.

Pikas and marmots lived in the talus that dropped away on each side of the stony ridge, no more shy than ever they had been, blessed with the ability to forget, during their long winter's nap, what they had learned of humans. Michael's heart lightened as he trudged north, following the trail as it twisted around outcroppings of crumbling rock the color of old parchment. Once he caught sight of a woolly fat bundle clattering over the rocks and thought he had spotted a mountain goat. But when he rounded the next pinnacle of rock, he found only a large flock of domestic sheep summering in the meadows above tree line.

It was a pretty scene, and innocent enough, but it plunged Michael into the depression he had been struggling to keep at bay. For it forced him to admit the truth: there was no place on Earth he could escape his fellow creatures, perhaps especially not here in the Rockies, washed over by successive waves of miners, ranchers, campers, and squatters in a tide that was still rising steadily after two hundred years.

Lunchtime under a close and merciless sun brought Michael's blackest moment. He seriously wondered whether he wanted to go on living in the world of men and women. Life's active round seemed fruitless, a meaningless frenzy of acquisition, achievement, gratification, failure, and death. By what objective measure—on the cosmic scale—could one distinguish the altruist, the hero, the murderer? Naming did not fix them, change them, affect them in any way. Humanity's fondest delusion was that the act of naming, describing, measuring, making fine distinctions, somehow invoked power over the universe. In fact, the universe did not care.

Monday morning, in Roger Crain's office, Michael had succeeded in describing an awesome mystery. Of course it had been an offhand sort of achievement, conceived out of boredom and laziness. Yet in the world of human affairs it should have counted for something.

Instead, when he had walked back to his own office an hour later, he had found his personal belongings stacked in the hall outside his door, with a curt note from the director informing him that: (a) the Mathematics Instructional Committee had no further need of his services and (b) his severance pay had been communicated to his bank. That was all.

Public humiliation was standard practice at the MIC; it had happened to others once or twice already in Michael's short period of employment. He remembered with shame how he had stayed tactfully behind his office door in those cases, waiting for the miscreant to creep silently away. He had not wanted to become involved. Now he saw that all the doors in the corridor were shut to him, as he had shut his to others.

Fury took him. He refused to go quietly, as was expected of him. He stormed into the director's outer office, past his startled secretary. But Muller's door was locked. Michael pounded on it, shouting imprecations at the top of his voice.

Muller's gracious secretary took pity on the distraught young man—when he stopped for breath, she explained in a sympathetic voice that Muller had been looking for him, had determined that he was away from his desk "without authorization," and could not be found, and had given the computer his personal orders to have Michael separated. "Apparently in a fit of pique," she confided in a whisper. She was terribly sorry; there was nothing she could do.

Michael had left his junk in the hall (only the books were valuable, and they'd been stolen from the library), had run to his car, ramming two of his ex-colleagues' cars in his haste to get out of the parking lot, and raced home at the Flyer's top speed of fifty kilometers per hour. To his horror, he found as he drove that his eyes were streaming with tears. He'd thrown some old clothes and Thermo-Paks into his backpack when he reached home, and ten minutes later was buzzing up Boulder Canyon in the protesting little car—running away.

He'd run about as far as he could in twenty-four hours—he'd reached the roof of the continent. It was all downhill from here. High noon on the mountaintop led him to Hamlet's choice.

Unless one is really committed, it is particularly difficult to sustain a suicidal depression when the means are close at hand—reality has a way of calling one's bluff. A few meters from Michael's picnic spot was the edge of a cliff so precipitous it was actually concave beneath the overhang where he now stood. Several hundred meters below, the cliff ended in a jumble of enormous boulders. Dirty snow lurked in the permanent shade of the crevices between them. Michael stared over the edge, while his self-pity fought a losing battle. Briefly he considered his medicine cabinet at home, replete with various painlessly lethal combinations. Then he sat down on the ground abruptly, laughing in scorn.

He wondered idly if his genes were undermining his courage. That mindless molecule DNA cared nothing for his self-esteem—it was still waiting for him to reproduce, which he had so far refused to do. (*How's that for cosmic purpose?* he mocked himself.) But whatever the root of his instinct for self-preservation, it did him another favor by turning him back in his tracks. Though the clear cobalt sky gave no hint of it, a storm was only a day away.

He camped that night in a dark forest of pine and spruce, beside a burbling self-important waterfall. As the sun dropped behind the ridge the wind rose in the branches. The wind and water hypnotized him to sleep.

He dreamed that the book of his future was opened to him: he could read each word clearly (though he could not pronounce it—and, oddly, no word was connected to the words on either side). The meaning of the whole was clear, profound, ineffable. He was deeply reassured.

He woke clear-eyed, refreshed, perhaps a bit sad. He began a mental list of his friends and business contacts. He would go home and start looking for another job.

As he walked, slid, scrambled in the mud—down through the spruce and aspens, hiding when necessary from the rain and hail of the darkening sky, trudging on again when the sun came out (the trail now gently descending through scrub oak and ponderosa)—he realized that the poor remnant of wilderness had given him all it could . . . and more than he had asked of it.

He parked his repaired Flyer outside the Bucket of Gore tavern. He kicked the door of the car shut irritably—that sly hick of a recharge station attendant had stuck him for a week's salary (which he no longer earned) to replace one worn bearing. He'd had no choice but to pay or abandon the creaky vehicle.

Soft wet snow, the first of the season, was falling all around him. He glanced up the face of the soleri that loomed darkly over the town; far up its side he could see his own window. He wondered how long he could afford to keep his desirable apartment on guaranteed income alone, before he'd be forced to move to the ticky-tack slums of North Denver. Long enough to find a new job, he hoped.

The interior of the bar was dark, and the Thursday night crowd had not yet gathered. In the corner, by the copper-hooded holographic fire, a University of Colorado instructor was pressing drinks on a bored co-ed. Angie, the equally bored waitress, leaned against the fake corral fence at the ear end of the bar, picking at the fringe of her ass-high owgirl skirt. Michael made his way to the bar.

"How you doing, Angie?" he muttered as he passed her.

"Hey, Mike Ward—where the hell have you been?" she sked, with real surprise.

"Oh, just took a day off. Went up to Heart Lake, walked round a little." He hitched himself onto a bar stool.

"Ain't you the cool one, though," she muttered to herself, ooking at him strangely.

The bartender was a new man Michael had never seen, a angy cowboy who'd doubtless been hired as an asset to the ar's Old West decor. "What'll it be, friend?" he asked, taking ceremonial swipe with his bar rag at the counter in front of Michael.

"Double Scotch on the rocks, thanks."

"Coming right up." The bartender scooped ice into a glass nd up-ended the bottle over it. He set the drink down in ront of Michael. "Name's Tex," he said heartily. "Started esterday. You a regular customer?"

"Yeah. I'm Mike," said Michael, briskly shaking the bar-ender's hand. "Good luck to you."

He brought the glass up to his face and stuck his nose in it, king a long sip. When he set the glass down again, he oticed that Tex was staring at him intently. "Something rong, Tex?" he asked.

"Not at all, not at all. Just, you sure look familiar. You ever hung around the old Time Machine down in San ntone, did you?"

"Never been to Texas," said Michael.

"Didn't think so," said Tex complacently. "I never forget a ustomer's face."

"Good for you, Tex," said Michael. "Excuse me a minute, have to make a phone call." He slid off the stool and carried is drink with him to the hooded phone, on the wall between e restroom doors in the back hall.

He tapped his own number, the charge code, and the umber of his parents' soleri apartment in San Francisco. Vith a drink in his hand he felt up to breaking the news to em.

His mother's face came on the screen. She stared at him.

"Hi, Mom . . ." he had time to say, before she burst into ars.

"Michael, oh Michael, thank God you're safe," she wailed.

"What do you mean? Of course I'm safe. Hey, Mom, take

it easy, will you?" Her naked emotion made him intensely uneasy. He turned away from the vidphone screen and took a quick pull on his drink.

"You're not in some kind of trouble, are you," his father's voice barked from the screen behind him. He turned to see his father shouldering his mother to one side. "Where are you calling from? That's not your apartment, is it, son?"

"Dad, for Christ's sake . . . No. I'm not in trouble. I'm calling from a, uh—a restaurant in Boulder. I just called to give you the news."

"We know all about it, and we think it's *wonderful* Michael." It was his mother again. "But you've had us all so worried!"

Michael was exasperated. "What's so wonderful? What's there to be worried about? Except the reason I called, which is that I've been *fired* again! What's so damned wonderful about that?"

His parents looked at each other. His father recovered first, pushing his mother aside a second time. "You say you were fired, son? When did that happen?"

"Monday morning. I didn't feel like talking about it, so I took off into the mountains for a couple of days."

"Without leaving word!" his father accused. "Do you know the Secretary of the Space Agency himself called personally, Mike? Called me at work. I was ashamed to tell him I didn't know where you could be reached."

Even as comprehension dawned, Michael found time to reflect that his father seemed downright satisfied every time Michael managed to disappoint him. "Would all this happen to have something to do with black holes?" Michael asked.

"It's been on the news every night, Michael," said his mother. "How you are going to make it possible for them to rescue those poor people. Oh, Michael, I'm so proud!"

"Except that no one's been able to find you," his father interjected. "You've caused your mother and me considerable worry and concern."

"Well, I'm sorry to hear that, but—" Michael began, but his father cut him off.

"Then I can rest assured you will contact your boss immediately?" he demanded.

"I don't have a boss, Dad. I just told you I was fired."

His father was momentarily stymied. Not for long: "Well, I'm sure that's all a mistake. In fact, I know so. I had quite a

ood little chat with Doctor Muller only yesterday. He has
othing but the highest regard for your abilities."

Michael couldn't restrain a giggle. "I would have liked to
ave listened in on that call."

His father seemed uncomfortable. "He was certainly quite
incere. It would behoove you to show a little more respect,
oung man . . ."

"Sure, Dad," said Michael, suddenly impatient. "I'll take
are of it. Sorry I worried you folks. Bye, Mom. I love you.
You too, Dad." And he hung up before they could protest.

He wandered back to the bar, his head aching. He wasn't
quite sure what he should do next. He would go home and
all Roger Crain, that made the most sense. But at the
moment he just wanted time to think.

As he climbed back up on the bar stool he noticed Tex
eaning over the far end of the bar while Angie whispered in
his ear. Tex turned and gave Michael an odd, rather goofy
ook.

Michael downed the rest of his drink and called out, "How
much do I owe you?"

Tex marched down the length of the bar toward him. "It's
on me, Mister Ward," he said with a wide smile. "Here have
nother!" Before he could protest, Michael's empty glass was
alf full again. "You know, Mister Ward," said Tex, still
ouring, "I met a few celebrities in my time. But never
nybody who has done what you have. I'm mighty proud to
make your acquaintance, sir."

He plunked the fresh drink down in front of Michael.

"You know, I knew for sure I seen you someplace before!"
ex whacked his thigh with glee. "Your picture's been on the
ews for the last two days. You must be the most wanted man
n the country right now, how about that?"

13

If general relativity is correct, spacetime is puckered and warped in an incredibly complicated way, on all scales from atoms up to at least clusters of galaxies.
—Michael Berry
Principles of Cosmology and Gravitation

Michael kept his face pressed to the window as the magneplane sped toward Searchlight Base, passing through the center of the town of Searchlight without stopping. The town was only two or three blocks wide, but it stretched for several kilometers beside the elevated magneplane tracks and the parallel two-lane asphalt strip of Highway 95.

Searchlight was like any military boomtown gone to seed, a dreary succession of dives: bars, massage parlors, tattoo parlors, pawn shops, triple-X movie houses, liquor stores, and amusement arcades—and those extra added attractions peculiar to the Nevada desert: wedding chapels, "escort services," and big barnlike casinos of garishly painted stucco dripping with neon that flashed on and off all night and all day, even under the direct glare of the midday sun. SLOTS, the signs proclaimed, GENEROUS SLOTS. BLACKJACK, KENO, GLAMOROUS GIRLS; FRIENDLY GLAMOROUS GIRLS; FREE STEAK DINNER AT DIAMOND BILL'S.

Behind the town's main street the gravelly desert was littered with the corpses of old cars and discarded washing machines, and the gaunt skeletons of hundred-and-fifty-year-old wooden mine lifts, blackened under the sun. Even further out, the sand and sagebrush bore the scars of abandoned housing developments—nothing left now but dirt roads scratched on the desert floor, and an occasional wooden signpost tilted crazily: LAKESIDE DRIVE, BOUGAINVILLEA LANE, MORNINGSTAR WAY.

Michael was too excited to be depressed by the view. He waited impatiently for the first glitter of sunlight on metal that would herald the approach of Project Cyclops' antennas. Beside him, Roger Crain kept his white head buried in a sheaf of papers, preferring to ignore the evidence of man's less than gentle touch on the once sublime landscape.

Crain would have been spared this close-up view if he'd accepted Joshua Rosenblum's offer of a government jet flight. But Crain refused to fly; he preferred to take his chances with magnetic levitation, even if it meant contending with fixed schedules. Michael stuck close by his side, not for the old man's benefit, but for his own: he looked forward to his first meeting with the legendary Joshua Rosenblum eagerly, yet with trepidation.

It was merely the latest in what threatened to become an endless series of emotional shocks. Michael had adopted a philosophical attitude, or so he pretended to himself—he was just going along for the ride. He had begun cultivating an air of nonchalance after his long phone conversation with Roger Crain the night of his return from the mountains.

Roger had persuaded him to take back his old post at the MIC, assuring him that he could have any price he cared to name. It was then that Michael realized the price he would have liked was impossible. There was no way he could humiliate Muller (and savor that humiliation) as he had been humilated. With this visceral pleasure denied him, he settled for the next best thing: the very next morning he had shown up at the MIC to receive a mumbled apology, an offer of twice his old salary, and a new office next to Roger Crain's (and with the third best view in the building).

He airily accepted, allowing himself only one outward sign of revenge: already that morning he had begun to grow a beard. Muller said not a word about the stubble on his cheeks and chin.

And now, only two days later, he was on his way to meet the world's most famous living astronomer.

The plane began to slow, and Michael nudged the old man beside him. "You can look now, Roger. We're almost there."

Crain looked up and peered out the window. A few kilometers away the horizon was solid with tall white metal towers—clean, precise, and dignified. Crain grunted, and began gathering his papers into his old-fashioned leather briefcase.

A neatly painted sign in blue and gold greeted them as they

stepped from the plane into the spotless little station: WEL-
COME TO SEARCHLIGHT BASE, HOME OF PROJECT CYCLOPS. A
JOINT FACILITY OF THE UNITED STATES SPACE FORCE IN-
TERSTELLAR COMMUNICATIONS COMMAND AND THE NA-
TIONAL SPACE AGENCY. BRIGADIER GENERAL BENJAMIN J.
TALBOT, BASE COMMANDER.

Underneath the sign stood a young Space Force captain
who grinned at them boyishly and thrust out a welcoming
hand. "Doctor Crain, Doctor Ward, I'm Ted Donner. Hope
your trip was smooth?"

Crain murmured "Pleased to meet you, Captain," and
Michael said eagerly, "Nice of you to meet us."

"My pleasure," Donner replied. "After all, you two are
definitely VIP's around here. I hope you'll give me a chance
to show you around after your meeting?"

"This is strictly a business trip, I'm afraid," said Michael, a
trifle self-importantly. "Maybe we could take you up on that
next time."

"Any time at all," said Donner. "Well, Doctor Rosenblum
is waiting, and I've got a tram standing by. Shall we go?"

Within a few moments they were humming across the
desert and through the main gate of Searchlight Base, toward
the deep shade of the rows of antennas. The trip from the
magneplane station to the Operations Building at the very
center of the array took only a few minutes, and Ted Donner
kept up an easy conversation with Michael all the way. Roger
Crain seemed to have withdrawn into his own thoughts, his
eyes fixed on the great antennas which marched by one after
another in a seemingly endless parade.

If Michael had later reflected on his talk with Donner, he
might have been uncomfortable at how much of himself he'd
revealed to the affable stranger in such a short time—his
former jobs, his former marriages, his tastes in food and
music, his favorite TV shows, what he liked to read, what he
did for exercise, his vague political views. Whatever Michael
said, Donner always had something apropos to add, which
coincidentally moved Michael easily on to the next subject,
and Michael stepped out of the tram unaware that he had
been fleeced by an expert mental pickpocket.

Donner whisked them past the guard at the door of the
Operations Building, through an airlock, down two corridors
and up a flight of stairs to Joshua Rosenblum's office. It took
a moment for Michael's eyes to adjust to the light, almost all

of which came through the huge window behind Rosenblum's desk, reflected from the dazzling surfaces of the enormous paraboloid dishes of nearby antennas.

When Michael's eyes did adjust, he found that Rosenblum was not behind his desk; he was not even in his office. Two people were rising to their feet beside a conference table in one corner of the big room. Ted Donner made quick introductions among Crain and Michael and Lynn Nishihara and Fred Walker.

"I suppose you people will be talking over my head, so I'll just disappear," Donner said. "But please let me know if I can be of any help. Any of these folks will know how to get ahold of me."

Donner slipped out of the room as Michael and Roger Crain thanked him.

"You both like coffee, don't you?" asked Fred Walker, moving toward the wall dispenser as Crain and Michael nodded. "Cream? sugar? Just black then," he said, tapping the unit's buttons, then handing them thin glass mugs. "Here you go. Josh should be with us any minute, he was called off to . . ."

Just then Rosenblum hurried through the door, loose coat and trousers flopping in the breeze of his passage. "Roger Crain, God it's good to see you in the flesh!" He extended a bony left hand and gripped Crain's right in a reversed handshake—meanwhile, with his free hand, he shook a sheaf of papers at the group. "Something most interesting here, people, most interesting—oh, pardon me, you're Ward, of course," he said, nodding once at Michael. "A pleasure. Sit down, sit down everybody, please."

Michael pulled out a chair between Lynn Nishihara and Fred Walker and sat, his eyes bright and his mouth shut tight. The easy braggadocio Donner had encouraged in him had departed. He was more than a little awed to be in Joshua Rosenblum's presence. He was also not quite sure that Lynn Nishihara didn't dislike him—she'd said not a word when they were introduced, and she'd kept her eyes grimly on the tabletop ever since.

In fact, now that his psychological armor had been pried apart ever so slightly, a flood of doubt rushed in to widen the chink. Wasn't Rosenblum ignoring him? Hadn't Walker been rather cool? Wasn't that fellow Donner just mocking them with all his talk of VIP's and such? Were they here just out of a sense of obligation on Rosenblum's part to his old friend Roger Crain? And were they going to get a few minutes chat followed by a polite brush-off?

The irrational fear that he was somehow *not worthy* rendered Michael momentarily unconscious of what was going on at the conference table. Suddenly he found himself holding a couple of sheets of paper—Rosenblum was dealing them out like playing cards—covered with irregular closed loops like ripples on the surface of a pond someone had just sprinkled with a handful of gravel. Arrows, Greek letters, and strings of signs and numbers crawled over the diagram like a colony of water bugs.

". . . finally getting results from the Farside link-up," Rosenblum was saying. "I read this as direct confirmation of the *Actis* data on the Tau Ceti system, at least as far as it goes. Have a look."

Michael stared at the papers. He recognized them as maps of radio signals, but their significance escaped him completely. He glanced at Roger Crain, desperately hoping that he was not alone in his ignorance, but the old man appeared to be studying his copies of the maps with interest.

"That's terrific," said Fred Walker, flipping back and forth from one page to the other. "Just the kind of shifting you'd predict from the reported mass values."

"Right you are," chortled Rosenblum. *"This* should prove the worth of getting Farside's cooperation. Even Washington can't ignore it." Rosenblum beamed around the table, flushed with satisfaction.

Then, to Michael's dismay, Rosenblum looked right at him and noticed his blank expression.

"Oh, forgive me for talking shop, you two . . . Am I making any sense at all?"

"Not yet, Josh," said Crain cheerfully. "But I assume you'll get around to it sooner or later."

Michael's heart lightened.

Rosenblum grinned at Crain. "Okay. What we've got here is solid evidence from ULB interferometry of planetary masses perturbing the path of the star Tau Ceti. Most of the mass seems concentrated in one orbiting point—not big enough to show a Doppler shift in the star until you stretch a parallax baseline from here to the moon, but damned big nonetheless. We've been after the Space Force for years to let us hook up with their radio telescopes at Farside to establish an ultralong baseline, but not until *Actis* could we persuade them to do it."

Fred Walker said, "That mass we've located showed up in the telemetry from *Actis* strictly in terms of computed deceleration, by the way. No visual record at all. Which means it's probably the black hole."

"The black hole at their end," Rosenblum specified. "If they went into one at this end, presumably they came out of one at that end. Which brings us to why you're here . . . it's time we took a close look at this wild theory you two have cooked up."

Michael cleared his throat nervously. *Why is he looking at me? Am I going to have to defend this "wild theory" by myself?* But before he could open his mouth, Crain spoke for him.

"It's good of you to take the time to meet with us and hear us out on this, Josh," Crain said.

"I wish you'd called me years ago," Rosenblum replied firmly. "I'd like to lure you away from that retreat of yours. By the way, are you hiding any more like this fellow out there?"

Crain smiled. "I'm afraid not. Michael is definitely a unique specimen."

Michael's face burned. Rosenblum chuckled, but Nishihara and Walker were silent.

Rosenblum cleared his throat mightily. "Well—we'll have to save the logistics of how we could work together until later. First, we have to get some of our major concerns on the table." Rosenblum knitted his long fingers together, cracked his knuckles, and grinned wolfishly at Michael. "It's a pretty picture you fellows have come up with, but it just doesn't work. Want to know why I say that?"

"Relativistic effects," said Roger Crain immediately.

"That's right, of course, Roger," Rosenblum nodded. He fixed his gaze on Michael. "What do you have to say about it, young man? Eh?"

"We're aware of the difficulty, sir," Michael stammered.

"More than a *difficulty*, young man," Rosenblum said sternly. If we can't explain the apparent absence of relativistic effects, we haven't got a model. Unless you plan to take on Einstein?"

Fred Walker was grinning, Michael noted from the corner of his eye. Michael felt himself becoming irritated. "We're not challenging relativity, Professor. We know we've got to enlarge our model to account for some missing elements. But we think the first priority is to explain the survival of the ship and its reappearance in Tau Ceti space . . ."

"Well?" asked Rosenblum impatiently.

"Well, let's first look at the problem from the point of view of those on board *Actis,*" said Michael. "Relativistic effects—while they certainly should be apparent from Earth—would not be apparent to the crew of *Actis.* If we stay with their reference frame for a moment . . ." Michael become uncomfortably aware that Lynn Nishihara had begun taking notes ". . . we see that the model we have developed *does* explain most of what happened to *Actis,* from *her point of view.*"

"Elaborate," Rosenblum ordered. Michael wondered if the man were needling him deliberately.

"Specifically, our model explains the absence of tidal effects, and the instantaneous transition from one region of our local universe to another, without traversing a unidimensional singularity." Michael realized he was gaining confidence as he listed the idea's advantages. "If ours turns out to be the only model that can satisfactorily explain those things from even *one* point of view—that of *Actis*—then we think it will be necessary to explain the absence of relativistic effects by somehow enlarging the model—not by throwing it out."

Rosenblum nodded soberly. "I assure you, Ward, competing models have been pouring in here at the rate of several a day. If yours weren't the only one that even halfway made sense, we wouldn't be sitting here." Rosenblum looked at Fred Walker. "Sorry, Fred. No prize at the bottom of the box."

Michael had only a moment to wonder what Rosenblum meant, when the astronomer went on: "Okay, here's our program. We'll spend as much time as we need fitting the actual data from the *Actis* telemetry to the Ward-Crain hypothesis . . ."

The Ward-Crain hypothesis! Sounds pretty good, Michael thought smugly.

". . . and perhaps by the end of the day we'll know whether there are any disastrous discrepancies. If not . . . we'll assume we're in business together. And *then* we can really start scratching our heads! Why did we hear from *Actis* in no more time than it takes a beam of light to travel from Tau Ceti to Earth?"

"Yeah," grumbled Walker. "That's the hook, all right. I

was really hoping you guys were saving something for us."
He looked sourly at Michael. "You know, Mike, according to
your model or anybody else's, that ship should still be sitting
there on the edge of the hole—frozen stiff."

It was dusk when Crain and Michael got back on the
magneplane for the three-hour return trip to Boulder, via Las
Vegas, Salt Lake City, and Denver. Michael thought back
over the day's events, as the mag-lev vehicle smoothly accelerated away from the towering antennas into the clear soft
blue night twinkling with its first stars.

When Rosenblum had finally given her the cue, Lynn
Nishihara had opened up, and what came out of her mouth
was a stream of numbers. She and Roger Crain had gabbled
at each other for what seemed like five hours straight, not
even stopping when they all ate a hasty lunch at the base
cafeteria. Crain had offered up the major features of the
"Ward-Crain hypothesis" (the phrase still made Michael glow
with satisfaction), specifying the parameters of the model in
precise mathematical terminology. Then Nishihara had attacked his equations from the data from *Actis*, all the
relevant automated telemetry the radio astronomers had been
able to collect in the short days before the doomed ship's
signals had faded forever into the cosmic background noise.
In every case the fit between prediction and observation was
reasonable.

Michael was sometimes hard pressed to follow their discussion, but luckily he wasn't forced to. Early in the afternoon
Fred Walker took him aside and, gingerly at first, launched a
separate line of inquiry.

"You're a topologist, Mike? If I've got it right," Walker
said tentatively.

"I'm interested in topology," Michael said honestly, "I can't
claim it as a specialty."

"Well, my interest is combinations. So my guess is we can
talk to each other."

"Try me," said Michael, curious.

Walker hesitated. "I'm not being coy, but I'd appreciate it
if you'd lay out how *you* see the relativity problems
first . . ."

Michael had. According to the model he and Roger had
developed, two singular masses spun around each other in a
dizzying spiral, dragging spacetime into a pleated funnel
around them. But this black hole system was no simple warp

in the local geometry of the universe. If it were, no human alive on Earth could ever had heard another whisper from *Actis*.

For the intense gravity of the black hole system distorted not just space, but spacetime: as *Actis* neared the orbiting hole she was accelerated to near light speed, just as she plunged into the event horizon. At that moment her motion relative to earth paradoxically slowed to nothing.

In the same instant she emerged from the hyperfold near Tau Ceti (presumably from a similar black hole system in Tau Ceti space): here gravity just as quickly decelerated her onward rush.

Yet on earth, what had taken the barest instant of ship's time had encompassed the rise of empires and their decay into dust.

That was what Fred Walker had meant when he'd told Michael that *Actis* should still be frozen stiff on the edge of the hole—dark and invisible, but in some mathematical sense, never having left the solar system at all. And if that were true, how could *Actis* have emerged in some *other* solar system?"

"That's how I see the problem," said Michael.

"That's pretty much how I see it too," Walker confirmed. "And I've been thinking about it for a few days. I'll tell you what I've concluded—*not* something I wanted to confess to while there was still a chance you guys had a really sensible explanation . . ."

Those earthly empires that rose and fell while *Actis* traversed the stargate—they were empires not only of the distant future, but of the distant past as well. Fred Walker realized (for his mind did not instinctively flinch from imaginary numbers) that *Actis* must have passed through a region where the direction of time's arrow is reversed. The ship had stayed there just long enough to compensate for the stretching of time in Earth's reference frame (the laws that governed this precise relationship waited discovery); *Actis* had reemerged in the neighborhood of Tau Ceti less than an eye-blink later.

Twelve light years in no time. On the cosmic scale, it was an achievement hardly more significant than a walk to the corner grocery. But the route *Actis* had taken had led through the dark wood of another universe altogether. Between the stargate's entrance and exit lay a labyrinth in superspace, with dark, twisting corridors of incalculable extent.

Michael and Fred Walker had spent the rest of the afternoon exploring some possible configurations of that labyrinth, laying out a program of research for themselves that would keep them busy for months.

As Michael rested comfortably in the seat of the magneplane beside the sleeping Roger Cain, it did not occur to him to doubt his own abilities. Proving himself was no longer a problem; solving the *problem* was the problem.

The magneplane reached Boulder long after dark. Michael drove a very sleepy Roger home to his little brick house in the heart of the old town. Then he retired to his own apartment.

As he pushed open his door he scraped aside a pile of papers: prepaid hard copies from the mailbox facscriber. Somehow people thought you would feel obligated to read their letters if they paid the post office to print them out.

But Michael already knew what to expect; a similar pile had greeted him for the last two nights. There would be fan letters, requests for interviews, solicitations, blunt sexual propositions, crank threats, and so on. He picked up the pile and carried it straight to the recycling chute. He had neither the time nor the inclination to read it all—he'd scan the computer's recording in the morning before he went to work, and catch anything important before he dumped the short term memory.

But as it happened, the next morning he forgot, and in the weeks and months that followed he became more and more consumed by the challenges of the black hole model, so that he rarely gave his mail or the TV news more than glancing attention.

Thus he had only the vaguest idea of the congressional hearings, the intense lobbying efforts and public relations campaigns, the contracts being solicited, the speeches at the United Nations. When the time came, he was ill prepared for his first meeting with Laura McCord.

14

She gave him of that fair enticing Fruit
With liberal hand . . .

—John Milton
Paradise Lost

One afternoon Franklin Muller's grandmotherly secretary (the only human secretary in the building, reserved for the most portentous communications) called Michael on the intercom. She asked with utmost deference if he would make himself available on the following morning to meet with a very important visitor. Michael agreed readily, and promptly forgot all about the call.

The next day was a cold, clear February morning, and the hour of the forgotten appointment found Michael huddled in the building's library, where the heat was always turned up just enough to encourage napping at the carrels. Michael was flipping through back issues of *Science* on the microscanner, searching for examples of particularly well-written research reports. With his theoretical work nearing a convenient summary point, Michael's thoughts had turned to publication. Fantasies of the Nobel prize had begun to creep into his daydreams, pushing aside the giddy quest for pure knowledge that had so long consumed him.

"Ah, there you are!" he heard Franklin Muller call out, in a voice cracking with joviality. Michael started guiltily from his reading, thrust for a moment back to the bad old days when he had used the library as a place to hide. He stood up quickly. Almost before he could remind himself that he had nothing to fear from Muller, he saw the director's gaunt figure swept aside by a formidable copper-haired young woman in Space Force uniform, who strode into the room escorted by two other officers, a man and a woman. The man looked vaguely familiar, but Michael paid him no attention. He was hypnotized by the red-haired woman's stare, like a bird before a snake. For a moment she stood there, Artemis with her hounds, booted and skirted and jacketed all in black and silver, regarding him with a satisfied smile, as the big-game hunter contemplates the freshly bagged trophy.

"So you're the man," she said.

He was naked before her expert appraisal, suddenly conscious of the flab around his waist, of the wrinkles on his hams from too many weeks in a soft chair, of the scruffy beard he hadn't trimmed in a month. *Ecce homo.*

Before he could dissolve at her feet, she smiled even more broadly and thrust out her hand. "Laura McCord. I'm honored to meet you."

He grabbed her hand with alacrity, trying to return her firm and confident grip. "Pleased, I'm sure . . ." *What the hell's her rank?* he wondered, trying to remember what those little birds on her shoulders stood for.

"Colonel McCord's been one of our most important supporters, Michael—" Muller began, but Laura rode over him.

"Call me Laura. I'll call you Mike. I feel I know you pretty well—I've been following your work closely. I'm curious to know what you think of *our* work so far."

"I beg your pardon?" Michael blinked.

She laughed. "Well, I'm disappointed, but not really surprised," she admitted. "Ted, you warned me he might have his head in the stars," she said, looking at her aide.

Ted—Donner, thought Michael. *That fellow from Searchlight. What's he doing here?*

Donner was smiling at her. "Well, there's enough time to fill him in on the plane. Mike picks things up fast."

The plane? What plane?

"We'd like to borrow Mike for awhile—with your approval, of course, Doctor Muller," said Laura, strafing the obsequious Muller with her gaze as she turned back to Michael. She did not wait for Muller's eager nod. "We're going into this space warp of yours, Michael. We intend to find the planet *Actis* found, and explore it. We're prepared to rescue any of the *Actis* people who're still alive. We've made a lot of progress since your theoretical breakthrough made it obvious it was worth trying."

"We have the specifications for the ship, we're putting the crew together right now," Donner added, "and the only thing left is to reassure a couple of webfooted congresspeople that we aren't going to violate any of Mother Nature's laws."

"That's why we need you," Mike," Laura said firmly. "To tell them that for us, in person. Whether you know it or not, your word carries enough weight to convince them."

A moment passed while he thought about what she was asking of him. Then he shook his head apologetically. "Doctor Crain and I aren't in a position to make predictions about the chances for success for a particular project, Colonel."

"Laura," she reminded him, with an edge of impatience. "Now look here, Mike—your results have established that any ship entering the hole will survive, right?"

"Well," he began cautiously, "the configuration of the null-gravity behavior surface would seem to make it probable that any object . . ."

"Yes, that's what I meant. And you've also established that the warp works both ways."

"Symmetry is an essential feature of our model, true, but it's not a simple four-dimensional symmetry . . ."

"Good enough. That's all we want you to say." She beamed at him.

"We can work it out in detail on the plane," Donner said. "Sorry we couldn't give you more time, Mike, but we didn't find out they were pulling this special session on us until just yesterday. We'll have you back here day after tomorrow for sure—if that's the way you want it."

Michael looked at the copy of *Science* in his hand. Then he replaced the little handsomely engraved microfiche card back in its binder on the library shelf. Resentment welled up in him.

He turned back to the woman. "I'd like to know where you get all your information," he flared at her. "Crain and I haven't published a word." His gaze slid off McCord to her partner Donner.

But both Donner and McCord were looking at Muller, questioningly.

Muller responded on cue. "Certainly you're aware, Michael, that periodic reports of our progress here have been sent to the Space Agency and other authorized parties on a regular basis?" He was acting surprised. "This was a condition of the research grant, and, I might add, quite a normal and proper requirement."

"Who wrote up these reports?" Michael asked, in a strained voice.

Muller turned a deep red. "You made it plain you wanted no interruptions. Therefore I took the liberty of—" He didn't bother to finish the sentence.

Michael turned back to McCord, expecting her to be dismayed by this revelation. But she regarded him openly, as if to say, "Now that we've got that insignificant business out of the way . . ."

Suddenly Michael realized what had not occurred to him earlier: this was *the* Laura McCord standing in front of him, last person on Earth to see the crew of *Actis* alive, Space Force prodigy, daughter of Senator Benton "Space-is-Destiny" McCord—unrecognized in the flesh, and virtually unchanged since the time Michael, as a teenager, had had a long-distance crush on the glamorous adventuress.

With that realization came another: the ivory tower he had been living in was a puppet stage of cardboard, and he, in his scientist's costume, was a marionette dangling from the purse strings of power.

Laura McCord heard in his silence what she apparently wanted to hear. "I'm glad you see it from our point of view, Mike," she smiled. She turned to Donner. "I told you that subpoena was a silly idea, Ted."

"Don't look at me, Colonel," said Donner cheerfully. "Sanders here was the pessimist."

For an uncomfortable moment Michael confronted the expressionless gaze of Laura McCord's other companion, a tall dark-haired woman who had stood just inside the library door since the beginning of the conversation, not moving a muscle.

"Okay . . . Laura," said Michael, sighing in resignation. "It's your show."

"Get whatever papers you need," she commanded with brisk good humor. "The car's outside—we'll swing by your place and pick up your personal gear. We've got a jet standing by."

Ten minutes later the little group was marching through half-melted slush toward a black staff car that waited outside the front entrance of the MIC building. Laura McCord was in the lead, and Michael followed behind her, flanked by Donner and Sanders. *Like a prisoner to the firing squad*, he thought. The cold dry air stung his cheeks, and his breath steamed in front of him.

Michael had made a hasty, last-minute attempt to locate

Roger Crain, with no luck. He'd been missing all morning; Michael wondered how Muller had managed to get him out of the way.

Behind Michael the windows of the building were lined with the peering faces of MIC staff members, solemnly watching the group's departure.

Donner held the rear door of the staff car open, and Michael bent to enter it. "Don't fight it, Mike," Donner whispered. "You know, if you play your cards right, there's a berth for you on our ship."

Michael was thrown off balance by his surprise, and bounced his skull off the roof of the car. Momentarily dizzy, he lurched into the back seat. Donner slid in after him, pretending not to notice Michael's confusion.

Donner was saying, "And I hope I'm the first to welcome you aboard."

The turbine whined and the car moved forward, its tires crunching and popping on the road's icy crust.

Michael looked at Donner, and the Captain gave him his patented freckled-faced-kid grin. Then Donner winked.

Michael turned away to peer back through the frosty rear window of the car. *McCord and her henchmen must have been studying me for months,* he thought. *Like a bug under a microscope.*

His thoughts went back to his first meeting with Donner at Searchlight Base. It had all seemed so casual.

He could not deny that Donner's insinuated bribe filled him with intense anticipation. What had the man said before? "We can get you back here day after tomorrow—if that's the way you want it." But Donner had already figured out that's *not* the way Michael would want it. He knew that Michael would be as persuasive before Congress as he could if he thought that by doing so he had a chance to break clean away from Earth . . .

Michael stared back at the receding MIC building, hoping to catch at least a glimpse of Roger Crain's face. He was suddenly unsure if he would ever see the old man again.

15

Oh, I have slipped the surly bonds of earth . . .
—John Gillespie Magee, Jr.
High Flight

His fingers tingle on the stick—it feels like a live wire with a low current running. He can smell his own sweat in the oxygen mask. He's got a crawling sensation in his groin, because he's sitting on top of a great big firecracker that's about to go off and kick him in the ass like he's never been kicked. He can't see a damned thing but glistering sunlight reflecting from scratches in the quartz canopy—that, and a few feet of shroud lines running to the balloon that towers invisible over his head.

He's hanging there thirty thousand meters above the Mojave Desert in a black and windless sky, waiting for the bottom to drop out of everything.

It does. His stomach floats up toward his heart. Then the rocket fires, slams him into his contoured couch with a force that knocks the breath out of him.

The limp shape of the huge balloon flicks down and away, barely visible for a split second in the tail of his eye. The needles of the dials on the instrument panel are all spinning: the altimeter and the airspeed indicator are going one way, the fuel gauge is going the other. But the engine cuts out well before the ship exceeds escape velocity. The point of the exercise is not to prove that the RAPLAR works going straight up—the test pilots established that a long time before he ever got near one. The point is to find out whether Michael Ward can land it in one piece.

Laura McCord stands at the edge of the long, wide, runway, squinting up at the sun. She could be inside the tower, but she'd rather be out here with nothing between her and the sky.

The distant bellow of the powerful rocket cascades almost gently from the cobalt reaches of heaven. The roar suddenly stops, and rolls away over the high desert in a long dying echo.

The loudspeaker on the tower behind her broadcasts the essential data: rate of descent, heading, airspeed, attitude, angle of attack, skin temperature, altitude, estimated time to touchdown. Laura can't see the black, dart-shaped craft with its stubby little wings and its white ceramic belly yet; it's still much too far away. But hardly anyone could imagine better than she what the pilot is experiencing inside the cockpit of the plummeting bird.

For fifteen minutes he's been a busy man. Despite its sleek appearance, the flimsy little ship has the glide characteristics of a brick. He's got to nurse it down, keep its nose up enough to give him enough lift to get within striking range. He can't see much through the window; he's got to put all his faith in his instruments.

Close enough to reach home in a shallow dive, now. Put the nose down just so—there's the marker. He's on the glide path.

Ground's coming up fast; not enough fuel in the tanks for a second pass. But there's plenty of dry lake bed out there if he needs it. He brings it in hot. At the last moment he lifts the nose ever so slightly . . .

The belly-wheel kisses the salt pan. It's a perfect landing. He's mildly surprised.

The black bullet shrieks past Laura in a cloud of yellow-white dust. She grins.

She's not surprised it's a perfect landing. From the beginning of Michael's flight training a year ago, it was obvious that the sky was his element.

II

ZETES

16

---

4 June 38

I met for two hours today with Dan Levine, over at Space. We were joined midway through by Hamlyn, for DOD, and Slater, for State.

Hamlyn was much subdued compared to yesterday. No more strenuous objections. Wonder who talked to him in the interim? Basically, he wanted reassurance that I'm not going to bust up his ships—he wants them back some day. I did my best to be polite. I reviewed the details of our plans for structural modification, safety precautions, so on. Hamlyn's only other concern was satisfied by Levine, that costs will not come out of DOD's budget. Space will pay the bills.

Slater was much exercised over my preliminary memo to Dan outlining crew composition. Although our thinking was still in the formative stages, Dan apparently thought it best to let State in on our thinking early, to avoid misunderstanding down the road. Slater thought Americans overrepresented, military in particular. "This is supposed to be a peaceful mission of the United Nations. We're just footing the bill," he kept insisting.

Over my objections Dan agreed to include somebody from L-5. But at my insistence he stipulated they be civilian scientists only. Hamlyn supported me on this. Slater was reluctant to commit himself without asking L-5's concurrence, but Dan reminded him L-5 was being included as a courtesy.

As for representatives, I suggested Hamlyn could track me down some good Jordanian pilots, or maybe Nigerians or Chinese. Most of them train here anyway.

Slater also wanted changes in command structure. He wants a civilian in the number two slot, to represent the scientists. This would bump Allison Sanders from Deputy Commander down to a number three position, although she would still be the second pilot, of course. Dan suggested a compromise on this: let Donner be the number two. He's military, but has long experience with scientists.

Sanders won't be happy with his, and I don't blame her. I

asked Dan for some time to think it over. But with Slater on his back, I think he will insist. State likes to think this is their show, and Dan doesn't want to disabuse them of that notion until we're under way.

The next meeting is scheduled for six ten. We'll finalize the schedule and crew. Dan and I will meet with the UN on six eleven.

After Hamlyn and Slater left I told Dan I wanted Dave as number three navigator. He was pleased at the suggestion.

(Signed) LMM/autoscribe

Michael's ears pricked up when the tinny speaker in the passenger cabin emitted an electronic ping. The shuttle pilot's bored voice filtered through. "Just in case any of you jokers are awake back there, take a look at the big screen. We have a nice clear picture of the mommy ship. And for anybody who cares, docking time is estimated at twenty minutes. So zip up your flies and say your good-byes. Smilin' Jack over and out."

A year and a half earlier Michael Ward would have been prissy enough to be offended by the pilot's casual obscenity. It no longer made any impression on him—he'd had plenty of time to accustom himself to the military's penchant for vulgarizing everything it encountered. He no longer winced even when he heard his shipmates refer to the "WC hypothesis" and its variants. After all, to Valeri Subotin, the only Russian in the crew, the phrase "black hole" was itself a dirty word.

Michael leaned sideways against his restraining seat harness to get a better view of the display screen down the aisle of the shuttle. The screen filled the forward bulkhead of the narrow cabin; across its width spread an image of Zetes, white and silver against the black of space. It was the first time Michael had seen the ship close-up and live.

Zetes was a monster, almost half a kilometer from one end to the other. Even though Michael had known every detail of her plan for months, the ship's nearness and the knowledge that he would soon be aboard raised goose bumps of anticipation.

The ship had not been built from scratch in the mere eighteen months that had elapsed since Congress and the Administration had given the go-ahead to the McCord plan (and the United Nations had graciously agreed to lend its name). The Zetes was actually two standard Space Force line cruisers joined nose-to-nose: once the *Calais* and the *Zetes* had been twins, but *Zetes* had stolen the identity of its sibling. Structural modification was surprisingly minimal; the only extensive changes were to the layout of the command-and-control decks, and to the crew quarters.

By pulling two proven ships of the line out of service Laura McCord had managed to decimate the Space Force fleet. Michael knew she must have enjoyed the screams from the commanders she displaced.

Despite the ship's ad hoc origins, *Zetes* had a compact, bluntly businesslike appearance, made vaguely menacing by the gaping magnetic blast nozzles at each end. Her double-stern design had one marked advantage: she could back up with as much force as she could move forward.

Clinging to her twin hulls like wasps to a hive were eight black dart-shaped objects that set *Zetes* apart from all other ships in the solar system. These were the RAPLARs—in bureaucratic jargon, "Retrievable Atmospheric-Planet Landing and Reconnaissance" vehicles. Unlike their near cousins, the ubiquitous space shuttles that plied back and forth between Earth and her nearby satellites, the RAPLARs were designed to enter the atmosphere of an alien planet, take on passengers, and return to space—without benefit of ground-base gantry rigs and rocket boosters. To achieve this they carried a strange cargo on the downward leg: colossal high-altitude balloons, neatly packaged and stored in the passengers cabins of the craft. Once deployed, the balloons could lift the RAPLARs above ninety percent of the density of an earthlike planet's atmosphere. From there, the RAPLARs' rockets had sufficient thrust to blast them free into space.

In only one respect were the landing craft dependent on the surface conditions of the planet: hydrogen to fill the balloons and recharge rocket fuel tanks must be obtained from water. But if the alien planet had no water, a RAPLAR would have no business being down there.

Michael Ward had firsthand knowledge that the RAPLAR scheme would work—like every member of the crew of *Zetes*, he'd earned his passage on the expedition by demonstrating that he could singlehandedly deploy the balloon, fill it with gas, let it carry the ship into the stratosphere, and effect a release and launch. Then, to complete the test, he'd piloted the RAPLAR back to a safe landing on Earth.

Now, as the image of *Zetes* and her planetary landers expanded in the shuttle's viewscreen, Michael idly wondered what it would be like to land a RAPLAR at a hundred and fifty knots, not on a dry lake bed, but in the open water. For that was the plan—though he knew he would not face that tricky task himself. His job, as navigation consultant, was to help *Zetes* find the planet. He was not slated to touch foot on its soil.

He slid forward in his seat as the shuttle's retro-rockets fired. For a moment he had the sensation of dangling head down from his harness. The flank of *Zetes* loomed large in the view screen, her docking port bright and open to the approaching shuttle. Beside the port, the big blue painted flag of the United Nations was briefly prominent in the glare of the shuttle's floodlights. Then the pneumatic seal of the port closed with a sucking "Whump" around the shuttle's nose.

The viewscreen went blank. Alarm bells sounded and were quickly silenced, as the forward hatch of the shuttle cracked open, allowing the shuttle's pressurized atmosphere to mingle with the atmosphere of *Zetes*.

Cabin lights came up full. A murmur of relief arose from the men and woman in the passenger cabin. Michael released the catch of his harness and floated gently up over the seat back in front of him, hooking gloved fingers into the ceiling webbing to prevent collisions with his fellow passengers. Even though the ride up from Vandenberg had taken only a few hours, he would be heartily glad to see the last of the shuttle. The military vehicle had none of the padded luxury of its commercial counterparts: its bare metal interior and worn canvas sling seats preserved the nervous-sweat smell of previous passengers, most of them Space Force recruits.

But he supposed he'd better get used to close quarters and the aroma of sweat, metal, ozone, and hot oil; he could expect nothing better aboard *Zetes*.

Michael and his fellow crew members emerged into the cramped tubular docking bay of *Zetes*. Donner and the watch officer were there to check them off, and Michael was pleased to see that Laura herself had come down to welcome the last contingent aboard ship. There was no ceremony, no salutes to the quarter deck; everyone knew everyone else intimately after months of training. Gloved hands brushed lightly, brief words were exchanged, and then the crew members headed through the inner lock to their quarters. No one needed to be shown the way.

It had been weeks since Michael had seen Laura, and the warmth the sight of her evoked in him was surprising. Ever since Congress had given the final go-ahead for the mission and he had been officially invited to join, he had felt her eyes upon him, testing, weighing, judging his fitness. Soon he had become part of the inner councils of planning, and had met with her often. But their relationship had been strictly businesslike. He had failed to notice how lonely he had been when she'd left Earth to supervise the final stages of outfitting *Zetes,* while he had stayed behind.

She surprised him, then, when his turn came in the perfunctory little reception line, by leaning down from her perch beside the inner lock, agile as a monkey, to put an arm around his shoulders and give him a quick, strong squeeze.

"Good to see you, Mike," she whispered. "Join us after the briefing tonight. Nineteen hundred, my cabin. A little going-away celebration."

He smiled, delighted.

She didn't expect an answer. She was already looking past him, to the woman next in line. Michael moved on through the hatch, toward his cabin.

He supposed "us" meant Donner, Sanders, and Laura herself, the expedition's ruling triumvirate. He found himself wishing Laura and he could celebrate without the other two. Odd thought, that . . .

Nevertheless, his heart was curiously light, and he did not think it was the absence of gravity that made it so.

17

Now entertain conjecture of a time
When creeping murmur and the poring dark
Fills the wide vessel of the universe.
                              —Wm. Shakespeare
                                Henry V

Laura McCord stood patiently in the humming, chattering darkness, her small erect figure tacked to the floor of the command deck by the Velcro patches on her heels. Michael Ward stood beside her, his bearing tense and nervous. The two of them watched the five-meter-wide viewscreen that dominated the bridge of *Zetes*, looking over the heads of a half dozen technicians who bent to their instrument panels. The viewscreen displayed an image of such crisp resolution that Laura and Michael might have been looking through a glassless window directly into space.

The velvet black was spangled with a thousand unblinking stars. Far down in the corner of the screen was the disk of the sun, a little smaller than if seen from Earth. Selectively filtered so as not to overbalance the rest of the image, the sun was surrounded by a pearly pink corona which seemed to reach up toward the white cylindrical shape hanging in the upper center of the screen.

That blunt cylinder was the last of the robot probes, which for the past week *Zetes* had been hurling like javelins into the heart of the black hole system. It pointed toward an invisible target.

With a telescope a knowledgeable astronomer might have detected several stars not exactly where they should be in that patch of sky directly in front of *Zetes*, and from their apparent displacement he might have calculated the strength of the gravitational fields that bent the paths of their distant light. But nothing in the unmagnified view from *Zetes*, several thousand kilometers away, betrayed the presence of the black hole system in the dead center of the viewscreen's frame.

"Launch in ten seconds," said a woman in the shadows.

"How long are we giving this one, Mike?" Laura asked.

"Thirty seconds on the other side to decelerate, another thirty to re-enter," Michael replied. "if we recover with less than two seconds error, we have a confirmed target."

Suddenly the room was washed in a dead white glare. The very rivets in the bulkhead panels sprouted deltas of inky shadow. Needles jumped, and the sensor circuitry gave out little whispered clicks of distress. Automatic override circuits suddenly adjusted the image to normal.

A searing bar of white light had sliced the star field from overhead to its center, and was fading slowly. Already the thrusting tip of the light pencil was darkening to orange, then red, then black, as the accelerating probe vanished from the universe, the last traces of its fusion exhaust Doppler-shifted beyond perception.

"Two seconds? That's not very generous," Laura complained.

"Hell it isn't," Michael grumbled. "It's a very big percentage for error. That probe's only a fraction of our length and mass. And *Zetes* is almost three times as big as *Actis* was when she went in. It would be nice to think the whole ship's going to end up in the same place, that's all."

"That's one contingency we never had a chance to test," she grinned, trying to tease him out of his edginess.

"I'm sure you thought of it," he said ungraciously. "Couldn't you figure out how to pull it?"

She was silent. She would humor him only so far.

"I can't read your mind, Laura," Michael continued, "but I swear I hope the next emergency is for real. It's bound to be something simple. Like an alien attack."

For months Laura had drilled the ship mercilessly to respond to every conceivable disaster. "If there is a next time, it will be for real," she said quietly.

"ETR fifteen seconds," said the voice from the shadows.

Laura and Michael fixed their attention on the screen. Seconds ticked away. A fleck of dark red appeared, and was instantly overwhelmed by a flare of corruscating white light which blossomed and died. From its heart appeared the scorched cylinder of the probe, limping toward them at a few hundred kilometers per second.

"Chasers?" Laura barked.

"Chasers away," a man in front of her confirmed.

The probe flashed overhead, disappearing from the screen. Invisible behind *Zetes*, chase ships sprinted to catch up with it.

"Retrofire positive," said the woman's voice.

"Chaser One has the target sighted. Estimated overtake two minutes," said the man.

"Readout," Laura commanded.

A technician punched a key. The ship's main computer spoke in a bland androgynous voice: "Performance fit: zero plus point zero zero three four seconds."

Laura relaxed. "Very nice," she breathed. She turned to Michael. "Make you happy?"

"Sure, I'm happy," he said, tonelessly.

"Good. You handle the recovery of the probe data, then." She paused; she thought she knew what was troubling him. "I don't see any reason not to start the final countdown. Do you, Mike?"

"No."

"Okay. I'll be in Communications," she said, loudly, informing the bridge personnel. She detached herself from the floor and floated toward the hatch. Just before ducking through, she turned her head toward Michael. "Trust yourself," she said, in a voice pitched just for him. Then she was gone through the hatch.

Michael stood silently, listening to the radio chatter that reported the recovery of the probe. He thought of the probes that had preceded this one into the black hole system.

Twenty-four had been sent; twelve had returned. Of the twelve survivors, the first seven had reappeared anywhere from several seconds earlier to many minutes later than planned.

One had emerged from the holes on a direct collision course with *Zetes* and instantly was ordered to self-destruct—with the consequent loss of its data. The others preserved charts of strange skies in their computer memories; the information had been relayed to Earth where, with luck, a few months or years of analysis might reveal from what vantage points they had looked on the universe.

Finally, a probe aimed by process of elimination had returned with evidence that it had visited Tau Ceti. More probes sent to the same locus along the fold confirmed the mapping. A ship entering just *there* would emerge in the new solar system; five consecutive successes were proof beyond the most extreme vagaries of chance.

Michael knew what had become of the others. It was possible to enter and exit superspace through double-hole systems, and survive the passage. But single holes also connected with superspace, and they were far more numerous . . .

The source of Michael's ill temper was simple anxiety.

Ship's time 23:00 hours:

Lights burned dimly in the corridors between the close-packed hexagonal cabins, one to a crew member, which made the living quarters of *Zetes* resemble a bee-hive. The dim lighting aided the fiction that it was "night"—the ship's clocks read 11:00 P.M., the time arranged to correspond with the time in Washington and New York.

Inside his cabin, Second Lieutenant David Levine impatiently scratched his chin with the microphone of his facscriber, hoping to find unhackneyed words to express obligatory phrases. He was not meeting with success.

"Dear Mom and Dad; Just thought I'd take the opportunity to write and tell you how much I love you both, since it looks like we're going to be pretty busy for awhile, and of course I won't have a chance to get in touch until we get back. Colonel McCord is a great commander, and . . ."

Et cetera. It might be the last letter he would ever write, of course. In view of that, he really ought to try a little harder. But meaningful thoughts were somehow out of bounds.

What if *Zetes* missed the right spot along the hyperfold, to emerge in uncharted space? The way back would be a matter of conjecture.

Or what if they somehow missed the null-tide behavior surface altogether, and fell directly into a singularity? They would never reach it, of course—long before that the fabric of the ship and the tissues of their bodies would have been ripped asunder; molecules, then atoms would dissociate; atoms would implode into their nuclei, nuclei would be mashed into colorless, flavorless quark soup. Grist for the mill of the gods, and no mill ever ground so fine.

Dear Mom and Dad: I'm afraid I'm going to die. I'm afraid if I don't die I'm going to be lost forever on the other side of the universe . . .

"I have absolute confidence in the ship," Levine said into the microphone. "We've tested the Ward-Crain theory with perfect results, so the whole trip will probably be pretty boring, probably . . ."

According to the data from the robot probes, and what could be gleaned from the *Actis* transmissions, nothing would happen when they crossed the warp. Almost nothing. The sun would redden and blink out. A new sun, Tau Ceti, would appear at a point mapped by the automatic cameras of the probes. The constellations might appear somewhat distorted, but the Milky Way would still stretch its pale band of light across the celestial sphere. *Zetes* would have shifted her perspective on infinity but little.

The ship would, of course, be utterly isolated.

"We can't wait to explore the planet and locate the survivors of *Actis*. In fact, communicating with the surface is probably the only tricky part of the whole mission. I'm not scheduled to be on any of the landing parties, so you can rest easy . . ." *But if we survive the trip through the holes, I'm going to do my damnedest to wangle a trip to the planet.*

Levine stared at the corrected copy of his letter, displayed on the facscriber's screen. There was really nothing more to say.

"Once more, I love you. So long. Dave."

He punched the send key. The letter would be batched and sent out early in the morning with any others the crew members had written. His parents would each get a copy— dad before he went to work, mother before she even got out of bed. He wondered if they were still friendly. Perhaps he should have sent separate letters, but he balked at it—he was reluctant to admit to himself that their relationship had changed.

Levine pushed away from his little desk, into the space in the middle of the tiny cabin. He reached out and flicked off the light, then began peeling off his uniform.

He thought of the girl in Biology, the one who'd been giving him encouraging looks at dinner. He'd like to get to know her better. He shouldn't be so shy; nobody else on the ship was.

If they made it through the holes, he'd be friendlier.

Ship time 23:20 hours:

Ted Donner watched from his bunk as Polly-from-Communications zipped the length of her uniform open down its front and slipped out of it quick as a fish. She was a lithe, smooth-muscled, efficient young woman, and Donner had only a moment to appreciate the play of the yellow night light on her bare skin as her shadowed body rolled over in midair, leaving the abandoned skin of the uniform floating in the gloom. Then she was too close for Donner to watch.

Her close-cropped brown hair brushed his cheek and he looked past her shoulder at the empty uniform hovering ghostlike in the dark. A shiver went through him . . .

The woman took it for passion and moved her mouth to kiss him. He rolled away from the phantom, gripping the steel bar at the head of the bunk—thoughtfully provided by the ship's designers for use in zero gravity—twisting his wrist to bring their two clinging bodies over and down into the sheets.

His open eyes stared into the near blackness of the bed-clothes. Half his mind was immersed in familiar pleasure; half skittered away, refusing to be seduced. His thoughts were jumbled, irrational. He heard strange noises; he thought he felt the ship move, though he knew it did not.

He imagined Laura's face grinning at him sardonically, seeing into his thirsty soul. He was afraid.

Ship time 23:45 hours:

Fire in Propulsion Control! A meteor punctures the hull! Explosion in Life Support; the computer suffers a nervous breakdown; a whole watch is poisoned at dinner; Zetes collides with a refueling tanker; explosive bolts self-detonate, hurling a RAPLAR into space . . .

And so on. Laura's imagination had quested far ahead of the ship on its months-long journey to the holes, creating obstacles and dangers from the extraordinary to the almost routine. Then, to the extreme limits of practicality, she had reified them. Emergencies were, of course, simulated when they had to be—she had no intention of aborting the mission through overzealousness—but they were always real to the harried crew, who never heard a hint or rumor of what would hit them next, or when.

What had she overlooked?

Laura lay on her bunk, still dressed in the uniform she had worn all day. She could not sleep—not that she was nervous; indeed, she was a little bored. Once the central computer had been instructed to start the final countdown, humans became superfluous. Only by their own insistence were they needed to confirm, in person, certain key commands.

Laura had given the command to proceed at five o'clock,

not long after the last probe had returned safely from Tau
Ceti space. Dan Levine had personally received the message
notifying the world that this step had been taken—after an
unavoidable forty-minute delay, Laura had received his reply,
alerting her to have the ship's company stand by in the
morning for speeches from the President of the United States
and the Secretary General of the United Nations.

Silly human rituals meant nothing to the computer at the
heart of *Zetes*. Even while the dignitaries spoke, the countdown would go on uninterrupted. Laura grinned—if the
speeches went on too long, *Zetes* would suddenly be twelve
light-years too far away to hear their conclusion.

What was it about the prospect of that leap that failed to
move her? Perhaps the very fact that Laura had fought,
schemed, worked for it for years—and in only a few hours, it
would be done. Done in an instant.

It smacked too much of final victory. She could not live in
a universe that did not constantly oppose her. When the
universe was lazy, she prodded it. Beyond the irreproachable
justification for her constant extreme drilling of her crew lay
this deeper motivation.

In a life replete with the love and admiration (and later,
the fear and respect) of those around her, she had never
stopped to ask herself what would become of her if she failed
to achieve some self-imposed goal. But neither would she
allow herself to contemplate some ultimate satisfaction—
certain victory and certain defeat were but opposite faces of
the same coin.

Only in constant motion could she fend off doubt—the fear
of seeing herself naked, her bare simple existence exposed to
an utterly indifferent universe. She would keep fate's coin
spinning to the end.

Laura shifted uneasily on her bunk. Ten hours to go—a
new sun, new planets awaited her. Worlds enough to con-
quer.

For no apparent reason she thought of Michael Ward. He
was unlike anyone she'd ever known, puppylike in his desire
for approval, bristling with defiance at any imagined insult, a
bright sloppy mind wrestling with an adolescent's emotions.
Yet she sensed steel in him, even discipline when something
touched him at the core. There was a word for that combina-
tion, one long out of fashion. Honor.

She knew he was a little bit in love with her. That was
certainly nothing new to her; she'd dealt with it hundreds of

times. But, she had to admit, she was attracted to him—in more than just a recreational way. He was different—different from the other sycophantic, pompous, or self-defeated men she was so familiar with in the service. Indeed, come to think of it, his type was almost completely alien to her.

She could not imagine why she chose to think of him at this moment. Perhaps it was a night to contemplate all things strange and mysterious and worthy of exploration.

18

Tiphys shouted at them to row with all their might, for the
Rocks were opening again. So they rowed on full of dread . . .
—Apollonius of Rhodes, *The Voyage of Argo*

Bright flame blossomed from her stern. *Zetes* began to move,
ponderously at first, pulling away from the cloud of tankers,
shuttles, and chase ships that had swarmed around her on the
long journey from Earth, like termites seeking a new nest.

Laura rested easily in the chief pilot's couch, on the control
deck above the bridge. To her right, Allison Sanders touched
gloved hands to the keyboard controls in the arm of the
co-pilot's couch. Like every other member of the crew both
women were suited, helmeted, and encased in webbing.
Across the wide viewscreen in front of them were projected
readouts from myriad instruments, superimposed on the star
field that was the view ahead.

Zetes bore down on her invisible target at an acceleration
of one-tenth gravity, impelled by her main stern engine.
Twenty seconds before entry into the warp the ship would
cross the point of no return: at that moment the full thrust
of her bow engine would still be just sufficient to halt her onward rush short of the black holes.

Laura wrapped her right hand firmly around the double-
contact dead-man switch planted in the arm of her couch. If
she relaxed her grip too soon, the mission would abort. Her
helmet radio was thick with the crosstalk of human and robot
voices assuring each other that all went well.

Laura believed them.

Below, on the bridge, Ted Donner stared at a similar
screen and listened to the same voices, but had no faith in
their calm assurance. The stars in the viewscreen did not
move; only the gentle pressure of acceleration against his back

gave him to understand that he was plunging straight up into a rip in the fabric of heaven. His body crawled with sweat. He stayed in his chair by an effort of will.

To one side of the bridge, in the auxiliary navigation cell, Michael Ward and David Levine lay side by side, still in their couches, their eyes fixed on a panel of meters, dials, and CRT screens. But for their cumbersome costumes they might have been a pair of ancient mariners, their attention held by a sliver of lodestone wandering on a straw raft in a bowl of water.

Into the comforting radio babble that filled Michael's helmet, the flat sexless voice of the central computer inserted itself: "Point of no return, at the mark plus thirty seconds. Mark."

Other robots kept talking, noting what suddenly seemed such trivia: acceleration, velocity, combustion chamber temperature, magnetic nozzle flux strength, radiation levels. But the human voices fell silent.

Michael stole a look at Levine, reclining beside him. He'd gotten to know the youth well in the last couple of years; he recognized a mind that grasped the intricacies of relativity more surely than his own. Levine's young-old face was shadowed inside his helmet, illumined only by the glow of the panel lights, oddly distorted in the curving plastic face plate. He seemed calm, alert, unconcerned. Michael took comfort from his nonchalance. Then Levine's tongue flicked out to moisten dry lips.

Ashamed to be spying, Michael turned his eyes to the instruments. As yet, nothing seemed in the least unusual.

"Point of no return, at the mark plus ten seconds. Mark."

If ghosts fled from *Zetes* as she plunged toward the netherworld, they were mere fictions of a feverish and over-rational mind. True, in a strict and mathematical sense, *Actis* lingered yet on the brink of the holes, moving slower than glaciers toward the rim of the world, still to make the leap that, just as surely, she had already successfully completed fourteen years earlier. The doomed expedition ships that had followed *Actis*, their ultimate fates unknown, were still time-locked beside her—as were each of the probes that *Zetes* had sent into the holes, even those which had already returned.

These things were all true in the frame of reference that *Zetes* was leaving behind, that local frame holding the sun and the spinning Earth (though no material clue remained in that frame to give tangible proof—the last packets of visible light had long since departed the falling objects, falling now like trees in a forest where no one watched). As *Zetes* approached the holes, the reference frame she carried with her begged to differ with the parochial view from Earth—*Zetes* moved in her own spacetime, from which dead stars and dead ships had long since fled away. No spirits remained to haunt her; no obstacles blocked her path. The way was open.

"Point of no return at the mark. Mark."

Michael caught himself holding his breath. He forced himself to inhale. They really weren't moving that fast. Still nothing on the instruments.

"We should be seeing something now," Levine said, his voice filtered of emotion through his helmet speaker.

"And there it is," said Michael. His fascinated gaze was fixed on the bank of gravitometer dials. Measuring the absolute strength of gravitational fields, independent of acceleration, the needles on the delicate gravitometers were climbing swiftly and inexorably toward maximum values. Only the meters that averaged the strength of competing fields hovered nervously at zero. The needles of all others leaned far to the right and bounced against their pins; and there they locked, quivering.

Michael's eyes had already flicked to the digital clocks—one that happily ticked off the seconds, driven by the master atomic clock where energetic atomic particles struck their target at a precise rate. Ship time. Beside that clock face was another, deriving its values from the first, modifying them by calculation of the ship's velocity. Earth time. Even as Michael watched, its numbers flickered, undecided between a choice of values. There it froze.

On the flight deck viewscreen, Laura saw *the stars redden and dart swirling away, like sparks from a collapsing bonfire.*

Her hand still gripped the now useless dead-man switch. She lifted her gloved fingers away from the switch: they moved a few millimeters, moved again from the same starting point, then moved again—the simultaneous visions overlapping on her retina.

Below, at the same instant, Michael turned toward Levine. Dials and lights smeared across his vision in triple exposure.

"We're in it," he gasped.

"We're in it," he gasped, his voice lingering in his ears, his tongue made thick by the collision of signals in his brain.

Nearby, Ted Donner saw nothing. His eyes were tightly

shut. If his heart beat three times on a single pulse, he was certain he had imagined it.

A wave of nausea swept up from the pit of Michael's stomach, choking him. The skin of his face tingled and a thousand droplets of sweat sprang out on his forehead and cheekbones, chilling him as they evaporated in the pressure suit's air conditioning.

His sickness passed; he forced bitter hot saliva down into his throat. "God," he whimpered.

"I half expected it," said Levine, weakly. "After all, your theory predicts it."

"Predicts what?" asked Michael, flushed, staring at Levine's pale greenish face.

"Time reversal," said Levine. "Twice in a row—backward, then forward again. Didn't *seem* like backward, of course—our whole universe went with us. But the nervous system's slow to react. We remembered each shift—they overlapped."

"Terrific," said Michael. "So that's what all those numbers feel like. Next time warn me."

Levine attempted a grin. The effect was ghastly. "It's *your* theory, sir—"

Laura McCord's voice broke in through their helmet sets: "Status report, by station," she ordered.

"Communications, all secure."

"Propulsion control, all secure."

"Navigation, all secure."

"Life support, all secure, except, uh . . . Joe threw up in his suit. Okay to open him up?"

"Affirmative," Laura snapped. "Bridge?"

Donner's shaken voice answered her. "All secure on the bridge."

The remaining stations reported. The robot monitors chimed in, unperturbed by the commotion. The ship was functioning.

"Have a look at the screens," said Laura. ". . . and congratulations!"

Michael turned his couch to look at the big screen on the wall of the bridge, behind him.

There was a new sun in the sky.

19

Witness this new-made World, another Heav'n
From Heaven Gate not far . . .
> —John Milton
> *Paradise Lost*

Wonderfully rich stuff—wish we had the time to really sit down and dig into it in detail. However, Captain McCord insists we move on to the inner planets without delay. Good reasons, of course. We've done just those measures we need, to be certain of what we're dealing with.

Thus: two singularities, combined mass of at least five thousand earth masses, orbiting each other at about eleven AU from Tau Ceti. And the interesting thing is, they both orbit Tau Ceti itself at a point right about where you'd expect a supermassive planet in the Dole-Sagan-Isaacman tables. Fantastic implications for star/planet formation theory! But no time to think about it now. We're off to find the planet *Actis* found. Detailed gravitometric measures entered below . . .

> —*Excerpt* from *Zetes* navigation log
entry time-coded 40:09:19:18:22:15-(David Levine, Second Lieutenant USSF)

Five hundred kilometers above its surface, *Zetes* orbited the fifth planet from the sun Tau Ceti. Dun-colored continents and pale turquoise seas rolled smoothly beneath the ship, seen through an atmosphere transparent and sparkling, brushed with high wispy clouds of ice crystal that obscured little of the planet's terrain. Dazzling ice sheets covered the poles, reaching to sixty degrees of latitude north and south. From above, the continental topography seemed deceptively gentle, rising in thin layered sheets of lava and sedimentary rock from the shores of shallow oceans, like an architect's model built up from flat pieces of cardboard. Yet in many places layer-cake mesas thrust fifteen thousand meters into the thin air, their tops and sides frosted with powdered-sugar snow, realms of cold light where no earthly organism could have survived.

Far down the terraced slopes of the super-mountains innumerable waterfalls glittered in the pinkish light, carving canyons and gullies with sides so sheer and bottoms so deep that sunlight never reached into them. Gradually these random lacy cracks in the continental crust ran together like veins in a leaf, to form great arterial rifts running outward to meet the sea.

Instruments aboard *Zetes* detected infrared radiation from lush growth in the canyon bottoms, and along the ocean margins. Toward the tropics the vegetation spread up thickly over the plateaus, and in the warm equatorial seas something very like coral had been at work building massive reefs. The reefs wandered unchecked over the shallow seabed to form an intricate maze of interlocking dikes, creating myriad lagoons—a mosaic of a thousand pastels painted by dissolved minerals and populations of microorganisms.

Even before settling into orbit, *Zetes* had detected something else: the distress call of automatic radio beacons, the kind that were standard equipment in ejection pods, designed to run untended for centuries on nuclear batteries. Five beacons formed a ragged V spread out over a hundred kilometers of tropical plateau, converging to the south, with the point of the V resting on the edge of a deep canyon twenty kilometers from the sea.

Zetes had turned her telescope on the site, which she flew over ten times in each long day. After only forty hours of inspection, the watchers caught sight of a thin trace of blue woodsmoke drifting above the dense canopy of trees in the canyon bottom.

The news electrified the ship. The crew of *Actis* must have survived their crash landing, and some of them at least were still alive!

Zetes beamed powerful signals to the apparent location of the survivors' camp, but there was no response. Undiscouraged, *Zetes* began to plot a landing.

The viewscreen in Laura's cabin displayed the spectacle of the terminator line creeping across the face of the planet, feeding on the long cold purple shadows of twilight that spilled over the shelving continents.

Laura stood in front of the screen, facing Ted Donner and Allison Sanders across the room.

Donner's reluctance surprised her. He had never balked at her slightest whim, before now. "Open up, Ted. What don't you like about it?"

His eyes shifted away from her. Allison Sanders regarded him impassively.

Laura persisted. "Do you think I'm endangering the mission in some way?"

Donner took a breath. "Nobody knows what's going to happen on the first landing attempt. The approach should be explored and cleared by the pilots who were trained for that job. Before you go down. The way it was planned."

Laura laughed, and Sanders grinned. "This *is* the way it was planned, Ted. Sandy's known that from the start."

"It's the Captain's prerogative to go first," Sanders said complacently.

Donner reddened. "Fine," he gritted, "but taking Ward with her—"

Laura pounced. "Is that what's eating you? *You* were slated to go originally; but you're the Second now."

Donner said nothing, but there was a strange look on his face.

Laura studied him for a moment, then turned to Sanders. "Well, that's all I need from you now, Sandy. Thanks."

Sanders nodded and pushed a foot against the floor. Within a second she had floated through the hatch and was gone.

Laura gazed at Donner, who'd found something to study on the Velcro rug. "You think you need Mike up here; is that it, Ted?" she asked softly. "You think that if something happens to us, you won't get back without him?"

Donner looked at her distractedly. "Where'd you get that idea? I never said—"

"You were terrified when I told you I'd wanted to take you down there with me."

"So what the hell does that mean?" he blustered.

She had found the raw place. "I mean your enthusiasm for this mission has waned steadily the farther we've gotten from earth."

Donner froze. "I've given you my total support, Laura," he said huskily. "I've done the best job I can."

"Ted, you've done an excellent job." She softened her expression and floated lightly across the room to lay a placating hand on his arm. "I need you to keep doing that good job while I'm gone. Face facts. David Levine knows that space warp better than Mike knows it himself. And Sandy Sanders is the best pilot in the Force. You couldn't get better support . . . hell, at this point you don't need Mike *or* me—we're ornaments. So we take the risks. As I see it, the mission is actually safer that way."

Donner tried to retrieve his dignity; he did not stop to analyze the sense of her argument. "I'm not afraid of reasonable risks, Laura."

"It doesn't matter that you're afraid." Her calm voice left no doubt that she read him plainly. "What matters is that you face the truth. Nothing to hide, nothing to be ashamed of between us, all right? You stay in the ship, you keep the crew in line and happy about it. That's what you do best. I'll take the risks. Just stay on my side, okay?"

"I am on your side, Laura," Donner said deliberately, "as much as anybody aboard."

"I trust you, Ted." She sought to convince him, fixing him with her green eyes. He said nothing.

She turned away from him, studying the viewscreen. The screen's image enhancers displayed the alien planet under the ghostly blue light of the stars. *Zetes* had entered the zone of night.

"See, it gets political again," Laura murmured, thinking aloud. "No matter how far you come from the world, the world comes with you. If Arnold Pratt's still alive down there, we have to persuade him to leave quietly. Even if he doesn't thank us for it."

"Why wouldn't he?" asked Donner, genuinely surprised at the direction of her thoughts. "Those people will fall down and kiss your hands."

"They used to call us zoomies, remember that? As if they owned space, and we were the neighborhood brats sneaking into the back yard." She turned to face Donner. "That's why it's even better that Mike's here to go with me. He's a civilian, he doesn't give a damn about all that. He's their savior, not me. If they want to be saved."

"I just don't follow your thinking," Donner said honestly. "They'll be eager to come home."

"I wonder how I'd feel if it was me . . ."

"And what about Ward?" Donner asked. "Is he going to be a willing volunteer?"

Laura smiled. "Oh, his problem is even worse than yours, Ted. He's as scared as you are—as we all are. But he's even more scared to let it show. He'll come cheerfully. His honor requires it."

Donner had nothing to say for a moment. Then, "Whatever works . . . when do you want to make the announcement?"

"Give me a half an hour to talk to Ward. Then you tell the crew. Schedule the launch in forty hours."

He grinned and started to throw her a jaunty salute, but she interrupted him. "You with me, Ted?" she snapped.

"I always was, Laura," he insisted.

"Okay, take off."

He turned and flew through the hatch with alacrity.

Laura could see that phony nonchalance for what it was. The man was terrified at the prospect of being left in charge, alone. Laura decided she'd better have a word with Sanders, privately.

"Mike, I've got some good news for you." She smiled at him from the viewscreen.

"Great, Laura. What's up?"

The RAPLAR's explosive bolts detonated, and Michael Ward felt like somebody had just given him a sharp slap on the top of his helmet. The great length of *Zetes* dwindled rapidly away overhead.

For a moment his impressions were confused. He could see nothing ahead of the ship through the quartz windows, and his ears were filled with the yammer of voices monitoring the launch.

Beside him in the left seat, Laura moved the stick forward. Pitch control rockets puffed briefly, and the nose went down. Now the planet's horizon lifted into view. Laura moved the stick back and the rockets compensated, fixing the ship in its dive. The thin transparent edge of the atmosphere was streaked with purple and gold, heralding the rise of Tau Ceti over the rim of the darkened planet.

Though the visible atmosphere was still many hundreds of kilometers below them, it would not be long before the speeding ship began piling into enough air molecules to raise the skin temperature. The trick was to slow down enough for the aerodynamic control surfaces to grab air without burning up in the process. Compared to the sturdy, chunky space shuttles of earth, the RAPLAR was a delicate, thin-skinned craft and must be lowered gently into its fiery baptism. Michael, a helpless passenger, could do nothing but silently anticipate Laura's fractional adjustments to the controls, twitching his fingers like a sleeping cat dreaming of the hunt.

For three hours Laura McCord gently coaxed the sleek RAPLAR down through thickening layers of air, skidding along the top of the atmosphere like a flat stone skipping across a pond, settling deeper at the end of each bounce. The white ceramic undercoating glowed cherry red and the cabin air conditioner labored to keep the inside temperature at a livable maximum.

They streaked across the sunlit hemisphere and back into the night. Overhead, the bright spark of *Zetes* pulled farther away into the night as the RAPLAR lost orbital speed and fell behind.

Suddenly the critical passage was behind them—the hypersonic regime, where rockets and control surfaces must work precisely in tandem to prevent the ship from tumbling out of control. All at once the ship was a functionally normal aircraft moving at mere supersonic speeds thirty thousand meters above the starlit landscape.

As they dived still lower the ground-sensing radar projected an image ahead of them on the quartz windows, of towering mesas to left and right.

Dawn again, this time not below them, but bursting all around the ship in a blaze of pink and orange. Flaming crimson in the light of the rising sun, stupendous sandstone cliffs rose off to both sides, their snow-covered tops flashing like mirrors. The jagged mesas were so huge that Michael could not adjust to their scale; they seemed to scrape the wingtips, though the radar informed him they were hundreds of kilometers away.

They were now only a few hundred meters above the twisted planet floor. Spires of pink and red rock towered up to clutch at them; they passed over a labyrinth of hogback ridges, wind-carved grabens, natural arches big enough for the ship to have flown through with ease. Bright water ran through the maze; thick clumps of trees, electric green in the dawn light, lined the water courses.

Suddenly the main rocket engine roared and the ship slid off to the right. Laura kept her hands off the controls, now;

the terrain-matching radar fed the computer with the information necessary to correct the RAPLAR's course and bring it in line with the landing pattern computed aboard *Zetes*. The rocket thrust for only a few seconds, while Michael reflected on the horrible racket they were leaving in their wake, a sound no ears on this planet had ever heard.

They swept out over a rolling, hilly plain, thick with matted growth. Michael had an impression of billions of hard shiny leaves glimmering in the light. And then he saw the sea, a silvery line on the horizon, reflecting the rising sun into his eyes.

Beaches of pink sand flicked away beneath their wings; they were out over the open water, and settling fast. Surf foamed against a reef only a few meters below them. The water was emerald green; Michael could see wave patterns on the sandy bottom of the shallow sea. Did a dark shadow move against the sand? They were past it before he could be sure.

Laura moved her hands gently to the controls. The RAPLAR flew itself, but in these final seconds she was prepared to wrench the ship out of its computer's control if she had to.

They entered the shadow of a looming cliff, two thousand meters tall, standing up against the sky ten kilometers away. It stayed on their right as they skimmed the sea at a hundred and fifty knots. A crevice of lighter blue opened in the dark purple face of the cliff, seeming to beckon them inward.

Then they struck. They bounced a hundred meters and struck again, harder. They skidded along the surface, raising a rooster-tail of foam; water seathed and hissed away from the hot ceramic plating of the wings and fuselage. Then a gout of sea water sprayed over the canopy, and Michael and Laura were thrown hard against their harnesses. They ploughed on for another hundred meters, blinded by flying foam. The ship began to slow, and their wake overtook them, rocking the ship violently.

Water drained slowly away from the windows. Laura touched a switch, and jets of air chased a thousand drops scurrying off the quartz plates. She touched another switch, and the tiny water jet under the plane's tail burbled merrily to life. The RAPLAR wallowed on, out of its natural element, but holding its chin bravely above water.

Laura's gloved fingers flew over the computer's keyboard,

anxious for the RAPLAR's health. Green lights flickered; the ship was undamaged.

She turned and looked at Michael for the first time since they had strapped themselves into the plane. She opened her mouth to say something, but he grinned at her, and she stopped herself and only laughed. It was so infectious that he found himself giggling with her.

20

Atmospheric content, Tau Ceti Five (combined spectrometry data, first approximation): nitrogen, 77%, oxygen, 22%, rare gases, .82%, carbon dioxide, .18% (average estimated dry weights). Water vapor by volume: polar, .0001%; equatorial, 7%. Elevated levels atmospheric dust, 70 to 40 degrees north and south latitudes; elevated levels salts in solution, tropical regions.

Remarks (hypotheses to be confirmed by on-surface observation): high levels of oxygen and carbon dioxide may be due to vulcanism, plus predominance of plant over animal species. Clearly an earthlike atmosphere.

—Excerpt from *Zetes* scientific log, entry time-coded 40:11:30:09:43:21 (Valeri Subotin, Chief Meteorologist, UNEF)

"... and we'll get back to you before we start up the canyon."

"Roger, Captain. Keep us informed."

Laura flicked off the radio. "What do you say, Mike? Can we have some fresh air?"

"No nasty beasties out there, according to the sniffers," Michael replied.

She cracked the canopy. The window plates swung back and away, and the alien atmosphere flooded the cockpit.

The air was cool and clean and sweet, heady as wine. Michael took a deep lungful. The chemical composition of the atmosphere was well known to them in advance, but shipboard analysis could not have alerted them to the delicate, delicious aroma that wafted down from the mouth of the canyon. Michael tried to identify it, but had to give up somewhere between a pine forest and a rose garden, spiced by the tang of an autumn afternoon in New England.

146

The ship swam on across a green lagoon, leaving a trail of hissing bubbles in its wake. The canyon walls opened wide before them, cliffs of striated sandstone rising precipitously in layer upon layer of yellow and white and gray and rust, streaked by vertical washes of shining spring water and festooned with hanging gardens of feathery greenstuff that might as well have been maidenhair fern. The cliff faces were spangled with delicate star-shaped blossoms of pale blue and bright yellow. Waterfalls dissolved into drifting mist above the heads of the voyagers, cooling their cheeks with fine spray.

The cheerful bubbling of the plane's little water jet was reflected and amplified by the walls of the canyon. Michael and Laura were serenaded by the echoing chorus of a thousand watery voices as they passed on between the high cliffs, beside the pink sand beaches where tall trees rose up on slender tan trunks, to sprout mops of fronds shimmering with round leaves the size of saucers.

The sun, Tau Ceti, crept over the edge of the cliffs, flooding the canyon with warmth and light. They pulled their helmets from their heads, to savor the mix of warm sunshine and the waterfalls' cool spray.

In Michael's eyes, Laura's gleaming coppery hair rivaled the sun.

For an hour they made their way slowly along the riverine lagoon, following its gently winding course deeper into the heart of the continent. Reminding themselves of their business, they set about to measure and record what they were seeing. Michael used a small camera to store electronic movies of the canyon, while Laura read geological and botanical observations into the plane's facscriber.

Finally they saw in the distance that the wide lagoon was dammed by a broad stretch of sandy beach. Over a jumble of lava boulders a river flowed down from the canyon, tumbling in a hundred silver waterfalls, hissing into the salty water of the lagoon.

Laura cut the plane's motor as they approached, and carefully steered the amphibian craft into the mouth of the river, grounding its nose against the sand where the fresh water would do its best to wash away the salt.

Michael sat up on the edge of the cockpit and threw a leg over the side of the plane. Then, on a second thought, he turned to Laura. "You mind?"

"Go ahead. We're about fifteen years too late to worry about who goes first."

Michael leaped from the cockpit into watery sand, and stood still for a moment with a hand touching the side of the plane, waiting to see if he would sink: it was an excellent place for quicksand. But his boots went in only a few centimeters.

He slogged around to the nose of the craft to fetch the lanyards that Laura released with a flick of a switch. He dragged the thin titanium cables up the beach, fastening one around the trunk of a sturdy tree, then bounded across boulders to the other side of the river. He looped the other cable around a half-buried lava rock as big as a small house.

He surveyed the mooring. The RAPLAR floated easily in the river's outflow, the broad expanse of the lagoon and the sunlit canyon walls stretching away into the distance beyond it. There were no tide marks on the beach; the moonless planet's tides rose only slightly above mean sea level. There was very little driftwood in the river mouth, suggesting that flash floods were rare: the river was fed constantly by springs and melting snow far upstream. The planet's thin air and light gravity encouraged water vapor to condense at high altitudes as ice and snow, not as rain. The landing craft would be safe from the elements.

Laura was standing in the cockpit, tossing their packs onto the sand. Michael went down to fetch them as she jumped from the plane. She turned and twisted the exterior lock that lowered the canopy. It snugged into place.

She came to join Michael. "We've already come about twelve kilometers up the canyon," she said. "If the growth isn't too thick it shouldn't take us long to reach our destination."

"Tell you the truth, I'm in no hurry," said Michael, shrugging the pack over his shoulders. "We've got the whole day ahead of us, and what a day!"

"You blaze the trail, then," she said, loosening the straps of her pack. "See if you can take me to beautiful places."

He smiled at her. "That will be easy."

He scrambled up a low dune to the moraine of lava boulders behind the beach. Jumping lightly from one rock to the next, he was soon under an open canopy of trees. Anchored to the sand between the rocks on multi-legged prop roots, pale trunks stretched to extraordinary heights, little hampered in their reach for the sun by the planet's easy gravity.

The grove of trees led away up the canyon in a cool maze of gray trunks. A thick carpet of mulch and big round yellow leaves lay softly under foot, filling the crevices between the rocks, deadening the echoes from the waterfall.

"Listen to that," said Michael as Laura came up beside him. His voice was hushed.

They heard the buzz and whine of what sounded like insects. They could see small dark shapes flitting between the trees; and now a fluttering dab of color, iridescent in the shadows, floundering through the air from one tree to another.

"It looks like a butterfly!" said Laura, delighted as a child.

"Yeah. With a thirty-centimeter wingspan," said Michael warily. "I hope it doesn't decide to perch on my shoulder."

They walked forward in silence through the living wood. They needed no path on the spongy, open forest floor.

They had gone deep into forest when Laura reached out to grasp Michael's arm. "Mike, look over there . . ."

Away through the trees they could see a long thin shape, resting on two piles of rocks: an upturned dugout canoe.

They hurried to it.

Michael ran his fingers along the smooth carved wood. "This is beautifully made," he said with admiration.

Together they easily lifted the boat and turned it over. Slat seats forced the curving gunwales apart; the sides were so thin that light shone through the rosy, veined wood. The boat was long: long enough to hold four or five people.

Michael stepped back and recorded several views of the craft with his pocket camera.

"Why do you think they keep it so far from the water?" Laura asked.

"I don't know. Sun and salt, maybe."

"You don't think there's something ugly in the lagoon, do you?" she whispered in mock alarm, her eyes twinkling.

Michael grinned. "Let's hope it doesn't have a taste for titanium."

They turned the boat back over and left.

The discovery of the human artifact reminded them of their purpose. They walked on silently and hurriedly, anticipating a greeting or a challenge at any moment.

The grove of tall trees ended a kilometer from the beach,

where the floor of the canyon rose up sharply. The ground here was a rich red volcanic soil well laid over with humus, carpeted with thick green grass. The trees were thicker too, a tangled mass of branches with hard, sharp, dark green leaves set close together. But for a narrow path of slick red mud the vegetation would have been impenetrable.

Michael and Laura trudged on for an hour, the trail leading them higher toward the north canyon wall. Gradually they passed into dry country where the bushes were only shoulder high, no longer shading them from the sun. They began to perspire freely; to cool off, they zipped their coveralls open down their chests.

The river ran somewhere off down the slope to the left, out of sight in a miniature gorge. They could hear its cool waters, but all they could see was a solid carpet of brush.

Still higher, the trail wound through chunks of sandstone, quarried from the canyon walls by the action of freezing and expanding water. Vegetation now was sparse and leathery, many of the plants covered with spines that looked capable of penetrating the soles of their boots. They climbed carefully.

Up ahead they saw a grove of green trees sprouting from a stone bench high on the cliff face. A waterfall spilled from the ledge, tributary to the river in the canyon below.

"Looks like the trail goes up in there," said Michael. "Want to take a break when we reach the trees?"

"I was going to ask you," said Laura. "Gravity's wearing me out."

They climbed in among the trees. The grove reached deep into a natural amphitheater in the canyon wall. They walked on for a hundred meters, back into the depths of the cool oasis, while black leafy shadows and dazzling patches of sunlight danced over their shoulders.

The amphitheater ended in a sheer wall. At its foot was a pool fed by a spray of water falling from somewhere high up the cliff: sunlight painted a rainbow in the mist. Fine powdery sand rimmed the pool; the water was clear, green and deep.

Laura let her pack slip from her shoulders. She collapsed gratefully on the sand, in the shade of a sandstone block covered with flowering creepers. The rock was overgrown with the gnarled roots of an ancient, leaning tree, in form similar to a weeping willow on Earth. Michael squatted down beside Laura, slung his pack to the ground in front of him, and dug in it for the canteen. He passed the plastic bottle to Laura.

"Pooh," she said, making a face as she sipped. "Water tastes like warm plastic." She looked at the green pool. "Bet the water here is better."

"I'll find out," said Michael.

He found the chemical analyzer in the pack. He stood up, went to the pool's edge, squatted again. Carefully he dipped up some of the water in the small vial of the analyzing kit. He waited a few moments, pushed a stud, and checked the readout on the liquid-crystal display at the base of the vial. "Clean and clear," he said. "There's a little . . ."

"That's what I hoped you'd say," said Laura, and her voice was loud and laughing—and right behind him.

He heard a whoop and turned too late to catch more than a glimpse of pale skin as she darted by him and dove head first into the pool. Cold water splashed over him and he gasped.

"Oh, oh, it's *cold*." she spluttered, teeth chattering, as she stroked vigorously through the water in an effort to keep up her circulation.

Michael watched her white limbs gleaming in the water. He blushed, covered with confusion. She was as beautiful as he could have imagined . . .

. . . And here, far from the bridge of her command, she was a different woman, all her stern authority dissolved in sunlight, clear air, and bright water. He sat down on the sand, put his chin between his hands, and stared at her, not daring to come closer, but unable to turn away.

She paddled toward him. "What are you waiting for?" she demanded, laughing. "It's cold, but not *that* cold. In fact, it's great when you get used to it. Come *on!*"

Michael blushed crimson. "Look the other way," he said.

"Not on your life!" she shot back. "Just get in here, and that's . . ." She couldn't keep a straight face. ". . . an order. Sort of."

Michael's face was hot with embarassment. "I . . . just can't."

"What's the matter?" she asked. Her feet found the sandy bottom. Her rosy nipples lifted from the surface of the water, and water streamed down over her belly. Michael found that his eyes were on a level with the dark red curls between her white thighs. He sprang hastily to his feet.

She marched straight up to him and leaned into his chest. She trailed the back of her hand against his erection.

"Just what I suspected," she whispered, as she covered his mouth with her lips. His heart pounded in his chest with such force that he ached. He was deaf from the surge of blood in his ears. He wrapped his arms around her cold wet skin and pulled her to him.

She moved her mouth from his. "I know how we can fix that," she breathed, and her hands moved to the zipper of his uniform, pulling it open.

Michael stepped back, wrestling to get out of his clothes, tugging with his toes against the heels of his boots. Clothes around his ankles, one boot still in place, he bent to free himself.

"Like this!" she shouted, and hooked his backside with her leg, sending him hopping and staggering into the pool.

"Aaagh!" He flopped around in the water. He plunged beneath the surface to emerge, after what seemed an eternity, with a wad of wet clothes and a soggy boot. He threw them to the shore.

He stroked across the pool as fast as he could, turned, plunged deep, came up, shook his wet hair, swam back to where Laura sat waist high in the water, grinning at him.

"Guess what?" he gulped, pulling himself up on the sand to sit beside her.

"What?"

"It didn't work."

She said nothing. She was no longer smiling. She reached out to touch his chest.

He bent over her, and her arms went around his shoulders.

"What a lovely world," she said. "Why can't we have it all to ourselves?"

Laura sat in the sunshine beside the pool, her legs pulled up under her. Michael lay back in the sand near her, his hands clasped beneath his head. His wet clothes dangled from the limb of the "willow" nearby.

"Don't be selfish," he said. He missed the earnest undertone in her words.

"We should have a name for this place, besides 'Tau Ceti Five,'" she said, almost petulantly.

"Maybe it's got a name. Why don't we ask the people who live here?"

She said nothing. Then she sighed. "You're right."

"Why do you sound so sad?" he asked, half turning to look at her. "You were happy a few minutes ago.',

"I was . . . yes, I really was." She gazed at him out of clear green eyes, an expression of faint surprise tugging at the corners of her mouth. "I think this world seduced me . . ."

He reached out a hand to take her shoulder, but suddenly her eyes widened, startled. "Look!" she exclaimed.

He turned to look.

The trail north away from the pool led between immense sandstone boulders, mostly overgrown with creepers and twisted tree roots. One of these boulders, the largest, was flat and relatively uncluttered on top. A figure stood on the boulder, watching them.

He was a boy, tall as a tall man, but with the long smooth muscles of youth. His skin was dark brown from the sun, and he wore nothing but an apron of string. His curly brown hair tumbled to his shoulders. A quiver of arrows was slung across his back—the arrows' vaned tips were visible behind his ear—and he held a long bow in his left hand.

With his right hand he gestured abruptly. A girl, as tall and brown and bare as he, joined him from behind the crest of the boulder. She too was armed with bow and arrows.

To Michael and Laura they seemed almost a part of the landscape of desert and jungle. The frank, interested gaze of the two children was no more threatening than that of a pair of kittens.

Unashamed, Michael sat up and raised his hand to wave at them.

The boy and girl waved back, tentatively.

"Hello," the children called.

And the boy asked, "Are you humans?"

21

I am sure the lizards told you many, many things, but you
were not listening.

—Carlos Castaneda
The Teachings of Don Juan

The jekyll croaked quizzically at Arnold Pratt, fixing him
with a round red intelligent eye. The little beast was perched
on its four back feet with its upper body cocked upright,
pointing off down the canyon with one of its three-fingered
front limbs.

Pratt wasn't fooled. The little lizardlike creatures always
looked as if they knew what they were saying. They were
gregarious things, always under foot, always clucking and
gesturing and waiting patiently for an answer. The children,
when younger, had tried to make pets of them, but the beasts
were so indiscriminate in their affections that they soon grew
tiresome.

Pratt brushed the jekyll off its rock. It jumped a meter
away to the shore of the pond, looked at Pratt undiscouraged,
and pointed in the opposite direction, croaking again.

Pratt ignored the animal. With a grunt of effort he lifted
the rock the jekyll had perched on, and wrestled it into place
in the weir. It was the last rock he needed to move; it had
taken him two days to muck the silt out of the pond, but now
the spillway ran clear again.

He stood upright in the knee-high water and arched his
back. The muscles were sore, but it was a good ache, a
rewarding ache. It was richly satisfying to Pratt to know that
as old as he was (he supposed he must be pushing sixty,
though it was impossible to know his exact age in earth
years), he was stronger than any of the rest of them: stronger
than Anton, who stuffed himself all the time; certainly

154

stronger than that sniveling Marston, who was overfond of the berry wine he'd learned how to make; stronger even than O'Connor, who was in good enough condition, but who seemed to have no inner drive, no sense of competition, nothing to give him spine.

Pratt waded out of the water, his tall, spare, sun-blackened frame naked except for a lioncloth of twisted homespun. His grizzled hair and beard dripped with sweat, and drops of sweat depended from his bushy eyebrows, clinging a second before dropping down to splash on leathery cheeks. His eyes glittered with fierce pride as he surveyed his handiwork, the newly repaired rock dam that held back the waters of the river.

On an impulse he turned and clambered up the rocky slope of the river bank to the top of a tree-covered promontory several meters above the level of the dam. From up here he could see a long way downstream—below him a whole series of fish ponds like the one he'd just finished working on stair-stepped down to the fields in the wide river bottom.

In the fields he could just make out two tiny figures, black in the noon light, bending over between rows of melon and pickleroot. Even at this distance he had no trouble recognizing the familiar movements of Anton Meerloo and Louise Chew. Pat O'Connor and Nancy were off hunting, he knew, and he supposed Marston and Rebecca Meerloo had sought the shelter of the longhouse. They were generally to be found somewhere in the shade during the hottest part of the day, Rebecca at her loom and Marston, like as not, huddled with a jug. No one knew where the children were, or would know until they decided to come back home for a visit.

Up the river bank from the fields stood the big windmill with its barkcloth sails, immobile now in the breathless heat of midday. Across the bare earth compound from the windmill, one end of the palm-log longhouse was visible to Pratt, standing cool in the shade under the south canyon wall. The rest of the building, and the paperwood domes of the out-buildings behind it, were hidden from his view by a tall grove of saucer palms.

On beyond the fields and the buildings stretched the great wide expanse of the canyon, its further reaches hidden in blue haze, its enormous red and yellow walls lifting into the sky. Strips of dark jungle followed the watercourses down to the central river, interrupting the tawny field of rolling sand hills.

"Cluck! Cluck!" insisted a jekyll beside Arnold Pratt's foot, pointing to the panorama that spread itself before him. Pratt pushed the animal aside. Startled, the jekyll nipped him on the heel—but its toothless jaws, good only for munching insects, made no impression on the thick hide of Pratt's bare foot.

But though he felt nothing from the jekyll's feeble bite, Pratt was suddenly seized with dizziness . . . his ears rang . . .

Abruptly he sat down in the sand, in the shade of a big old water-willow that grew out of the red rocks. Pratt gritted his teeth, and the vertigo passed. Indeed, within seconds he had completely forgotten the incident. He felt only a vague sense of irritation, almost of anger, for no reason he could pin down. He should get back to work—he wanted to get started on that next fish pond down stream. But he'd rest a few moments first.

He watched Anton and Louise at work, far below him. After a few minutes Anton put down his hoe and walked toward the compound. Evidently he said something to Louise, for she lifted her head, but then she went back to her cultivating.

Louise was a good woman, uncomplaining, a hard worker—a credit to her sex. Not like Rebecca Meerloo, a hysteric who was always bursting into tears. And even Nancy had her female moods. Not that it wasn't a hard life for women; hell, it was rough on all of them. But the challenge of building a whole new society, a new world, really—that challenge had rewards of its own, which (Pratt supposed) a woman could never really appreciate.

For his own part, Arnold Pratt had realized almost immediately what an incredible stroke of luck had befallen the crew of *Actis* when they had stumbled on this planet. Everything they had been trying to achieve in a paltry and imitative way with the colony at L-5 was here handed to them—endless, bountiful space, and total freedom from the government of Earth! The only price was a bit of labor.

No refinements, of course—and none of that pretense of equality between the sexes that a complex technology made possible. He supposed that's why the women tended to resent the situation—the women plus that rather sissified male, Marston Smith-Jones. Even an aimless guy like Pat O'Connor could pull better than his own weight when prodded to it, whereas the women were obviously only at their best with the children.

The children, now—they were something to be proud of! Pratt only wished there could be more of them. (Indeed, the fact that there were no others was a little puzzling—unless the women had gotten together in some sort of conspiracy. Now there's a thought that had occurred to Pratt before—but he'd never been able to prove it.)

None of that would matter in the long run. The children would soon have children of their own; it was obvious the day could not be far off. And with the second generation of humans born on the new world, Pratt would have no trouble whatsoever inculcating his own certain principles of right and wrong.

. . . *right and wrong.*

What was that? Pratt shook his head—it seemed logy. Something about the children . . . gone now. Didn't matter. It was time to get back to work.

"Yes! We *are* humans!" Michael called, delighted at the question, and delighted to answer in the affirmative.

Without hesitation the tall brown boy jumped from the boulder, landing lightly in the sand. In the same move he sprang to his feet, one hand just brushing the ground for balance on the way, and stepped boldly toward Michael and Laura. Behind him the girl too leaped to the beach, an arc of golden flesh in the bright sun.

Such grace, such careless audacity of action moved Michael's heart, lifted it with the spectacle of pure beauty. These perfect children, tall as angels, surely were creatures of paradise.

Michael scrambled to his feet to meet the boy's out-thrust hand. "I am Adam," said the boy.

Of course you are, thought Michael.

And simultaneously the girl presented herself to Laura. "I'm Virginia," she said.

There followed an elaborately polite moment while they all introduced themselves to each other, shaking hands all around.

"You are very beautiful," Virginia said to Laura, speaking frankly. "Your skin is very white. Do you live in the world?"

"We're from the planet Earth, Virginia," Laura replied. "We've come to find you and your parents."

"To find us? Do you know us? Do you know my parents? Do you live on Elfive?" The girl's tone was one of intense curiosity, but only mild surprise. Her questions tumbled out without waiting for answers, as if she must say them all while they were still fresh in her mind: "How did you come here? Are you marooned? Do you plan to live with us . . . ?"

"Wait!" Laura laughed. "We'll tell you everything, but it will take awhile." She glanced at Michael. "Right now we have to put our clothes on."

Michael, entranced by the beautiful bare, brown, grainless skin of the children, had forgotten his own nakedness. Reminded, he blushed, and the tingle of the blood in his face alerted him that his skin was hot and dry. "I guess so, before we burn to a crisp," he said, walking toward his drying coveralls.

Adam came with him, while Laura and Virginia went in the other direction. "Your clothes look very heavy—too hot for much walking. Why do you need them?"

Michael bent and hopped around, pulling on his underpants. "Partly to protect our skin from the sun," he said, reaching for his coveralls and pulling them on. "Also, we need pockets to carry things. But mostly from habit, I guess; because we're used to them."

"Yes, Marston says everyone on Elfive wears heavy clothes. But we don't need them here." Adam reached out and took the cloth of Michael's sleeve between his fingers. "My mother makes cloth much softer than this on her loom. I'll have her make some for you."

"Thanks, Adam." Michael sat down and began to pull on his boots. "How far away is your home from here?"

"Half a day, up the canyon," Adam replied. "But we walk a lot faster than you do."

"You've been watching us?" Michael asked, looking up at the tall boy, and thinking how curious it was that that thought did not disturb him.

"Yes, we followed you from the lagoon. We saw your boat." Adam hunkered down and addressed Michael man to man. "That's a very strange boat, Michael. It seems heavy and slow, even though you don't have to paddle. It looks impractical."

"Impractical," Michael repeated. Practicality must be an important concept to Adam and his family. "Well, you're right. As a boat, it's not too practical. But it does very well as an airplane. Are you familiar with airplanes?"

"Marston has described them to us," Adam replied. "They look different than I expected. Why do you have an airplane?"

"To travel to our ship. We came here from Earth in a spaceship. It's circling the planet now . . ." Michael waited for a flood of questions that failed to materialize. Adam continued to regard him steadily. " . . . and we flew down from the ship in the plane. Later we can go back up the same way." Michael deliberately held back from mentioning the rescue aspect of the mission—Adam clearly needed no rescue.

But the boy surprised him. "Will you take my parents away with you? They used to say all the time they hoped someone would come. Marston, too. But Arnold gets angry when he hears them talking that way."

"I don't know what we're going to do, yet," Michael said, treading cautiously. "Whatever's useful, I guess." Michael picked up his pack and got to his feet.

"Mike," Laura called, "from what Virginia tells me their home is still twenty kilometers away. The smoke we saw was just a campfire."

"I guess we'd better get moving, then," said Michael. "I'm glad we have guides."

"Do you want to get there tonight?" asked Adam, as if it were a matter of perfect choice to him and Virginia when they got home.

"Yes," Laura replied. "We're eager to meet your people."

"Well, you'll have to walk very fast," said Adam, and it was clear he had doubts. Michael had doubts of his own.

"In that case, let's not waste any more time," said Laura. "Let's go."

Adam and Virginia looked at each other. Adam nodded. Virginia turned and ran up the path. The rest of the odd foursome followed, leaving behind the green pool beneath its cliffs and misty waterfall.

Through the long hot afternoon the tall naked children guided Michael and Laura deep into the endless canyon. It seemed a protocol of travel that one of the children was always far out in front, running ahead through stippled shadows of tall cane, leafy palm, and feathery trees resembling willows, acacias, and mesquite; or through the gloom of immense vine-draped hardwoods near the river bottom; or across sun-blasted, cactus-covered hills of rock and sand standing between the strips of jungle that followed every tributary stream down from the cliffs to the river.

The children never seemed to tire. Sun and shadow played

over their golden skin and flashed from their golden hair. At first, Michael's spirit was lifted out of his straining body by the mere sight of them running ahead.

But as they walked on for endless hours, under a sluggish sun creeping slowly across the sky of a lazy planet, the heat of the afternoon grew intense—magnified by reflection from the canyon walls. Adam and Virginia had a trick of dipping cupped hands into every stream they crossed, scooping up mouthfuls of water without breaking stride. Michael and Laura sipped just as often from their water bottles, but nonetheless their skin seemed continually dry and feverish, and Michael's tongue was thick in his mouth.

Stumbling down a rocky slope toward the dark growth of the river bottom, Michael felt cactus spines tear at his shins, felt his weary legs twisting under him, felt his head grow light—and knew he had to rest again.

"Let's stop," he gasped. "I've had it."

No one answered him. Laura was too tired, and Adam had already accepted the suggestion without comment. Virginia had disappeared somewhere up ahead; Adam put his fingers to his lips and whistled shrilly.

Michael and Laura and Adam entered the deep shade of the trees, where vines grew thick and the air was chill. Michael's ears roared louder as he walked; he wondered if he were on the verge of losing consciousness.

But suddenly there was space among the towering tree trunks, as they came upon a clearing, formed by a deep pool that shown clear amber with the color of the pebbles on its bottom.

A white torrent fell crashing and foaming into the far upstream side of the long pool—the full force of the river descending from the lip of a major stratum of rock twenty meters above their heads. And above that ledge, Michael could see another fall, higher still, its top lost to sight above the trees.

Michael and Laura folded to the ground in a heap on the gravel bank. Adam squatted on his haunches, watching them. A shadow detached itself from the others in the green, gold, deep brown glade—Virginia, appearing silent and abrupt, high up the trail beside the waterfall. She darted silently down the path and came up to them, and hunkered down beside Adam.

The water's roar was dull in the background; Michael tried to tune it out of his head. All he could hear was his own ragged breath. All he could see were the faces of the children, watching him and Laura silently, watching with naked curiosity.

Michael shivered, and sought to avoid their gaze. His eyes fixed on something white, which gleamed against the dark earthen slope on the far side of the pool. A narrow path led to it.

Michael sat up. "What's that?" he demanded of Adam.

The boy turned to look. Laura said in Michael's ear, "It's a gravestone. There's something carved on it."

Adam turned back to face them. "Angela's grave," he said. "She died before we were born. When they were climbing down into the canyon from where they landed."

"This is Two Falls Glade," said Virginia. "This is where we had the fire you saw two days ago."

"How many hours do you count in a day?" Laura asked, wearily, looking away from the white gravestone in the dark glade.

"Twenty-four, of course," said Adam. "But hours are different for you, aren't they? Marston said once, 'The days here never end.'"

"I know what he meant," said Michael. "How much farther?"

"I could run there in an hour," said Adam.

"I couldn't run for five minutes," said Michael.

"If you walk so slowly, it will be evening when we come," said Virginia. "Do you mind walking in the dark?"

"Why do you ask?" said Laura, suddenly alert.

"The others don't like to be out after dark," the girl replied.

"Because of what happened to Marston," said Adam.

"He wasn't listening," said Virginia, almost primly, as if referring to a careless child.

"What happened to Marston?" Michael asked, glancing at Laura.

"A nightglider slashed him," Adam informed him.

"Nightgliders?" Laura asked, interested. Suddenly she seemed less tired.

Michael looked at her, noting with surprise that the hint of danger seemed to have revived her.

"Nightgliders can't see very well," Adam explained to Laura. "So they slash anything that moves. But they're very stupid. All you have to do is listen for them—when you hear one coming, stand still, and it will go right past you."

"You'll see them," said Virginia cheerfully. "They come down from the cliffs when the wind rises, as soon as the sun goes over the edge."

Michael got to his feet. "Suddenly I don't feel so tired either."

Laura laughed. She stood up and adjusted her pack.

"Isn't there anything dangerous on earth?" Adam asked, reluctant to get started right away. He knew Laura and Michael would be too tired to answer questions when they were walking.

"Oh, a few things," said Michael offhandedly. "Drunk drivers, jealous lovers, political fanatics, dedicated scientists, good soldiers, religious nuts, bureaucrats of any kind—"

"Mike!" warned Laura. "You must be exhausted ... You're not making sense."

Michael broke off. Looking at the puzzled expressions of the two perfect children, he realized he'd been spouting phrases they'd never heard before in their lives.

"Sorry," he said. "People is what I mean. Other people are dangerous, on earth. Maybe you won't ever have to find that out."

"But you are people," said Adam. "And you are no more dangerous than we are."

Laura laid a restraining hand on Michael's arm, before, in his fatigue, he said anything else undiplomatic.

"That's right, Adam," she said gently. "We're here to be helpful. We are not at all dangerous."

22

Stars above
Fire below
Coal in the hearth
The soul in the eye
Cloud smoke and death.
          —from a Fang creation myth, Gabon

Enough for one day. Time for dinner and a long, deep sleep.

Arnold Pratt waded out of the lower fish pond and stood on the sandy bank for a moment, letting the cool water drip from his skin. The pond was almost in shadow. The far wall of the canyon was already orange in the light of the lowering sun.

Soon the nightgliders would drop from their holes high in the cliff face to go hunting insects along the river bottoms, riding the night breeze on long silky double wings.

Pratt walked toward the compound on the path that ran down through the groves of saucer palms. He walked slowly, savoring the cool blue shadows of the grove. Then he became aware of excited voices drifting on the evening air.

Virginia appeared at a turn in the path, running silently as a forest sprite on her tough bare feet. She stopped when she saw him.

"What is it, Ginny?" Pratt asked.

"People. People are here, Daddy." The girl's eyes shone with excitement. "They come from the other Earth."

They were all gathered in the courtyard, the newcomers shockingly obvious in their white uniforms: everyone else looked suddenly naked to Pratt.

In the motion of her copper hair, in the gaze of her green eyes, he knew her. "You . . ."

She walked boldly to him, extending a hand. "I'm very pleased to find you looking so well, Captain Pratt."

In his confusion he could do nothing but respond automatically. His hand came up, and she took it.

"I'm not the woman you may remember, Captain," she said quietly. "I hope you'll give me the opportunity to prove that."

He stared at her. "It was a long time ago, wasn't it?"

The windmill across the compound groaned; its barkcloth sails, stretched on wooden frames, began to turn slowly in the rising breeze.

She was the very image of the woman he had confronted on L-5 so many years ago. How could she have changed?

Pat O'Connor tossed a length of palm log into the fire. Flames erupted and sparks showered. Red light flickered over the smoke-blackened rafters, the roof of woven rushes, the log walls of the longhouse, the bronzed faces of the men and women at the long table.

Pratt brooded silently at the table's head. He could not keep himself from imagining how the strangers must see this scene. Despite the building's many ingenious devices—the palm oil lamps, the pottery basins running with sun-heated water, the cooking utensils and metal hooks of the big sandstone fireplace, fashioned from the wreckage of the ejection pods—the room gave at best an impression of barbaric splendor.

As did the dinner: baked fish from the ponds (heads, four fins, and forked tails intact), steaming bowls of shoots and tubers, piles of triple-lobed fruits—all long familiar to Pratt, though the play of expressions on the stranger Ward's face was enough to remind him of how subtle and haunting their not-quite-identifiable flavors had once seemed.

The McCord woman (a colonel now—hard to believe) had been chattering away like any housewife, with Anton and Rebecca hanging on her every word. She gossiped about the Meerloos' friends and relatives on L-5, their work, new babies, family crises, all the trivial events that had occurred since the disappearance of *Actis* and the granting of independence to L-5. Pratt didn't know whether to believe any of it; the woman could have made it all up to fool them.

But Rebecca was certainly lapping it up. The look on her face was pathetic, that once pretty face sucked dry of its sweetness by the lines around her eyes and mouth. It infuriated Pratt to see the way Rebecca kept reaching out to pluck at the McCord woman's sleeve with arthritis-gnarled fingers, as if to reassure herself that the woman was real.

And Anton seemed to have abandoned any notion of curbing his wife's behavior. He just sat there, red-faced, and pot-bellied, looking for all the world like an overstuffed owl, with those two tufts of gray-blond hair sticking out from the sides of his balding head.

Marston, his tall frame stooped more by depression than physical hardship, had a feverish gleam in his eye that did little for his wild appearance. The livid scar where he had been slashed by the nightglider was made more obvious by the shaggy unkempt beard that refused to grow over the scar tissue. Marston bore down intensely on the Ward fellow, forcing him to lecture on advances in physical and mathematical sciences, though it was apparent that Ward was more interested in the mysterious origins of the food he was eating with gusto. But with Marston's insistence, Ward had given a thorough account of the discovery of the space warp between old Sol and the local star.

Used to be Pratt's field, astrophysics. He didn't quite follow everything the newcomer said, but then he hadn't been paying close attention. He was a bit contemptuous of Marston's excitement, though—it didn't seem that impressive a theory. They'd had plenty of time to work it out.

It was too bad they *had* worked it out.

Well, at least Marston hadn't drowned himself in his fermented berry juice; by this time of the night he was usually unconscious.

Pratt looked at the others: Louise, as usual, had managed to find the darkest shadows in the room. Though her skin was as smooth as the day she'd boarded *Actis*, she seemed somehow shrunken, withdrawn inside that shapeless homespun kaftan she favored.

And Pat—outwardly he was the picture of health, hard-muscled, carefully shaven, his wavy blond hair chopped short. But there was something vague about him, something unfocussed about his eyes—had been, ever since they'd landed on the planet. O'Connor had hit hard that day—Anton had had to cut him out of his ejection pod, which the rest of them hadn't been able to reach for almost two days. Physically, Pat had recovered in no time; but something seemed to have gone out of him.

Pratt caught himself wishing that Nancy were here so that he could show her off. He was proud of her; she was a handsome, fearless woman, fit to be his wife and the mother of Virginia. But she was still away hunting. She stayed away for days at a time, and her trips seemed to be getting even longer of late. She was as bad as the children.

The children being here made up for Nancy's absence. There was an echo of her in Virginia's long smooth face. The others in the room, the adults, might be marked with the strain of their years, with the terrors of the struggle for survival. But the children were uncorrupted by memory.

The McCord woman had been telling them there were recorded messages aboard her ship from their friends and relatives on L-5. There were even some people on the ship, she claimed, who were Fivers themselves.

But all this was temptation; the past was gone.

Only once had McCord spoken directly to him, after Rebecca had told her of Angela's death during the terrible descent into the canyon fifteen years earlier.

McCord had said she was sorry, as if such paltry sentiments had meaning. "It was a long time ago," Pratt had said; it seemed that was the only thing he could find to say to the woman. She belonged to the past; she was tempting them with the past.

Now Louise and Pat were cleaning away the remains of the dinner, helped by Adam and Virginia. Pat paused to stoke the fire, and Marston brought out his jug and, uncharacteristically, offered it around. Ward tried it with interest.

Then they all sat around in the semidarkness, fighting off fatigue, waiting for someone to speak. It was Pratt himself who finally broke the silence, with a false attempt at jocularity.

"So, what do you two have planned for us?" He was taken aback by the harshness of his own voice; he'd hoped to be subtle.

McCord answered him as if she'd noticed nothing amiss. "As far as the mission of *Zetes* is concerned, the primary objective has been met—to find the 'survivors' of *Actis*—I hesitate to call you that—and to determine your condition, which is clearly excellent. Of course we're prepared to render any assistance that may be required." She smiled. "By the way, thanks for a delicious and quite extraordinary dinner."

Pratt grunted, trying to pretend he appreciated the flowery compliment. Rebecca stared bright-eyed at the woman; Pratt knew she was waiting for McCord to state the obvious: that Zetes would take them all off the planet without delay. But for some reason Pratt could not comprehend, the woman dissembled.

"Our secondary objective is to survey and explore," McCord was saying. "There's a lot the United Nations wants to know. Our ship's crawling with 'ologists—biologists, geologists, all kinds—who're eager to get down here and start poking around."

She paused, but no one said anything. Rebecca's disappointment was plain.

"I don't know how much of a look you got at this planet as you were orbiting," she continued (was she trying to draw them into remembrance of those terrible hours?), "but you've done some exploring since. You'll be able to help our research immensely."

There was another silence, suddenly broken by a strange choked whimper from Marston. The man's face was distorted by fury. "*Help* you! Help *you?* God, Colonel McCord," he groaned, "it's us that needs the help. Can't you see that?"

"Marston!" Pratt snarled. "Get a grip on yourself."

"You all sit here like it's some damned tea party! When do we *leave,* that's all I want to know . . ."

"So far as I'm concerned, you can leave tonight, and the group will profit by your absence," Pratt snapped.

Marston's rage collapsed instantly; the relief on his face was pathetic, as if he'd been afraid Pratt would try to stop him from going.

Pratt saw that Anton was gripping Rebecca's arm tightly, warning her to keep silent. So he was one of the weaklings; well, what did it matter if the fools wanted to throw away their heritage? Let them all go.

Michael Ward piped up, his voice thin in the awkward silence. "Excuse me," he said carelessly, "but what do you folks call this place? It feels funny just to keep referring to 'it' in the abstract."

Even Pratt had to grin at Ward's ludicrous attempt to restore cheer.

"What do *you* call it, Mister Ward?" Pratt asked him.

"Tau Ceti Five," Ward replied, "which—"

"—hardly does it justice," McCord finished for him.

"*We* call it the world, that's all," said Marston, bitterly. "And this is the *compound,* in the *canyon.*" His tone was mocking. "And the sun was just the sun, until you two came. Anton, you guessed it was Tau Ceti . . ."

"Thank heaven I did," Meerloo said. "But I had no way of knowing for sure. There was not time for accurate calculation . . ."

Pratt felt the darkness closing in again. It wasn't the fire; the fire burned as brightly as ever. But it seemed far away. Anton's face seemed far away, a pinched little pale blur in the middle of the room. And the shadows were darkening all around.

"You also may leave any time you wish, Meerloo," Pratt said contemptuously, interrupting whatever Anton was talking about. Something about those radio messages to Earth, fifteen years ago. Pratt should never had allowed that. But at the time, of course, he'd had no inkling . . . "You and your hysterical wife and your weakling friend. But you will not take anyone else with you, anyone who does not want to go . . ."

Anton glanced at Adam, his son. "We will discuss this later, Arnold. You are tired."

"We'll take anyone who wants to return to their home," said the McCord woman; she had no ends of words. "I admit we expected you'd all want to come. It seemed a very human, natural thing to expect. But I won't interfere in your personal affairs."

"What interest does the United Nations have in this planet, Colonel?" Pratt asked. "Aside from their touching concern for our welfare?"

"There are no territorial rights in space, Captain Pratt," McCord said quietly.

"The crew of *Actis* discovered this world," Pratt said flatly.

Rebecca Meerloo's eyes clouded with tears, and Anton and Marston glared angrily at Pratt. But Pat O'Connor looked at him as if waiting for some kind of guidance, some kind of signal. And Louise and the children watched from the shadows, quiet, wary, uncommitted.

"Tau Ceti Five, discovered inadvertently by you and your shipmates aboard *Actis,* will be administered by the United Nations. We might both wish it otherwise, you and I,"

McCord said to him, and her voice was no longer warm. "But we have no right to protest."

"Thank you for your answer," Pratt said abruptly. "I have no time to waste on protest. Will someone please show our guests a place to sleep when they get tired? As Anton has recently reminded me, I'm an old man. I've had a hard day. I want to get some sleep."

Pratt stood up and walked away from the table, disappearing behind the woven rush screen that separated the main hall of the longhouse from the sleeping compartments.

For awhile no one said anything. Then Pat O'Connor got up and walked like a zombie to the main door opening onto the compound. He drew back the bolt and went out into the darkness.

Anton went to the door and replaced the bolt, which O'Connor had failed to slide shut from the outside. Anton spoke for those remaining in the room. "Arnold is older than he would like to think. And tireder. His life here has been harder than anyone's. We owe him our survival."

"I understand, Anton," McCord replied. "Maybe we should all go to bed now. We can talk about what to do next in the morning. Things have a way of looking different in the morning."

Listening from behind the rush screen, Pratt sneered at Anton's feeble attempt to apologize on his behalf. What did weaklings know?

Pratt moved down the hall into the darkness.

23

> Oh it is hard to give in! But it is worse
> To risk everything for stubborn pride.
> —Sophocles, *Antigone*

Laura's cheerful voice came over the speaker in the communications center: "... done wonders here, come through better than anything we imagined. It's truly been an inspirational experience."

Donner glanced at Sanders, wondering if she noticed the odd tone of Laura's voice. But the taciturn co-pilot betrayed nothing.

"Must have been inspiring, Captain. You don't sound like yourself at all. When will we be seeing you again?" Donner asked.

The speaker hissed, and a second later Laura's voice replied, "We'll be arranging details of our schedule in the morning. Lots of things to think about. I'll have more for you then. I calculate the new orbit will bring you over the horizon at ten thirty-two ship time, right?"

Donner grunted, and looked at Sanders again. She gave him a confirming nod. "Plus or minus a few seconds, Captain. Will that be your next transmission?"

This time the delay was a hair longer than the propagation time of radio waves required. "I should be snoring during your next three passes. I, uh, snore in a very interesting manner. So I've been told."

"Well, maybe I'll listen in," said Donner. *What a weird thing to say,* he thought. "A shame to pass up such a rare opportunity."

The speaker hissed, Laura laughed. "Do that," she said. "Over."

"*Zetes* over," said Donner. The communications officer at his console flicked off the radio. Donner turned to say something to Sanders, but she had disappeared.

For almost twenty minutes Pratt and O'Connor had been watching the bright fleck of light arcing slowly across the heavens, cleaving the star-strewn sky on a line parallel to the north rim of the canyon.

They sat in the shelter of a shallow natural cave, scooped out of the sandstone cliff twenty meters above the longhouse. It had often been used as a lookout during the early days, before the settlers had learned that dragons rarely came down into the canyons, and it was still a convenient place to get away from other people while staying within earshot of the compound.

"Must have changed their orbit to get us in line of sight," O'Connor had offered, when first he saw the wandering star; but Pratt had not replied, and O'Connor rarely pursued any subject unless encouraged to do so.

From time to time the two men heard the susurration of wind in a nightglider's winds—the black shadow of the beast would sweep down over the smooth pale stone of the starlit cliff, and over them, and on into the dark canyon. Nightgliders meant nothing to them; they simply sat still and talked in quiet voices.

"Mere symbolic revolution will not work again, if indeed it worked before, as the woman claims," Pratt was saying in his droning voice, "Not with the prospect of a whole virgin world spread open before them."

O'Connor nodded solemnly.

"Therefore simply to resist is not sufficient. We must effectively destroy the ship. It must never return to Earth. No one must ever know what became of it."

"There are thirty of them," O'Connor said tonelessly.

"Half of them are scientists who know nothing of flight. It's the others we must eliminate. We do so by drawing them down to the surface . . ."

O'Connor listened patiently as Pratt continued. For twenty minutes now Pratt had lectured him on the meaning of history: the attempt to build a second Earth in space, called "L-5"; the mission of *Actis,* which was to have saved the L-5 dream; the unique destiny that had brought them to this place; Pratt's dawning realization that the space colony had never been more than a half measure, compared to this, the true heavenly Earth. *Actis* had been fated to win this world; ergo, the crew of *Actis* must hold it.

O'Connor was stirred, deeply if vaguely, by the urgent conviction of his captain's voice. Pratt's argument was persuasive to the ultimate degree—although O'Connor could not have repeated two words of it in sequence. O'Connor waited to be told what to do.

" . . . deception will not work," Pratt mused. "Pretending to cooperate will bring the scientists down, but not the soldiers. The bait must be real." He paused for breath, then continued in the same monotonous, hypnotic key: "We capture the woman, and let it be known. So long as their captain is alive, they continue to try to save her. We ambush and dispose of them at every turn. The man, of course, is of no account. He may be put to use as an example of what will happen to her; as an added inducement to rescue . . ."

Above their heads, the heavenly spark that was *Zetes* slid below the rim of the starlit cliffs.

Laura snapped the flap of her pack down over the radio, securing it. She moved across to the bunk where Michael sat, threw her arms about him, gripped him with a compelling grip, pulled him down into the homespun bedding. She buried his head under her flowing hair. "Oh darling," she moaned, louder than she had to, "hold me."

Startled, he did as he was told. His arm shielded her face. She pressed her lips against his ear. "I'll let you up if you promise to keep your mouth shut," she offered in a whisper.

"Okay."

She sat up slowly, trying to be quiet. He sat up beside her, not quite so carefully. She kept her eyes on the door of the narrow cubicle and listened hard.

Hearing nothing, she turned back to Michael; their noses were almost touching. "There's a door at the end of this corridor," she whispered, almost inaudibly. "It's unbolted. They're careful to bolt their doors. So Pratt must be out there with O'Connor. He lied about going to bed."

"So?" Michael breathed, puzzled.

"Pratt will move against us, probably before morning. We have to get out of here right away."

"Are you crazy?" he hissed, staring at her.

"I'm deadly serious. *He* may be crazy—crazy enough to try to kill us immediately. If not, he'll try to hold us hostage. In the long run it will amount to the same thing."

Michael glared at her, his face suffused with anger. "Can't you see life as anything but one long war?" he croaked.

She flushed. "You may have a right to say that, but this is not the time or place. Our lives are in danger; this whole mission is in danger."

"It's your imagination," Michael said—quietly enough, but forgetting to whisper until she dug her fingernails into his wrist. "So he's a rude old man," he went on, husking the words. "So maybe he's a little crazy. With what they've all been through, it's no wonder. You're blowing it up."

"That's what I despise about *honorable* men," she spat. "Willing to maintain everybody's perfect sainthood until you get stung personally—and after that, no forgiveness. Get it through your head I don't blame Pratt. But I don't have any delusions about him either."

"What he is, you helped make him."

"I'll be responsible for that. And if you don't come with me on your own, I'll be responsible for you too."

"What the hell does that mean?"

In an instant she had flipped open her hip holster and drawn her dart gun. She held it up high at arm's length, where he could see it plainly enough if he shifted his gaze. "I'll shoot anybody who comes through that door," she said. "After I've shot you. That's one way to handle it without taking any chances. The other way is for you and me to get out of here now. That way nobody gets hurt unless they want to come after us. To me, that looks like a fair test. Will that convince you?"

He thought about it for a long moment. "What about Smith-Jones? What about the Meerloos?"

"If they're on our side, they'll do us more good if we leave them behind and come back for them later."

Again he was silent. Then, "What about nightgliders?"

And then she knew she had him, for his mind had turned from ends to means. "We just have to keep our ears open, according to Adam and Virginia. And we've still got these . . ." She waggled her dart gun.

"All right," he said. "When? Now?"

"Yes, if it's clear. We'll try the way Pratt and O'Connor went. With luck, they're still in powwow."

He moved as quietly as possible to put on his pack, while she did the same. Ready to go, he paused by the door, looking back at her. "You know, Laura, I think this is nuts. I think you were right earlier, when you said everything looks different in the morning."

"Maybe it will, Mike. I won't be disappointed."

"Yes you will," he said shortly.

They listened for awhile, but heard nothing outside the thin rush door. They eased it open. The corridor was dark. Nothing stirred in the shadows.

They made their way quickly to the end of the hall, past the sleeping compartments of the others. They came to the wooden door at the end of the hall, in just a few short steps. It still stood ajar. They pushed it outward. It creaked on its hinges, but they had no choice but to keep pushing.

They could see most of the courtyard, and the base of the cliff behind the longhouse. The sails of the windmill swung sluggishly in the breeze. Tall cane in the creek bottoms sighed and rustled in the gentle night wind. Bright starlight, almost as bright as the full moon back on Earth, outlined the path leading down the canyon, a path of silvery blue disappearing into the darkness of the palm groves.

They ran.

Pratt broke off in the middle of a sentence. "Look there," he commanded. He pointed to the canyon floor.

O'Connor turned his head; even as he looked, the two figures in white vanished into the shadows of the saucer palm grove.

"I misjudged her intelligence," Pratt said. "I won't do that again."

"Shall I go after them?" O'Connor asked.

"No. I will. You do as you were told."

"Yes, Arnold. But won't you need help? They have those dart guns."

"I'll take a bow. They'll never see me."

"What about their radio? Will they call for help?"

Pratt swore softly. That would indeed be premature. He should have thought of that, not O'Connor. . . "The radio is useless until the ship returns. That should be at least two hours. And they will exhaust themselves quickly; they're not used to gravity."

Pratt stood up. Close and wide behind him, the Milky Way

spread a band of crystal starlight. He listened for a moment, but nothing moved in the night breeze. "I'll catch them," he said.

He began to climb down the path carved in the face of the cliff, toward the canyon floor.

24

Slash'm with a beak
Rip'm with a claw
Bring on the meat wagon
Raw! Raw! Raw!
—football cheer
US Air Force Academy

Michael threw himself sideways to the ground, tearing his ribs against cactus spines, grinding his cheek into the sand. He was almost too late.

The creature's razor-sharp beak had ripped open the shoulder of his coveralls, leaving a three-inch gash in his upper arm. It stung like fire.

"Don't move," Laura snapped. She stood rigid as a statue on the path a few meters from where Michael lay gasping on the ground. From the corner of his eye he could see the dark shape of the nightglider flapping its compound wings, circling back over them, swinging its beaked head from side to side.

Good Lord, the thing's as big as a sailplane!

The head swung in swift regular arcs, back and forth like a radar antenna. Silhouetted black against the starry sky, Michael glimpsed what were presumably eyestalks jutting from each side of the leaf-bladed spear point of a head. Its bulk darkened the sky as it flew over. Short three-clawed legs trailed its gaunt body.

It flapped its wings again, an awkward looking but coordinated motion, like sheets blowing on a clothesline. It rose higher into the air and drifted away up the canyon.

"How badly are you hurt?" Laura asked, moving quickly now to kneel beside him, pulling apart the tatters of his torn sleeve.

"Stings, but it's superficial. Not much blood."

"We'll fix it quick enough." She readied a patch of Medi-plast from the kit in her pack and clamped it to his arm, holding it in place until it conformed. "Anywhere else?" she asked, as he sat up.

"I may have some cactus spines in my side," he said, grinning through clenched teeth. "Forget about them for now. They'll make their presence known." He brushed sand from his scraped cheek.

"Damned clumsy beast," Laura mused, "lucky for us." She looked in the direction the nightglider had flown. "Brain can't be much bigger than a pea. Computes trajectories, but can't cope with discontinuous movement. How do they survive?"

"No competition, that's how. Introduce some birds on this planet and nightgliders will go out faster than dodoes."

"I don't think I'd want to do that," said Laura. "They're rather magnificent, aren't they?"

"Right now it's hard to be charitable."

She looked at him, smiling her sympathy. "Ready to go on?"

"Okay." He got to his feet a bit unsteadily. His heart pounded in his chest. "But I'm tired, Laura, I've got to tell you. I can't run."

"Neither can I. Too dangerous anyway. Can't hear them coming over the sound of your own breath."

Michael sighed. "Is this going to work?" he asked wearily. "Say you're right about these people—it can't be long until they find us missing. They're in good shape, they know the ground, they're hunters."

"I don't think they'll want to run at night, though. So maybe our stupidity's given us the edge." In the dim blue light he could see the worry on her face. "We've got to hold out until we can radio the ship. An hour and a half. We can do that."

She loosened the flap of her hip holster, turning from him as she did so. She struck off down the path, walking steadily.

He trudged after her, hurt, tired, and bitter. A fine way for the representatives of the human race to behave toward one another. But certainly typical.

He reached the crest of a sandy ridge and turned to look back up the length of the great starlit canyon. The walls rose up high around him. Nothing moved against all that expanse of sand and rock and starry sky, except the steady wind and the whispering unseen water in the river, far away.

He wondered how in the world they were going to explain why they'd run off in the middle of the night, terrified, when it turned out that the survivors of *Actis* had never dreamed of doing them harm.

Arnold Pratt moved silently along the path in a loping stride, his sandaled feet skimming nimbly over the sand. In his right hand he carried his long bow, its wood polished and darkened with age. A quiver of arrows rode lightly across his back.

He had an urge to run that he continually suppressed. The fugitives had had only a few moments head start; he surely should have had a glimpse of them by now. Had he taken longer to fetch his weapons from the longhouse than he'd realized?

He knew where to look, too—he knew every turn in the path, where it was hidden by the rocks and dales, where stretches of it were visible a long way off, crossing the dunes and ridges. The man and woman should be easy to spot in those white uniforms of theirs.

They must be far ahead of him. They must have continued to run. They wouldn't be able to keep that up for long—they were already exhausted just by their day's walk from the lagoon. Their faces had made that plain enough, when he first met them.

If the running didn't bring them down gasping, a night-glider surely would. Nothing moved in the canyon at night that a nightglider didn't find sooner or later.

For his own part, Pratt felt fine. Although he'd worked hard, dinner had restored him. The whole planet was on his side, its gravity pulling the intruders to their knees, the nightgliders attacking from the air, its geography as familiar to Pratt as his own body. And he had fire in his belly.

He crested a high rocky ridge. To the south and east the canyon curved away to the right; he could see more of it here, across the arc of the curve, than from any other point along its upper reaches. He could see almost as far as Two Falls Glade, which he knew to be just out of sight beyond the distant promontory jutting from the southern wall.

He waited, resting easily. If the fugitives were still on their feet, it could take no more than a few minutes before they'd reveal themselves to his vantage point, climbing up out of one of the arroyos. Even at a dead run they could not have gone far enough to escape detection from here.

He was right. There they were, two specks against the gray-blue landscape. Not that far away, either; maybe a couple of kilometers. Walking, not running. He couldn't tell if they were really stumbling along as slowly as it seemed from here, or whether that was just a trick of the distance and the starlight. But it didn't matter. He was obviously gaining on them, and that without pushing himself.

He looked up at the night sky. Decades of familiarity with the circuit of the stars told him the time exactly. He'd have no trouble at all catching up with the fugitives before their ship reappeared.

He started to move again, but then he heard it.

It was the telltale whisper of wind in a nightglider's wings. He froze. He moved his head ever so slightly, scanning the sky for the ominous shape.

But with the return of tension, the blackness came. He could see nothing in the sky; the stars themselves were like grains of mica on the bottom of a fishbowl, dim, pinched, upside-down and far away.

And the wind shifted too, carrying the faint warning sound of the nightglider away from his ears.

He'd just have to stand here for a few minutes and give the monster time to go about its business. He'd have to wait until his head cleared. No great loss. He had plenty of time to spare, before he had to get on with what he was doing. Whatever that was.

On the bridge of *Zetes* Ted Donner sat sweating in his couch, his eyes glued to the display screen that showed the face of Tau Ceti Five. It was daylight down there, on the side away from the survivors' compound. The shadows were growing longer, but they seemed to be taking forever to do it. Still an hour to go before *Zetes* would be in position to catch the next transmission from Laura's radio.

Something had gone wrong. That much was obvious, and nothing more. On that last transmission she'd sounded quite uncharacteristically giddy. Unless she was exhausted, that could only have been a performance for eavesdroppers. The only thing that had come through plainly was the message to "keep listening . . ."

Donner dreaded the next message. It could only be a call to take some kind of direct action. He prayed that her orders would be clear, direct, and unambiguous. And that they wouldn't entail a risk to the ship or vital members of its crew.

He hadn't shared his worries with anyone. After all, if you only listened to Laura's *words,* there was no cause for alarm. He didn't want his own fear spreading through the crew.

But Sanders knew something was up. He wondered where she'd been in the half hour after the last message; he'd called all around the ship, casually, of course, asking for her. No one claimed to have seen her. And that meant that some of the crew were lying, unless she'd gone straight to her bunk with a migraine.

But she'd reappeared an hour ago and gone up to the flight deck, without a word to him. She was there now. No bulkheads separated the flight deck from the bridge; by craning his neck back and looking up through the honeycomb deck flooring, Donner could see Sanders' couch. She herself was invisible, except for the tips of her toes and the fingers of one hand resting lightly on the control arm of the couch.

It wasn't her couch. It was the left seat, the command couch, the one Laura usually occupied. And Sanders wasn't doing anything in it; there was nothing for a pilot to do when the ship was in orbit. But the left hand seat was the station of ultimate authority on a spacecraft. Sanders meant Donner to know that she was looking over his shoulder, figuratively and literally.

It was partly the Space Force's hybrid tradition that had put Donner in this fix, a bastard offspring tradition of the Navy and Air Force of a century before. Ponderous naval ships had helmsmen and engine rooms and big crews; the captain's job was to make strategic decisions and order people around. His place was on the bridge, where Donner sat now. Airplanes, however, were frail craft (even the biggest of them), unforgiving of mistakes; there was no delay between the moment of a command decision and its consequences, reassuring or disastrous. Therefore the commander of a plane had always been (theoretically) the person best qualified to fly it.

Spacecraft were really nothing like airplanes or ships, but new technologies are traditionally mismanaged according to old rules. Laura had precedent on her side when she left the crew of *Zetes* hanging in space while she personally piloted the first RAPLAR to the surface of Tau Ceti Five—no less a precedent than the first flight of men to the moon. By so doing she divided the command she left behind and put both her crew and her vessel in danger.

But of course Laura was really harkening to a much older

tradition, that of Alexander when he pushed aside his Companions to set first foot on the shores of Asia.

For whatever reason, she was not with them. That's why Donner hoped her next communication would be unambiguous. For without clear and specific orders Donner might very well find himself having a difference of opinion with Allison Sanders.

Sanders was fiercely loyal to McCord. She was also accustomed to decisive action in a crisis. And she was not above jealousy that her prerogatives as second in command had been usurped.

Donner, on the other hand, was a politician and a mediator, more accustomed to persuasion than command, and—as he had recently and reluctantly admitted to himself—a coward.

Under the circumstances, a "difference of opinion" might quickly grow into something more sticky.

Laura lowered herself to the ground as gently as she could. She gasped for breath. The world swam in front of her eyes, glittering with ghost motes that exploded on her retina in rhythm with her heartbeat. The linings of her nose and throat were raw with the forced passage of the planet's thin dry air. She was too sick and exhausted even to quench her thirst from the nearby pool.

A few seconds passed, and she could hear nothing but the seething blood in her ears, indistinguishable from the hiss of the waterfall.

Then Michael stumbled out of the darkness, his knees buckling under him. He sat down hard beside her, hanging his head down onto his chest, his mouth slack. He sobbed with the effort to draw air.

Whole minutes passed while they said nothing. Finally Laura crept on hands and knees to the edge of the pool, cupped water greedily into her mouth, and splashed it over her burning face.

Michael did the same. They sat on the soggy beach, Michael with one boot in the water, too tired to move it.

"How long now?" he gasped.

She pawed at the sleeve of her uniform, drawing the cuff back just far enough to read the digits on her watch. "Fifteen minutes." She breathed rapidly, then took another gulp of air. "Better stay here. Take cover in trees. Just need time for two words."

He nodded, thankful for the decision to rest. He leaned back on his hands and rocked his head back between his shoulders.

"Two Falls Glade," he said, after a moment.

She followed the gaze of his half open eyes. Angela Pratt's grave. Its white stone, high on the sandstone bench opposite the pool, was open to the sky through a natural clearing in the tall hardwoods. It seemed to glow in the starlight.

"We could have done worse," she said.

Painfully she staggered to her feet. They had pushed themselves harder than their bodies would permit. She hadn't felt this sick for twenty years, since her first summer at the Air Force Academy. But they weren't in bad condition, basically. They'd recover in fifteen minutes, with luck. Half an hour at worst.

They couldn't stay here by the path, though. They had to make an extra effort, enough to reach cover, and to set up some defenses.

"You okay to climb back up to the top?" she asked the still-seated Michael.

"Do I have to?"

"Yes."

"Okay." He rolled to his hands and knees, and then, by stages, pulled himself to a standing position.

"Let me see your gun," she said.

He looked at her resentfully, but said nothing. He fumbled at the catch of his holster for a long time before opening the flap and getting a thumb and a finger around the butt of the gun. He pulled it out and handed it to her upside down.

She checked the chamber, pumped the slide once to bring a hypodermic dart into firing position, checked the magazine. She handed it back to him. He let it hang limply from his hand. "Hide where you can get a good look back along the trail," she told him. "If anyone comes before I get back up to you, shoot them."

"Just . . . ?"

"Just shoot them. Don't stop to talk. Don't give a warning." She pinned him with a stare; her breath still came in ragged gasps. "Mike, you can't hurt anybody with these. Put 'em out for a long time, that's all."

"Needles are four centimeters long. For big animals. Hit an eye, they'll go right in the brain."

"You're not good enough to aim for the head, so aim for

the widest part of the body. Safest for everybody." She paused. "Will you do it?"

He said nothing.

"If they're out there, they're after us, Mike. Don't you see that?"

He nodded glumly. "All right."

"Okay. Don't miss. I'll come for you as soon as I've sent the message."

She turned away from him, surveying the pool, the cliff face, the trees. She chose her spot and started to move.

Michael faced back up the path, which climbed steeply beside the waterfall. Grimly, he trudged uphill.

Pratt was sweating, as much with apprehension as with hard work. It could hardly be more than ten minutes until that spaceship would be back in position to receive radio transmissions.

Already the fugitives had reached the cover of the trees at Two Falls Glade. Maybe they'd be dumb enough to keep going, but he doubted it. And they must be dead on their feet.

Those damned nightgliders had pestered him every fifteen minutes for the last two hours. It was like he was attracting every one of the stupid beasts in the whole canyon. Almost like they were on the foreigners' side instead of his.

Pratt started to run. To hell with nightgliders. Better to go that way than overrun with foreigners.

He hadn't exactly forgotten that the foreigners had guns. But running, he'd make a hard target. The woman would be preoccupied with her radio, and that Ward fellow looked like he couldn't hit the broad side of a barn with a guided missile. He'd bet on it.

Michael was not thinking clearly at all. Two hours ago he'd been arguing with Laura about whether she was impugning the motives of a collection of innocent castaways, and now he was lurking in the shadows waiting to blast somebody—man, woman, even innocent child.

Although Michael hadn't realized it yet, he'd already botched the job. He'd sat down behind a rock just high enough to rest his gun hand. Behind him the tall trees of the glade rose up over the edge of the cliff that formed the break in the watercourse; in his white uniform, Michael's whole upper body was starkly outlined against the blackness of the trees. And he was too near the waterfall: its sound masked all others.

His head swam with fatigue. His sense of time was confused. He was even a little uncertain of just where in the world he was. Roger Crain seemed to be trying to tell him something, although Michael recognized it for just a scrap of remembered conversation. What would Crain think of him sitting here with a gun in his hand?

Surely there was a more important question, if only he could pin it down. Oh, yes. What should he himself think of what he was doing? What *did* he think? Maybe after he got some sleep he could figure it all out.

He'd promised to defend Laura, and he wanted to keep that promise. That might mean firing the first angry shot on a world that had known only peace. Surely there was another way.

If only this ringing in his ears would go away. He raised his left hand to his eyes, rubbed them, willed the fatigue to leave him.

When he dropped his hand there was a man on the path, running, not fifty meters away. For a split second, as he came over the ridge, he was silhouetted against the stars. Michael did not even think about it. He tried to shoot him.

The gun leaped in his hand and the "thok" of its expanding gases slapped his eardrums.

The running figure broke stride and crashed sideways heavily, falling away from the path.

"Damn it! Damn it!" Michael screamed. "Who is that? Are you hurt? Did I hurt you?" Yet though tears of pity and self-hatred burned in his eyes, he was not fool enough to jump up and run to look.

Pratt had been right about Ward's lack of marksmanship. The glass dart had splattered against a rock at least two meters past him. But Pratt forgot to congratulate himself.

He lay there in the sand on his back, looking up at the swirling sky, trying to remember what he was doing out here. He really wasn't very comfortable. He was hiding, wasn't he? Somebody was shooting at him.

Pratt rolled over, across the hard bundle of arrows that had fallen beneath his shoulders. His bow was still in his right hand.

He was glad to find that he was armed. Swiftly and silently

he pulled an arrow from the quiver and nocked it to the bowstring. He inched forward on his belly until he reached the cover of a big cord plant.

Is that the one who's trying to kill me? Just sitting there, like a white paper target pinned up against a black wall. Less than fifty meters away. Wind is light, steady, straight toward him. Couldn't be ... he isn't hiding. Too easy to kill.

He's yelling something. Am I hurt? Am I hurt? He's looking for me. He wants to help me.

Pratt watched from beneath the broad rubbery leaf of the cord plant as Michael shouted again, "Captain Pratt! It's you, isn't it? Are you hurt?"

But Pratt would not reply just yet. He didn't want whoever was shooting at them to know his position. Then Michael moved, slowly getting to his feet. For a moment Pratt was in agony, wanting to shout a warning, but not daring to risk it.

"Captain Pratt, let me talk to you," Michael was saying, as he walked slowly in the direction of Pratt's hiding place. "Just tell me what you want from us. Maybe we can work something out."

No one attacked Michael. The bushwhacker must have gone. Pratt supposed it was safe to show himself. He stood up; he still held the arrow ready in the bow.

Michael stopped. "You're not hurt, are you, Captain?"

Pratt could not reply; he swayed on his feet dizzily.

Who is that man? Anton wouldn't help me like this. Marston's afraid of the dark. And I sent Pat on some errand—he wouldn't defy me. It must be ...

Michael started walking toward him again. "I guess I must have missed you, or you'd be out by now. Thank God. Obviously, this is all a horrible mis ..."

Michael was only ten meters away when Pratt raised the bow, drew and released the shaft, and began to run.

The arrow struck Michael in the right forearm. It wasn't a clean hit. The head stuck in the flesh, and the shaft flopped over and hung from his arm. He yelled, more surprised than afraid. But he didn't drop the gun.

Pratt was already past him and down the path. Michael was still staring at the arrow, the words shocked out of him.

What came over me? I let the man almost talk me into submission! And as it was I almost missed him—it was like I hadn't meant to kill him at all! What sorcery is this?

He nocked another arrow as he ran. Within a few seconds he had reached the edge of the trees, where the path went down the face of the cliff. Just then he heard a "thok" behind him, and at the same instant, an insect bit him in the calf.

He hit me! Did he? No . . . nothing there. Must have been a damn little humbuzzer. Fine time.

Go careful, don't pitch over the cliff. The woman couldn't have heard him yell, with the noise of the falls. She'll be hiding, of course. I'll find her—not many places to hide with that white suit. I've still got time. Must try not to kill her. More valuable alive. There's still time.

Pratt bounded down the steep path a meter at a jump. From the level of the first pool he could see almost the entire glade below. He paused there, pressing himself into a crevice in the sandstone quarried open by the gnarled roots of a huge tree. From this hiding place he could scan the darkness below.

Above him he could hear Michael stumbling down the trail, kicking rocks over the edge to crash down through the foliage. "Laura, watch out!" he was yelling, "Pratt's past me. He's got a bow and arrows!"

Pratt didn't move. He was invisible in the shadows, his sun-blackened, stringy body blending with the tree roots and the night. When Ward passed him, it would be a simple matter to kick the man over the edge of the trail. Meanwhile, if the woman moved in response to Ward's cries, this was an excellent place to spot her.

Legs are heavy—almost numb. Maybe Ward nicked me after all. Couldn't have been a clean hit, though.

What's that? White on the hillside!

Pratt estimated how far above him on the path Michael must be. He still had a second or two. He stepped into the path and swiftly raised his great bow.

But it's not the woman at all! It's Angela's grave . . . how could I make such a blunder?

His vision was going now, and he knew it. Shapes blurred and melted and ran together. Utter darkness closed in from all around.

It is moving! It's splitting in two. The woman is behind it . . .

But Pratt had run out of time.

He'd been right, though. Laura, realizing that her white uniform was an easy target, that her pale skin would be no better, and that she had no time to change that situation, had collapsed in hiding behind the only white object in the glade.

When she heard Michael's shouts her watch was showing oh-one hours, eleven minutes, and thirty seconds—the earliest moment *Zetes* would appear above the planet's horizon. She needed only a few seconds in which to transmit a simple message of two words: "Send help."

As she lifted the small radio to her lips, her foot moved in the soft earth. She threw out a hand to keep from falling. She recovered almost immediately.

Almost.

Michael was two steps away when the arrow flew from Pratt's limp fingers. He watched in stunned horror as the pale shaft floated in what seemed like dreamlike slow motion, out across the liquid depths of the dark clearing above the pool, to strike Laura in the neck.

Without a sound she collapsed onto her hands and knees. The radio fell from her grip and tumbled down the steep slope into the pool. For a few seconds she stayed in that ungraceful position, staring wide-eyed at the ground. Then she slowly pitched forward onto her face.

25

Oh doe not die, for I shall hate
All women so, when thou art gone . . .
　　　　　　　　　　—John Donne
　　　　　　　　　　A Feaver

They had checked everything. They had checked and re-checked for half an hour. The equipment aboard *Zetes* was functioning perfectly. There were no unusual weather conditions below. There was nothing, in short, to prevent any message from the surface from coming through, had any message been sent. None had. Not even snores.

"I'm putting the crew on alert," Sanders informed Donner.

"You really think that's advisable?" he asked.

"I do. Any objections?"

"Not if you want to take the responsibility," he shrugged, trying to suggest that she was acting more than a little prematurely. On the other hand, he wanted his own nose clean if trouble developed and all this came before a board of inquiry some day.

After another fifteen minutes of silence, Donner attempted to divert Sanders' attention. "I can tell you're on edge, Sandy. Why don't you go get Carson and Washington ready to take R-3 down in the morning? And get the plotters started on flight path calculations. If we can't wake up Laura on the next pass, we'll schedule a launch to put them down there at daybreak."

"That will take me about five minutes," she replied tersely. "When I get back I want a word with you."

"Sure, Sandy, whatever you like."

She left. Donner brooded. He stared at the back of the communications officer's neck. The man had been flipping switches fruitlessly for almost an hour.

"How much longer will our window be open, Fuzzy?"

"Shut down half a minute ago, sir. We're over the horizon."

"Okay. If Captain Sanders comes looking for me here, send her to Colonel McCord's office."

"Yes, sir."

"Prefer you didn't repeat anything you've overheard between us, Fuzzy." Donner said lightly.

The communications officer's ears glowed red. "Understood, sir."

Donner went straight to the captain's office, a small room connecting with Laura's cabin. He couldn't bring himself to sit in Laura's desk chair, which is where he should have been for maximum effect when Sanders came in. He barely had time to make the preparations he needed to make before she rapped on the door.

He tacked his feet to the Velcro rug beside Laura's desk, clasped his hands behind his back, and said—cheerfully, he hoped—"Come in."

Sanders floated through the hatch and swung it shut behind her. She turned to him.

"Sandy, I ought to tell you I'm recording this," Donner said easily. "For the record, you know."

"Suits me." She floated a few inches off the floor, relaxed and ready, a fish in her own pond. "For the record, and as a matter of fact, it's my opinion that Ward and the Colonel are in serious trouble and need our immediate assistance."

Donner smiled indulgently. "What makes you think so?"

"It was clear from her last transmission that she was worried . . ."

"Come now. She scheduled a transmission for ten-thirty this morning. She said she was going to sleep. I'd hardly say she sounded worried."

Sanders cool gray eyes inspected him. Plainly she knew he was lying about his feelings. "The Colonel was obviously worried about eavesdroppers when she said that. She told us to listen for her snores . . ."

"A joke," Donner insisted.

"And yet she hasn't responded to a direct page. The alarm on that radio would wake the dead."

"Only if it's turned on. Doubtless she turned it off before she went to sleep, for that very reason." Donner continued quickly, before she could contradict him: "But I'm just as anxious as you to cover all the bases, Sandy. That's why I told you to get that plane ready for the morning. You've taken care of that as I suggested?"

Sanders' lip curled in a sneer.

Donner realized he was playing it for the record a bit too obviously. He hurried on. "I'm confident we'll raise Laura and get a countermanding order before we have to launch an unscheduled RAPLAR." He willed himself to put steel in his voice. "Under the circumstances, there's nothing more to be said."

Sanders reached slowly into the pocket of her uniform and just as slowly drew out a piece of Laura's personal stationery. "I want you to read this," Sanders said. "For obvious reasons, the Colonel didn't put it into the computer."

Donner stared at it. "Bring it here."

Sanders floated toward him, holding out the paper. When he took it, she slowly floated back toward the wall.

"Ted," the note read, "if Sandy shows you this, it's because of an emergency situation she'll be better trained to handle than you are. I want you to follow her suggestions and make them your own. Consider this an order. Yours, Laura."

He had hardly finished reading when Sanders started talking: "First, put *Zetes* into low orbit so we will have radio contact at frequent intervals. Second, launch three ejection pods, each with a crew of three; one to touch down near the main camp, one near the mouth of the river, one halfway between. Under parasails they should be able to make it into the canyon." Sanders paused for questions, but Donner was silent.

Sanders continued, calmly laying out the battle plan. "If Laura and Mike escaped the camp, they'll be heading down river for their RAPLAR. Once this has been established, launch three RAPLARs at dawn, with landing patterns computed to bring them well up into the lagoon. The canyon is wide, there'll be no risk. On the other hand, if Laura and Mike are being held at the camp, we launch the second wave in ejection pods if necessary. Or if they're okay, we cancel the second wave altogether."

Donner stared at her, his fear a coppery lump at the back of his throat. "That would strip virtually every competent Space Force officer off this ship," he croaked.

"The computer can fly an orbit as well as anybody," she replied.

"But if something happens to them!" he quavered. "We'll never get back to Earth!"

"What will happen to them?" Sanders asked contemptuously. "Trained officers with guns against a handful of half savages with bows and arrows! You have Laura's orders. It's your duty to act."

"As for this," he said, holding the paper at arm's length, "my guess is, it's a forgery. Even if it is authentic, it is an ... illegal order, under the circumstances. Your proposals would endanger the ship, the crew, and the mission. I forbid that," he squeaked. "Now tell me you concur."

"That's your decision?" Sanders asked calmly.

"It is, and if you don't immediately give me your concurrence I must reluctantly order you to report to your cabin and place yourself under—"

Alarm bells rang in the corridor. *Zetes* was preparing for deceleration.

Donner had his gun in his hand already, but somehow she knew it, for she sprang from the cabin bulkhead with a strong kick and was halfway across the room toward him before he had brought it from behind his back and raised it to aim at her.

Michael was thinking clearly at last, but he was a bit late. It was the clarity born of a crisis that had already passed beyond despair.

Pratt had shot Laura and stumbled around drunkenly and fallen backward against the cliff. He did not register Michael's presence. Nevertheless, in a flare of anger Michael tried to shoot him in the face from a range of less than a couple of meters. Michael was a hopeless shot: the dart struck Pratt in the shoulder. He fell heavily to the ground.

The sight of the glass dart protruding from the flesh of the man's arm brought Michael to his senses. He did not shoot again. He reached down and snatched the hypodermic away, wondering whether the doses from both darts would combine to stop Pratt's heart. He could not say that he really cared, though he supposed he would feel differently about it later. Anyway, he doubted it—if he'd hit him at all with the previous shot, it could have only been a mere scratch.

He stepped over Pratt's sprawled body and hurried as quickly as he could down the steep path to the edge of the pool. He leaped stones over the river and scrambled up the far side, along the thin track that led to Angela's grave.

He did not touch Laura at first, but bent his head down to where her mouth and nose were twisted toward him, pushing into the earth. Her eyes were closed. She was breathing.

The greater length of the vaned shaft protruded into the air, from under the right side of Laura's jaw. He could not see the arrow head.

Gently he took her by the shoulders and twisted her body sideways, until she lay on her back against the slope of the hillside. His arm bled all over the front of her coveralls, a spreading black stain. He knew he would have to stop his own bleeding quickly if he were to be of any use to her.

He shrugged off his pack and opened the flap of the pocket that held the first-aid gear. He wrapped a gauze tape around the wound, tearing it off with his teeth, then shakily sealed the crude bandage with porous Mediplast. The bundle was darkly splotched, and the wound throbbed mightily, but he wasn't losing any more blood.

He looked at Laura. He could see the arrowhead now, sticking out under her left jaw by perhaps five centimeters. It was a bright bit of aluminum with sharpened edges and one set of barbs, the whole thing less than two centimeters long and a centimeter wide. For fish, or small animals maybe, not for big game. Not for humans. The arrow had passed through the flesh of her throat above the larynx.

Michael fumbled for her pulse, and felt her hands and forehead. He wished he knew more about anatomy; with his free hand he explored his own throat: glands, stringy muscles, floor of the mouth—what's in there? Root of the tongue, he guessed.

God, it hadn't missed the artery by much—but it must have missed; there was very little blood. Her skin was cool and clammy; her fingers in particular were cold. Pulse was damned hard to find, and when he found it, it was light and fast. Her breathing was light and fast, too. She was in shock; he didn't know how severe.

He did what he could. He pulled the Mylar blanket from his pack and spread it over her. He knew he was supposed to keep her flat, but the position of the arrow meant he had to keep her head up. If he remembered his training, he was also supposed to get fluids into her when she came around—how the hell was he going to do that? And, Lord, what if she vomited? The thought almost panicked him again, but he fought it off.

Oh yes, the most important thing: get the patient to a hospital. He sat in the darkness, his back against a gravestone, holding the cold hand of the woman he thought he loved and knew he needed to get him out of trouble, who was now unconscious, unable to speak if she were awake, and possibly dying. The radio he needed to call for help was at the bottom of a black pool of water. His arm was pounding with pain, his shoulder stung, his side was on fire where cactus needles had worked into his flesh, he was weary, he wanted to cry, and he couldn't shoot a gun straight to save his life.

And out there in the darkness, more of *them* were coming.

Two of them were already close. They were running, and they could run a long time without stopping; the breeze was with them, they knew nightgliders attacked upwind, so they knew they could see them coming. Walking and listening were for adults.

They were thankful they didn't have to talk. It would take them a long time to find words; what they had seen still burned in their brains.

They thought a dragon was loose in the sleeping quarters. First it was Marston's voice, starting with a question, ending with a scream. Then Rebecca shrieked.

By then Adam had the steel hook from the fireplace in his hand. He had come awake instantly, and Virginia beside him. He gestured her to stay back where she could cover him with her bow and arrows. He crept toward the screen at the end of the hall.

There was a bellowing cry and the screen exploded out into the room. Anton and Pat were locked together, covered with slick red blood. A knife in Pat's hand—it flashed in the dying firelight. Anton fought desperately to keep it from his throat. "For God's sake, help me," he cried. "Kill him. Be quick."

Adam stood frozen by the unimaginable sight. Pale frightened faces, Louise's and Rebecca's, appeared in the dark hall.

The knife's point nipped at Anton's skin. Adam struck hard with the steel hook, catching Pat behind the ear, jerking him away. He was utterly surprised by the insult; he lay on his back, his mouth working like a fish.

Louise rushed out of the shadows and knelt beside him, her twisted hand reaching for his cheek. Anton pulled himself to his knees and glared at her. "Marston first," he grated.

"The living first," Louise said. "Marston's dead."

Later Pat told them, a word at a time, what Arnold had

ordered him to do to them, to Marston and Anton. He'd done half of it.

The children would never forget the lesson of the fire and the shadow and the blood and the hatred and the tears.

As they neared Two Falls Glade they saw a sight of extraordinary beauty: two streaks of red fire in the sky, blazing brighter than the stars, and growing brighter still just before they faded. They knew what they were, of course, for Marston had told them about meteors; but they'd only seen a few of them before, none this dazzling, and Marston had said they weren't as common here as they were on the other Earth.

Two at once! And so bright! One of them was almost over their heads. For awhile Adam was to wonder whether the shade of Marston had not summoned them : . .

David Levine's pulse raced with excitement. To his left sat the other two occupants of Pod Beta, Lieutenant Taras, the pod's pilot, and a woman named Ross from propulsion control. Levine had gotten his wish to wangle a trip to the surface; only he hadn't had to do much wangling, since Major Sanders had given him his orders in person.

Levine gripped an automatic repeating dart thrower between his knees—tightly, hoping he wouldn't lose control of it when the pod hit. Several centimeters from his face the alien landscape twisted and swung in the sensor screen's reconstructed image: the brown cliffs yawned and dropped away, revealing a winding strip of phosphorescent blue that was the river; trees and bushes resolved into individual splotches of flat, phony-looking green; and a blob of the glowing red that denoted animal life sliding between the descending pod and the ground.

Taras had miscalculated his descent trajectory rather badly, fooled by the planet's thin cold air, and hampered in his ability to maneuver within the confines of the tall canyon walls. The pod was coming down fast several kilometers farther up the canyon than intended. But there was little time to be concerned about just where they were going to land at the moment; the ground was coming up fast, and Taras was trying to steer the pod under its parasail to any place that looked a little flatter than everyplace else.

They struck hard. The pod rolled a couple of times and came to rest on its side. Levine and the others were hanging face down from their webbing. Levine still had a hand on his gun, though. And from the looks of things, he was the only one of the three of them who could reach a hatch—the auxiliary hatch operated by explosive bolts that took most of the electrical system with it when it was blown.

"Go ahead," said Taras, in a strangled, impatient voice below him. "You don't have to pay for it."

Levine reached up and twisted the safety locks. The hatch popped with a bang. Awkwardly, he struggled out of his harness and up onto the rim of the hatch.

The reality of the world was a lot different from the sensor screen's simulation. He was momentarily carried away by the beauty of the distant blue cliffs and the starry expanse of night sky. But he remembered himself, and turned to reach a hand down to Taras.

From the corner of his eye he saw a great black shadow spread across the sky. He turned, startled.

The great beast bore down upon him. He screamed.

Laura sighed, a long, deep sigh, followed by a strangled gasp. Her eyelids flew open. She stared into the darkness. Then her eyes slowly turned toward Michael.

"Don't," he commanded. "Don't try to talk. You can't."

She stared at him, mute.

"I'll ask you questions," he said. "You can feel my hand. If you want to say yes, push once. Twice for no. Understand me?"

He felt the pressure of her fingers. Once.

"Do you feel any pain?" he asked.

Twice.

"Okay, no pain. Are you cold?"

She thought about that. Then she squeezed once.

"You're cold. I'll try to wrap the blanket around you a little better . . ."

She squeezed twice.

"No?" He looked at her, trying to guess her thoughts.

She swung her eyes from side to side, forcing them down. *Oh, God, she's looking at the arrow.* "You've been hit, Laura. But I don't think it's too serious. If we leave it alone."

She squeezed his hand hard, twice. No!

"Laura, I don't think we should try to pull it out."

Yes!

"Laura! Laura, it won't help. It might make it worse."

Yes!

He stared at her, wondering what to do.

She stared back at him, stark and wide. Then she pulled her hand away from his and reached for the arrow.

"God, no!" he yelped, restraining her. "All right, all right, I'll do it. I will do it, I will, I promise. Just let me . . ."

He rummaged in his pack. What could he use? He had to cut the head off without moving the shaft.

There's a saw in here somewhere a little coiled up piece of saw-blade wire where the hell is it why didn't I inspect this pack but she didn't give me any time I left the ship before . . . there it is. Now he had to immobilize the arrow. Clamp it between a couple of rocks, maybe.

He held the wire saw up where she could see it. "I'll cut the head off with this. First I have to find some rocks. You won't move, okay?"

He felt for her hand and found it. She squeezed once. Her hand was so cold.

As he moved away from her he heard the footsteps. There was no way he could have heard them over the sound of the waterfall, but somehow, with some primitive part of his animal brain, he did. The sound came to him with the force of all his senses, as if he could smell them and see their bright bloody faces all at once. He snatched up his gun and held it level across the dark maelstrom of the falling water.

"I'll shoot you!" he screamed. "I'll shoot if you move! I'll shoot until you're dead!"

The roaring silence of the water. Then, "Michael, it's us. Adam and Ginny. Are you hurt?"

"Damn you to hell, you tried to kill her. You shot her . . ." He stopped screaming. No, it wasn't them; of course it wasn't them. They didn't do it. He had to stop thinking like a wounded animal.

"All right, what do you want?" he called, warily.

"To help you," Adam called. "Can we come to you?"

"No weapons," he shouted. "Come slowly."

"Yes, Michael. We're coming. No weapons."

Michael still held his gun pointed at them, the two vague shapes in the shadows. Then he thought better of it, and lowered the gun to his lap.

Then he heard a cry: Virginia's voice. "Is he dead?" she wailed, and he heard the tears.

"No, he's asleep, that's all. He'll be all right," Michael shouted back to her, hoping it was true. "Laura's hurt bad," he shouted again. "Can you bring someone to help? Can you bring Louise? Isn't she a doctor?"

"She's coming, Michael," Adam said. He was down by the lower pool now, jumping lightly from boulder to boulder over the stream. "Pat told us what happened. Arnold was sick. It was a—an accident."

Michael said nothing. There were no accidents, only excuses. The boy came quickly up the path to Angela's grave, and then he stopped, staring at Laura.

"Arnold did that," he whispered.

"Yes," said Michael. Then he sighed, forcing himself to say more. As the words came out he realized they were true, a truth he had not admitted. "He . . . probably didn't know he did it. He may not have meant to, he may have been confused. He was sick . . . and he was drugged. You see, we fought."

But Adam had simply tuned him out. The boy was on his knees beside Laura, inspecting her. Laura looked at him, but her eyes were unreadable.

Adam said, "Michael, this looks serious, but I don't think it really is."

"She wants me to pull it out," Michael said.

Laura moved her hand to Adam's and fumbled for it. She squeezed it once.

"That means 'yes,' " said Michael. "Two for no."

Adam looked at her and said gently. "You'll get blood in your throat, and if you swallow it, you'll vomit. That would be worse than letting it stay."

He shouldn't tell her those things, thought Michael. *They'll make her panic. The doctor should be here, the woman.*

But Laura squeezed the boy's hand hard, twice.

"I want to wait for Louise," said Adam. "She'll do it well."

"How long will that be?" Michael interjected.

"An hour. No longer."

Laura's brows knitted, and she squeezed Adam's hand twice, quickly.

"Is it starting to hurt?" asked the boy.

Yes!

He paused to think. "All right," he said to Laura.

Michael interrupted. "Do you know what you're doing? You're not . . ."

Adam went on talking, ignoring him, but ignoring him so

simply it was as if he'd never spoken. "You're strong, aren't you?" he was saying to Laura. "Strong and brave. You feel warm, now. You're heart is strong. We will take it out, because that's the way you want it. Now listen: you must breathe through your nose. When the arrow is out, sit up, and let the blood out of your mouth. Don't swallow before then. Promise me that?"

Yes.

"Michael, let me see what you've got in your kit," Adam said, and Michael moved with alacrity to show him the first-aid supplies.

As Adam was inspecting the kit, Michael became aware of Virginia standing over them; she had silently materialized from the shadows. If he had not been drained of emotion already, the look on her tear-stained face would have broken his heart. "Is there anything we could do for him?" she asked.

"Just let him sleep," said Michael, and turned away.

Adam seemed to know exactly what he wanted. Michael thought of how broad the children's education must have been. Louise, a doctor, had taught them their medicine. The boy's manner was confident and loving. What would the universe be like if all its inhabitants were like him?

"Do you need this?" Michael asked, showing him the wire saw. But Adam shook his head. The boy looked up at Virginia, held her eyes for a moment, and then nodded to her. She moved soundlessly, to support Laura's head and shoulders with her hands. The boy drew his knife from the sheath on his hip, leaning forward.

No weapons, he'd said, thought Michael. But to him a knife was not a weapon.

With its razor edge Adam sliced through the cord that bound the head to the shaft. The bit of aluminum came away in his hand. With automatic thrift, he slipped it into the pouch at his belt. He trimmed away the remaining cord, and gently shaved off a minute splinter, his left hand all the while touching and supporting the shaft to precisely counterbalance the pressure of the knife blade. The shaft never moved. At last he poured disinfectant from the vial in Michael's kit liberally over the wood.

Laura's eyes were closed; she was somewhere deep inside herself. Adam's fingers flew over her throat, delicately probing, estimating the precise linear path of the arrow. He lifted his eyes to Virginia. Her responding nod was almost imperceptible.

Adam paused in calm suspension. The thumb and fingers of his right hand lay firmly along both sides of Laura's jaw; his left hand, immobile, was wrapped around the shaft of the arrow. He watched Laura take a deep breath through her nose.

At the height of her inhalation, his hand moved. The arrow was gone, tossed into the darkness in the same motion.

Laura's eyes flew open, but she made no sound. Blood welled from her wounds. Cradled in Virginia's lap, she rolled her head to the side and let the blood flow from her mouth. Adam's hand rested on her stomach, alert to the spasms that did not come. Reassured, he brought swabs to clean the wounds and soak up the blood in her mouth. His hands moved swiftly and certainly, flickering in the darkness like fish under water.

That was the last image Michael remembered, for his own head began to swim and the darkness took him.

26

They heard the soldiers shouting out 'The sea! The sea!' and
passing the word down the column. Then certainly they all
began to run . . .

—Xenophon, *The Persian Expedition*

The cliffs were silent in the dawn light; the lagoon was cool
and placid. From the mouth of the river lazy miniature swells
spread slowly across the green surface of the water.

Half a kilometer from the beach where Michael sat
propped against a half-buried lava boulder, the RAPLAR
that had brought him to Tau Ceti Five was about to leave the
planet's surface. Its towering balloon bulged with hydrogen
from the RAPLAR's nuclear-powered electrolytic generator.
Then, like an eagle making off with a fish, the balloon
suddenly plucked the craft from the sucking grasp of the
water, and lifted it with accelerating swiftness straight up into
the calm air of morning.

Laura, Arnold Pratt, and David Levine went with it,
resting sedated in acceleration coughes, in the passenger bay
lately occupied by the folded balloon. Lieutenant Taras
would pilot the craft back to the womb of *Zetes*; the third
member of Pod Beta's crew, Lieutenant Ross, stayed with the
party on the beach.

Michael watched the balloon recede overhead. He shifted
his gaze to Adam, who stood beside him on the beach, staring
after the vanishing craft.

"Thanks for what you did for her, Adam," Michael said.

The boy said nothing.

After a moment Michael added, " . . . and for me," probing
for a response.

Adam looked at him. He was as calm as ever, but Michael

saw the anguish behind his eyes; "I'm sorry, Michael," he said. He had nothing more to say.

Michael nodded glumly. He looked over at the little knot of people standing on the pale pink sand of the beach, Louise with her arm around Virginia's shoulders, Lieutenant Ross talking into her radio. He looked back up into the sky. The balloon and its hanging burden were too small now to distinguish from the bright swimming motes in his eyes.

In the viewscreen of the bridge Allison Sanders watched the winged black RAPLAR creeping cautiously closer, a dark speck against the planet's bright background. According to Ross's report the wounded aboard were in fair-to-good condition—even Levine, who'd been cut up badly by the night-glider he didn't know he wasn't supposed to fight, before his companions had managed to find one of its vulnerable spots with their guns.

It seemed that thanks were due Adam Meerloo and Louise Chew. When the RAPLAR docked, the passengers, who were in better condition than chance would have predicted, would be taken straight to surgery—there the equipment was the finest, and recovery should be swift. But although the immediate crisis was over, Allison Sanders was concerned about the fallout. For a mission of rescue and peaceful exploration, the tally sheet was perversely impressive . . .

Smith-Jones was dead; McCord and Levine and O'Connor were severely wounded; Pratt was psychotic; Ward and Meerloo were pretty well beaten up; Nancy Duquesnes Pratt was still missing.

And the crew of Pod Gamma was stuck on top of the plateau—with the wind against them they'd been forced to make a choice between that and the middle of the lagoon. Adam and Virginia had volunteered to guide them to the canyon floor; Sanders lacked the sense of irony to appreciate the situation.

For herself, there was no doubt she had committed technical mutiny. Donner had been right when he'd said Laura's note was an illegal order. Donner had a good case if he wanted to press it. Which reminded her—she supposed she might as well let him out of his cabin, now, if he wanted to come out.

But it was Laura that Allison Sanders pitied. Even if Laura could not be held accountable for Pratt's madness, she was the last person who should have been there, vulnerable hostage to his wrath. Though Laura had worked hard to drill the crew of *Zetes* for every conceivable mishap, she had been blind to the one factor that made all her preparations a mockery: her own pride.

The RAPLAR was close in the viewscreen now; the controllers on the bridge talked it toward rendezvous in brisk emotionless voices. Laura McCord was returning to the command she never should have left.

She slept around the clock. The machinery in the surgery worked to accelerate all the body's natural healing processes. Michael sometimes sat beside her, holding her hand.

He told her about his life, all the things they'd never had a chance to talk about. Some of the stories he made up. Perhaps he was telling them to himself, to occupy his imagination while she slept.

He told her about his friend the writer, who lived in a house on a mountainside in Colorado. A couple of years before, the writer's wife had borne him a beautiful boy, their first child. The writer's reputation, by the way, was based on daring stories of sexual confrontation—he'd been published in all the best-paying men's magazines; he'd won prizes for his uncompromisingly realistic novels.

But having the little boy around (especially when he grew old enough to walk) made it hard for him to concentrate. The problem was, the curious little fellow was always crawling into his study, or tottering into his study, or lately running into his study, wanting to play. The writer couldn't say no.

Underneath his house was an unfinished basement, just a tiny space between the house's supporting pillars and the steep side of the hill. With the help of a carpenter the writer built himself a kind of cell in this space; it had no windows and no door, and was accessible only by a ladder reached through a trapdoor overhead. Here the writer installed his bookshelves and his desk and his autoscribe. He also used one corner as a wine cellar—he had some excellent vintages from the past stacked against the cool roots of the mountain.

This was the arrangement of his house: the top floor could be reached from the road, and it was above the tree tops, so it was light and sunny and there was a good view out over the plains; this floor had the living room, the kitchen, and the dining room where he liked to entertain his friends. The next floor down had the bedrooms (his wife had chosen the big soft ornate bed in their room), and the bathroom with its large comfortable tub. It was in the floor of the bedroom, not far from the edge of the bed, where the trapdoor was located that led down to his private hiding place.

Every day when it was time to write he would come down the stairs from the living room, past the big bed, and open the trapdoor in the bedroom floor, climb down the ladder, and close it over his head. There, in the small dark privacy of the deepest part of his house, he wrote stories for children.

Michael told this tale to Laura as she lay sleeping, but she smiled when he finished. Maybe she really did hear it, and she was smiling because she thought Michael was making it up. But he was telling the truth.

The test probe came back with a comical image; a warning buoy, orbiting in space to mark the locus of Sol's companion black holes, beeping shrill caution to wayward spaceship pilots.

Reassured, the navigators of *Zetes* set their sights on the entry point of Tau Ceti's local star gate.

Adam and Virginia, dressed in ill-fitting coveralls (no one on the ship came close to their height), lay in their acceleration couches and watched the big screen in the wardroom of *Zetes* with apprehension. Michael had tried to explain what would happen in a reassuring tone of voice, but he was obviously as nervous as they were about the time-reversed passage of the black holes.

They felt the ship begin to move. The speakers in the room babbled with many voices, confusing but somehow comforting. For a long time the screen in front of them showed nothing but a black sky full of stars.

Suddenly the stars turned red and darted away.

EPILOGUE

27

McCORD FOUND GUILTY OF NEGLIGENCE, ANNOUNCES RESIGNATION

Washington DC (USI)—The century's most sensational military trial ended this morning when Colonel Laura M. McCord of the United States Space Force was found guilty on a single count of "negligence in the pursuit of official duties," and punished with a reprimand and a reduction in rank to the permanent grade of Major. The announcement was made by Brigadier General Carl Becker, presiding judge of the military tribunal. This relatively favorable outcome for McCord—at one time she had been accused by her military superiors of inciting a mutiny, although this charge was never formally brought—is seen by legal observers here as evidence of a compromise worked out behind the scenes by Col. McCord's father, the well-known retired Senator Benton McCord of Missouri, and high officials in the administration, possibly including President Culp himself.

Immediately after the adjournment of the Court Martial, Col. McCord informed reporters who were assembled on the steps of the Pentagon that she intends to submit her resignation from active duty and "has every confidence my resignation will be accepted without delay."

The charges against McCord grew out of the United Nation's *Zetes* expedition to the planet Tau Ceti Five, an expedition Col. McCord herself was principally responsible for organizing. During the course of the mission Col. McCord (according to the trial transcript) "required assistance on the surface of the planet," and, subsequently, "a dispute arose between two of her officers over the best way of getting help to her and her companion, Dr. Ward" (who is the well-known mathematician). The prosecutor at the Court Martial continually referred to this "dispute" as mutiny, over the objections of Col. McCord's counsel. Last week the two officers in question, Major Theodore Donner (designated Second in Command of the *Zetes* expedition) and Major Allison Sanders (designated Third in Command) were put on the witness stand by the defense, and both testified to the effect that there had been "a temporary confusion in orders," and that while this had resulted in "an unfortunate public disagreement," the whole thing "was quickly straightened out." USI has learned that this is far from the whole story, and that for a period of time there did exist a state of rebellion among the crew of *Zetes* that might well be labeled "mutiny" (see following item).

McCord's sensational trial has overshadowed the numerous substantial accomplishments of the expedition, and it is the opinion of experts in many fields that the Court Martial will fade to a minor historical footnote in years to come. The proof of a practical means of travel among star systems surely must stand as first among *Zetes'* achievements. However, the rescue and recovery of the lost survivors of *Actis* should also be noted. *Zetes* brought back to Earth all of the original crew who disappeared from the solar system in 2026 except Angela Pratt and Marston Smith-Jones, both of whom died on Tau Ceti Five (see following item). In addition *Zetes* brought back those two charming teenagers born on Tau Ceti Five, Adam Meerloo and Virginia Pratt, who are by now familiar to newspaper and magazine readers and television audiences everywhere (see following item). Many of the *Actis* survivors made public statements in support of Col. McCord during her trial. Included among these is Nancy Wilson Duquesnes Pratt, who married *Actis* Captain Arnold Pratt after the death of Angela, his first wife. Although Nancy Pratt was absent on a hunting trip during the period of the events in question, she offered to testify that Captain Pratt had been suffering lapses of rational behavior during the weeks prior to the arrival of *Zetes*. (Subsequently doctors on L-5 have diagnosed Captain Pratt as suffering from a brain tumor.) For unexplained reasons, Col. McCord did not avail herself of this offer of friendly testimony. This had led to speculation that the willingness of some persons, both on Earth and on L-5, to use the events of the *Zetes* expedition to open old wounds between the United States and L-5 was a deciding factor in the Administration's decision to settle the McCord trial in a noncontroversial manner (see analysis by USI commentator Peter Bergdorff, below).

In addition to these accomplishments, *Zetes* returned with a wealth of scientific data on the planet Tau Ceti Five, including impressive motion picture tapes and recordings available to the public at the Smithsonian Institution in Washington, along with the display of the carcass of the even more impressive creature, native to Tau Ceti Five, known as the "Night Glider" (*Pseudoreptilia, Noctaura pterocomposita*).

In view of this record of achievement, it seems unlikely that

Laura McCord's public career is ended, despite today's events. But when asked about her future plans, Col. McCord was noncommittal. "I look forward to having my privacy back," she said. "I have no plans except to get away for a long time . . ."

Michael Ward saw her for the last time on a windy April day shortly after her separation papers had come through. He'd been an overnight guest at the Washington home of Senator McCord, where Laura was living these days. Their bedrooms were on separate floors.

They sat in the back of the senator's limousine on their way to Union Station, where Michael would take the magneplane that would eventually bring him to Searchlight Base.

As they swung past the Tidal Basin the breeze flung a million pink cherry blossom petals in their path. The streets were thronged with pedestrians, and a few little turbine and flywheel cars; the white marble of the old neoclassical buildings gleamed in the rays of the sun; flags snapped on every pole; troops of fluffy white clouds marched in review through the blue sky. Proud marble trophies, carved armor piled on the beaks of triremes, greeted them when the car pulled to a stop in front of the station.

The chauffeur jumped out and opened the door on Michael's side, but he didn't get out at once.

"I can't change your mind?" he asked. "You'd like the desert, Laura. A few minutes' plane ride from my place I know canyons would make you swear we were back on Tau Ceti . . ."

She laughed. "You'll be too busy to take me there. Rosenblum's going to keep your nose glued to the CRT until you've come up with a workable map of the near corner of superspace—you know that. I'd feel like a fifth wheel."

"What else are you going to do?" he protested. "I can't imagine you sitting around Washington writing your memoirs."

"Okay, I'll let you in on the secret," she said, her voice low and husky. "I'm going to work for the railroads."

"The what?"

She smiled. "It's traditional for us explorers who get themselves busted out of the ranks. Look it up in your history book."

"I was never too good at history."

"Me neither. I wish I'd studied it more carefully. Maybe I wouldn't be repeating it." She leaned forward. "Look, this is confidential, promise?"

"Sure, Laura."

"Trans-Continental Transport wants me to head up a study group— 'prospects for commercial development of interstellar traffic.' I'd say the prospects were good, wouldn't you? Now that there's someplace out there worth going."

Michael looked dubious. "I'm not sure I'm glad to hear it. Except I'm glad for you, of course . . ."

Laura's smile was sad. "I'm a leopard who can't change her spots, Mike. Nothing you or I can do will stop people from spilling out of the solar system—we both had a hand in that. But from what we experienced, maybe we learned enough to help soften the impact a little."

"I doubt it," said Michael, "but then, I always was a pessimist when I stopped to think."

She was silent. She knew they were going their separate ways.

He looked at her, trying to get it all—to sum up the totality of her in the space of a glance—to capture the essence of her, as if he were a master photographer.

But she was already changing under his inspection. In her smile, he saw the lines of experience radiating from the corners of her eyes. Her eyes no longer flashed with the pure green fire of ambition; like her voice, they had become smoky and deep. Pity, and love, and the knowledge of her own human weaknesses, swam in their depths.

"No matter what you say, you did change, Laura," Michael said at last. "More than I did."

"I had farther to go," she said.

"So . . ." He cleared his throat. "I guess it's good-bye. It was too short, wasn't it? Paradise, I mean."

She said nothing. She reached out and took his hand, and squeezed it.

Yes.

OUT OF THIS WORLD!

That's the only way to describe Bantam's great series of science fiction classics. These space-age thrillers are filled with terror, fancy and adventure and written by America's most renowned writers of science fiction. Welcome to outer space and have a good trip!

FANTASY AND SCIENCE FICTION FAVORITES

Bantam brings you the recognized classics as well as the current favorites in fantasy and science fiction. Here you will find the beloved Conan books along with recent titles by the most respected authors in the genre.